"If I get any happier, I think I'll explode,"

Alanna admitted.

"You deserve some happiness," Matt returned. "Come on, let's go to bed."

She turned within the security of his arm, and he walked her through the dark, silent house. At her door, he leaned down, kissing her lightly on the lips. "I'll see you tomorrow," he whispered.

Alanna caught the gleam of humor in the depths of his gray eyes. "I have a feeling I won't be safe after tonight."

He kissed her lingeringly. Then, raising his head, he murmured, "You won't be."

Dear Reader,

Welcome back to another month of fine reading here in Silhouette Classics. Once again we've chosen two top-notch books for you, written by authors whose new work continues to bring you pleasure.

"Sandi Shane" did only two books, and *No Perfect Season*, a Silhouette Intimate Moments, was her first. However, you may know this author better as Bay Matthews and Karen Keast, because these two women combined their talents under the Sandi Shane name before moving on to solo careers. This book showcases their fine command of plot, character and, of course, emotion—all the elements they continue to capture so well. We hope you will enjoy this look back at their collaborative beginnings.

Lindsay McKenna is virtually synonymous with the word "excitement." She excels in all kinds of action and is particularly well-known for her use of military backgrounds. *Captive of Fate* was her first Silhouette Special Edition, and we think you will see all the excitement for which she is known as well as characters who will touch your heart. Quite an accomplishment for such a new writer.

A special note regarding the future: In July, Silhouette Special Edition will publish *Thorne's Wife*, Joan Hohl's long-awaited sequel to *Thorne's Way*, one of our most sought-after early titles. And if you missed *Thorne's Way* the first time around, you will soon have another chance to find it, because it will be available in April, only from Silhouette Classics. If you missed this book before, be sure not to miss it again next month.

Leslie J. Wainger
Senior Editor

Lindsay McKenna

Captive of Fate

Silhouette Classics

Published by Silhouette Books New York

America's Publisher of Contemporary Romance

SILHOUETTE BOOKS
300 East 42nd St., New York, N.Y. 10017

Silhouette Classics edition published March 1989

Silhouette Special Edition edition published March 1983

ISBN 0-373-04634-0

America's Publisher of Contemporary Romance

Printed in the U.S.A.

Books by Lindsay McKenna

Silhouette Intimate Moments

Love Me Before Dawn #44

Silhouette Desire

Chase the Clouds #75
Wilderness Passion #134
Too Near the Fire #165
Texas Wildcat #184
Red Tail #298

Silhouette Special Edition

Captive of Fate #82
Heart of the Eagle #338
A Measure of Love #377
Solitaire #397
Heart of the Tiger #434

LINDSAY McKENNA

enjoys the unusual and has pursued such varied interests as fire fighting and raising purebred Arabian horses, as well as her writing. "I believe in living life to the fullest," she declares, "and I enjoy dangerous situations because I'm at my best during those times."

To Dave, my husband—
Once a Marine, always a Marine

Chapter One

"*A*lanna, I want you to fly down to Costa Rica right away." Senator Jameson Thornton frowned darkly, pushing a yellow legal pad around on the top of his large, mahogany desk. He peered up at his special assistant, his bushy gray eyebrows drawn together. "You're my South American expert, and this is your chance to investigate something big."

Alanna suppressed a tired sigh. It was late Friday afternoon, and it had been one hell of a trying week. Well, now she had an explanation for that long-distance phone call from the Costa Rican minister. Thornton had been the ambassador to that country at one time and had maintained a parental interest in it ever since. She sat down, flipping open her notebook. "Big in what way, Senator?"

Thornton pushed his heavy, aging body forward, resting his bulk on the desk. "An earthquake hit the heart of Costa Rica two days ago. Several mountain villages in the coffee district have been devastated—the

7

loss of life has been terrible, and the number of injured is constantly rising. Our government has sent down a medical relief effort headed up by our mutual enemy: Colonel Breckenridge."

She looked up, her green eyes widening at the mention of the name. Her heart skipped a beat as she allowed the information to soak into her fatigued brain. In nearly two years' working for Thornton, Alanna had rarely heard the Marine officer mentioned without undisguised anger and animosity. After all, Colonel Breckenridge was responsible for the death of the senator's only son, Tim. And over the years, Alanna had grown to loathe the phantom military officer almost as much as her boss did.

A catlike smile graced the senator's fleshy features. "That's right, Alanna. I've got him exactly where I want him this time. And you're going to fly down there tonight and confirm the evidence already in our hands. God, how I've waited for this."

She pushed her dark, walnut-colored hair away from her face, sending the shoulder-length tresses back across her shoulders. "I don't understand. . . ." she said, trying to keep her voice neutral. She had already put in nearly seventy hours this week, and all she wanted to do was retreat to her Georgetown apartment for a well-deserved forty-eight hours of rest and relaxation.

"That earthquake occurred yesterday near Chirripo Grande, the highest peak in Costa Rica. A little village by the name of San Dolega was severely hit, and nearly three thousand people are cut off and homeless. There are reports of a high death rate among the injured, and the government is fearing an epidemic on the heels of the devastation. Apparently the Organization of American States has mobilized to send relief. The U.S. will participate, of course." He hesitated, his brown eyes narrowing. "Some fool assigned Colonel Breckenridge as our representative to the relief effort, and he has been placed in charge of all field operations."

"Is he qualified?" she asked.

"Who knows? It's just another ploy of the Defense Department to build a closer alliance between our military and the Costa Rican police force. If you ask me, a civilian agency should have been put in charge. . . . But that's neither here nor there. Did you see the gentleman who just left?"

Harried, she gave a quick shake of her head.

"He's a missionary from Costa Rica. He flew up here with evidence that a large part of the medical supplies intended for the relief effort is being stolen. Look here," he urged, pulling several splintered wooden crate slats from behind his chair. He pointed to the black lettering. "The missionary obtained these from their sister mission in Nicaragua. The crates were found in the abandoned camp of a leftist guerrilla organization. Looks like our Colonel Breckenridge has started a little black market racket selling supplies meant for those hungry and sick villagers."

She cringed inwardly, knowing her next question would probably aggravate him. "Senator, are you sure Colonel Breckenridge is involved?"

"Couldn't be more positive, Alanna. And that's where you come in. I've got you scheduled on the next available flight out of Bolling Air Force Base aboard a MATS C-130. It's due to take off for San Jose in two hours, and you're going to be on it. Peggy's processing all the papers you'll need as far as introduction goes. I've informed the right people in the government you're coming, and you'll be given carte blanche to get up to San Dolega and begin your investigation. The fact that you speak Spanish is a plus, as is your familiarity with the political and economic environment of Central America." He smiled with satisfaction. "I made a wise decision in hiring you as my special assistant, Alanna. I know you've sometimes chaffed at the more mundane duties around here on the Hill, but I think you'll jump at this chance to get right into the middle of the action. If I didn't have this filibuster coming up on Monday, I'd be flying down there with you."

She blinked. "You want me to investigate Colonel Breckenridge and his relief efforts by myself?"

"Yes, I do. And I know you'll do a thorough job. I've got my chauffeur out front. You had best hurry home and throw some clothes into a suitcase. Peggy will have a travel package waiting for you at the airplane. When you get to San Jose, call me."

This isn't happening, she thought dully, leaning back against the rough corded cargo netting. The throbbing hum of the four prop jet engines lulled her close to sleep. She was cramped into a small space with twenty-four other passengers, military personnel who were also flying down to Costa Rica. Everywhere she looked in the wide-bodied fuselage, huge wooden crates were stacked to the ceiling. There was a tense quiet among the others, and Alanna had pulled herself into a tight ball, discouraging any talk. Her head ached from the events of the day. It seemed as though the entire situation had toppled on her without any warning.

Absently, Alanna rubbed her left arm where she had been given several vaccination shots before boarding the plane. Damn you, Breckenridge, she thought. You've got to be even more of a monster than Senator Thornton's said. She leaned against the webbing, closing her eyes. She knew very little about Colonel Matthew Breckenridge, she realized. She had been told that he worked over at the Pentagon. And, of course, she knew that he had been responsible for Tim Thornton's death when Tim served in the Marine Corps during the closing days of the Vietnam War. But that was all really, though he had often been the subject of the senator's angry discourses. She moved stiffly, unsure of the task looming before her. She was being sent down to prove once and for all the Marine's guilt and catch him in the act of breaking the law. Once she was able to establish his part in the ploy, Thornton would undoubtedly smear Breckenridge's career from the Pentagon to the Senate with the greatest of pleasure. . . .

Alanna awoke with a jerk, sitting up wide-eyed as an Air Force officer leaned over, touching her shoulder. "We're here, Ms. McIntire. All personnel have been ordered to disembark so we can start unloading the supplies. Could you—"

"Sure," she murmured, rising unsteadily. My God, how long did I sleep in that contorted position? Turning, she saw that the entire rear area of the C-130 had opened like gargantuan jaws. The boarding ramp was already in place, and a small group of men waited miserably in the rain for the unloading to commence. Grabbing her briefcase and one small bag, she stretched in an attempt to feel more alert, giving a cursory glance down the boarding ramp where two men were engaged in an animated discussion. As Alanna approached, she recognized the copilot and heard angry words being traded between him and another man dressed in olive green fatigues.

A curtain of rain covered the airport in the washed-out morning light. Alanna regretted wearing her leather shoes and wished mightily for boots instead. Well, at least she had a raincoat and slacks on—they would help keep her dry as she made a dash for customs.

"Just who is this McIntire?" a voice demanded loudly.

Alanna halted, raising her chin, her eyes moving to

the two men at the bottom of the ramp. The copilot turned and pointed directly at her, and she felt her heartbeat automatically quicken.

"That's her, Colonel. And I suggest you talk to her instead of me. I had nothing to do with bumping your man from this flight. Maybe she can give you more information." The copilot saluted and made an abrupt about-face, his features contorted with barely concealed anger.

Alanna remained frozen as the officer in jungle fatigues turned menacingly upon her, taking four swift strides to where she stood. A hundred sudden impressions bombarded her, ripping away the exhaustion that had followed her from Washington, D.C. His face wore the countenance of a hawk, with gray eyes that looked extraordinarily merciless and cold. He was not tall but lean and wiry and moved with the boneless grace of the panthers that roamed the Costa Rican mountains. The deep bronze of his skin only emphasized his rugged facial features. His mouth was compressed into a thin line of displeasure, and Alanna stared fixedly up at him, completely stunned by his demeanor.

"Are you McIntire?" he demanded.

She opened her mouth and then closed it, blinking. Why did she feel like a child reporting to a teacher? Rapidly, she regrouped her forces, noting the black insignia on the collar of his uniform. Unfamiliar with the military, she had to search her memory for what the symbol meant. "Yes," she answered, her voice softer than usual.

"Just what the hell is going on here? Where's Sergeant Haskell? Who gave you permission to bump my man? Don't you realize we've got three thousand people up on a mountainside who are starving and in need of medical attention? Who in the hell are you, some damn reporter?"

She groped to find her voice.

"Show me your papers," he ordered tightly.

"Papers?" she repeated stupidly. Her heart pounded like a caged bird. She cringed inwardly at the utter masculinity of the man who stood over her with his hands resting tensely on his hips. She could smell the dankness of the jungle around him, the musky scent of his body, and realized his uniform was drenched thoroughly by the rain. Muddy red clay clung to his black, booted feet, and the lower part of his bloused trousers. Despite the harshness of his features at that moment, she saw dark circles of exhaustion beneath his eyes. His hair was a raw umber color, typically short in keeping with the military fashion. The cap he wore rested low on his forehead, the bill half-concealing his fiery, silver eyes. As he stood there for those long, interminable seconds, she saw his mouth lose its imperious line and soften somewhat. Idiotically, among all her colliding thoughts at that moment, Alanna found herself thinking it was generous and well shaped. She had expected his mouth to dip harshly at the corners, but to her surprise the lines there curved upward, indicating that he laughed or smiled a great deal. It made the planes of his face less threatening, and she sighed inwardly, realizing on a gut level that he might be human after all.

"Papers," he repeated levelly, taking great pains to control the obvious anger in his voice. "Your passport, for instance. Because if you're a reporter, I'm hauling you—"

"I'm not a reporter," she blurted out, becoming used to his abruptness. She dug in her purse, searching for the letters of authorization, her hand trembling as she found them.

"What, then? A photographer? God, I've got enough of you damn people up there at the base camp right now. I don't need a woman on top of everything else."

13

Alanna felt a sliver of courage returning. This man's abrasive manner was like a bucket of cold water, and she was beginning to come alive beneath his blistering salvo of demands. She opened the letters of authorization and showed them to him. "I'm Senator Thornton's special assistant, Alanna McIntire, and I'm down here at his express direction. Who are you?"

He looked up from the papers, studying her with a renewed intensity that made her shiver. What was happening? She felt lightheaded and at the same time panicky beneath his glare. His mouth thinned.

"I'm Colonel Matt Breckenridge."

Alanna's eyes widened. So, this was the man. The Marine who caused Tim's death by allowing his company to be overrun. But he didn't look inept. He exuded confidence and masculine authority. No one could possibly mistake him for anything less than a man who was very much in control of the situation. And other people's lives. Hers, for instance. She quickly jammed the papers back into her purse.

"You're the person I want to see, then," she explained.

"Lady, as far as I'm concerned, you can make an about-face and return to Washington on this bucket of bolts. Your friend the senator obviously pulled a hell of a lot of strings to get you aboard this plane because my radio communications specialist was the one you bumped from the flight." He sucked in a deep breath, gripping her arm and giving her a little shake. "Do you understand what that means, Miss McIntire? Without Sergeant Haskell I'm going to continue having radio transmission problems between San Jose, the base camp, and San Dolega. That sergeant is a genius. He could establish communications despite this perpetual rain and fog. And he could find a way to train these imbecile police officers as radio operators. Let me put it in terms you politicians up on the Hill might understand a little more clearly: numbers. Not numbers of voters, granted. But numbers of wounded and sick people who need to be med-evacked out of that Godforsaken village. I have sporadic radio relays. I might as well fly carrier pigeons. At least they'd stand a chance of getting through." He released her, taking a step back. "Dammit!" he snarled. "Haskell also speaks Spanish, and I desperately need an interpreter."

Her arm tingled from his grip. Somewhere in the back of her confused, stunned mind, Alanna realized he could have hurt her. Instead, he had monitored the amount of pressure he'd exerted. She gulped, the importance of Sergeant Haskell sinking in. Maybe Colonel Breckenridge had a right to be upset under the circumstances. A wave of guilt surged through her, and she felt her face grow warm with a blush. She frowned, uncomfortable that, despite her twenty-nine years, a blush could give her away. More than anything, she wanted to hide all her reactions from this man.

"I'm sorry. I didn't know."

"Civilians and politicians *never* know before they act. I don't accept your lame apology, Miss McIntire. You are unessential personnel as far as I'm concerned. Excess baggage. Useless." He jerked off his cap, running his long fingers through his hair. Alanna had expected a crew cut. After all, Senator Thornton had painted him as a gung-ho Marine officer. Instead, his hair was neatly tapered to the base of his neck, and a rebellious strand dipped momentarily down across his forehead.

Alanna compressed her full lips. "I said I'm sorry, Colonel. I'm as confused about all this as you are. I had no idea I was coming down here until the last minute. . . ."

Breckenridge jammed the cap back on his head,

exhaling and glancing out the open bay at the continuing pall of rain. "Yeah, I bet you are, but not half as sorry as those poor souls up there on that damn mountain."

Her heart wrenched as she heard a note of anguish in his tone. For a brief instant, the official mask of the Marine Corps slipped away from his features, and she saw a man who was beyond fatigue . . . beyond hope. Alanna chewed on her lower lip, suddenly at odds with herself. Senator Thornton had accused him of being a machine. A ruthless automaton bent upon destroying anything and anyone who got in his way. But he didn't appear to be that robot right now.

"Look, maybe I can be of some help. I do speak Spanish quite fluently and—"

He shot her a flat look of disgust. "An aide to Senator Thornton offering help? I'd rather take a peace offering from an enemy carrying a grenade."

Alanna's temper flared. "I'm not your enemy!"

"Aren't you?" he asked wearily, standing with his shoulders slumped forward, his head down for a moment. "God, this is all I need." He gave a helpless, bitter laugh. "Well, I guess I should be thankful that the old man didn't come down here himself. At least you're beautiful. You're the only thing I've seen in the last two rotten days that makes me feel like there's still some hope left. . . ."

She bridled, confused again by his sudden change in manner. One moment he was ripping her apart; the next, complimenting her. The man was unfathomable. Alanna gripped her bag tightly and muttered, "You're stuck with me, Colonel, whether or not you or I like it."

Matt looked at her. "What?"

"I'm down here to investigate reported losses of medicine and supplies from the relief efforts."

He shook his head, a cold smile replacing his sadness. "There's always some pilferage, Miss McIntire. That's to be expected."

Alanna steeled herself. "I'm not talking about petty theft, Colonel."

Matt rubbed the back of his neck in a weary gesture. "Yeah, I'm sure the senator would like to pin my hide to the wall by accusing me of some stupid black market ruse. Well," he said, "you're barking up the wrong tree. Whoever told him we were losing substantial amounts of supplies is inflating numbers."

"That's for me to decide," she answered firmly.

"Not on my time it isn't."

"I'm not asking for your time."

"Good. Then be a smart girl and stay in the capital here for a few days, go shopping, and then take a jet back to D.C. I don't have time for a meddling woman in any way, shape, or form. Especially one that thinks she is a detective out to prove I'm somehow involved in peddling relief supplies needed by those poor earthquake victims."

Alanna inhaled sharply. "I didn't say that."

He came forward, standing scant inches from her to examine her closely. "The senator has an ax to grind with me. Our quarrel goes back a long way, and I'm sure you're just as aware of it as everyone else is. He sent you down to do his dirty work, Alanna. I don't think you realize what he's handed you. He hates me enough to concoct stories to try to get me court-martialed or publicly embarrassed." His voice became husky, coaxing, an invisible balm to her shredded composure. He had used her first name, and it sent an unbidden shiver throughout her tense body. "I wouldn't have been without sleep for the past thirty-six hours if I didn't care what was happening to the survivors up there on that mountain. Every case of medical supplies is being delivered, I can promise you that. No one knows better than myself the value of morphine and penicillin in this kind of situation, and I wouldn't jeopardize people's lives for a little cash on the side. Money doesn't mean a damn thing to me when it's measured against people's lives. Now, why don't you do us both a favor and find a hotel, get some sleep, and take the next flight home? There's no story down here."

She was mesmerized by the sudden change in him: from tyrant to warm, responsive man whose virility seemed to affect her like a heady wine. Gone was the anger in his gray eyes, his mouth more relaxed, and a hint of a tired smile had replaced his earlier grim look.

For an instant, she was caught within his web. But Senator Thornton's voice reverberated through her head: "He's a hawk, Alanna! A cold-blooded monster who feeds on war and chaos."

She fixed an icy smile on her lips. "The answer is no, Colonel Breckenridge. The senator's sources are impeccable. You are going to take me along with you, one way or another."

A cold, impenetrable mask dropped over his features. Alanna shuddered at the ease with which he resumed his military bearing. "Have it your way," he whispered. "You're out to slit my throat for your misdirected boss. All right, Miss McIntire, the ball is in your court, but just stay out from under foot." He turned to leave and then halted, turning slowly back toward her. "If you get in a jam with Costa Rican officials, don't come crying to me. I have no authority down here except for delivering medicine and supplies."

"I have a letter from the senator, Colonel. I'm sure no one will give me any trouble except you."

"Don't be so sure. A beautiful woman up in the mountains with a bunch of men. You're taking your chances. I'm afraid they may not take time to read your precious letters. That's if they can read at all."

Her eyes flashed with anger. He was deliberately trying to scare her into not going! "I'd rather take my chances with them than you," she flung back.

Matt grinned momentarily. "Contrary to popular opinion, I don't rape women."

"I'm afraid your Marine image leads one to expect something of that sort, though," Alanna retorted.

"Typical civilian remark. I can't say it's been a pleasure meeting you under the circumstances. Too bad we never met in D.C. before this. It would have been interesting. . . ."

She blushed scarlet at the innuendo. How dare he! She called him a few expletives in her mind as she watched him stride down the ramp and back out into the rain, issuing crisp orders to his men.

"Damn you, Colonel. You're going to get everything that's been coming to you. I promise. God, how I promise." She pulled her coat tighter, walking quickly out of the plane and heading with determination toward the customs building.

Alanna waited impatiently for the phone connection with the senator's home to be completed. She pushed her damp hair away from her face, still boiling with rage over the impudence of the Marine officer. Thornton's voice came over the phone line, faraway and slightly distorted by distance.

"He's everything you said, Senator."

"Met him already?"

"Unfortunately, yes. What an arrogant—"

"A monster, Alanna. Look, can you start finding out about his supply routes?"

"Yes. I just persuaded the police commissioner to allow me aboard the next helicopter flying to his staging area at the bottom of the mountain. It's pouring rain here and getting colder. They're having a lot of trouble with fog in the mountains, and the supplies are backing up at the base. I'll start my investigation there."

"Good girl. Give me a call the first time you stumble upon something, and remember, Alanna, don't trust Breckenridge. He can be suave as a fox when he wants to. Don't fall for any of his tricks. Be on guard."

"Don't worry, Senator, I'll be on my toes. He's an easy man to dislike."

"But a clever enemy. I don't trust him under any circumstances. Remember what he did to Tim." She nodded, recalling vividly her own clash with the officer.

"I will. Good-bye."

It was early September, the beginning of the rainy season, and San Jose lay drenched in the wake of the tropical storm. Alanna spoke in fluent Spanish to the commissioner's aide, thanking him. He motioned for her to board the awaiting helicopter. The Costa Rican at the door offered his hand, pulling her aboard. She sat crouched in the doorway, searching for a space to crawl into. There was a small niche behind the pilot's seat, and she struggled to wedge herself down between it and a large wooden crate. Looking up, she saw Matt Breckenridge staring stonily at her from the copilot's seat.

"I'm impressed," he said, raising his voice above the roar of the helicopter. "You've managed to twist one of the local officials around your little finger and wrangle your way on board. What did it cost you, Miss McIntire?"

She glared back at him. "Not a damn thing, Colonel. Some people occasionally do nice things for free."

He grinned wolfishly. "Nothing in life is free, lady. Your senator has influence down here because he was once an ambassador. Don't kid yourself."

Alanna crouched back, unable to meet his laughing

gray eyes. God, how she wanted to slap his ruggedly handsome face! He was such a know-it-all. But a voice nagged at her. There was an ageless wisdom in his eyes, whether she wanted to recognize it or not. He was probably in his mid-thirties, and from what the senator had said, he had been all over the world. And he had come out of the war highly decorated, a proud symbol of the Marine Corps. She was not half as well traveled, but she had studied and got a master's degree in political science—the world had opened up to her just as widely in other ways.

Alanna grudgingly found herself watching him as the helicopter flew through the murky mist of rain. At times he conversed with the pilot over the microphone, or consulted the map and plotter which rested across his thighs. There was a sureness in each of his movements: none were wasted or appeared unnecessary. His hands were spare, long, and callused, with several small white scars on the backs, and she idly wondered how he got them.

Alanna studied his face, watching his eyes narrow with intensity as he talked on the radio or looked out the cockpit window, staring into space for minutes at a time. He always seemed to be thinking. She found herself secretly smiling when he smiled. There was a noticeable camaraderie between him and the pilot, and she enjoyed watching his mouth lift upward, hearing the resonant laughter that came from deep within his broad chest as they joked with each other. With a set of earphones on and without the cap, he looked younger, more boyish. If he put the Marine cap back on, would he resume his "superman" image?

Alanna watched as the dull green of the jungle below them gave way to the lowlands that skirted the Cord de Talamanca mountain range. Fixing her stare out the cockpit window, she wondered where, in those lush, verdant mountains, San Dolega was nestled. According to her limited knowledge of the topography, Chirripo Grande, a twelve thousand–foot mountain peak, hovered over the important coffee-growing area that surrounded San Dolega. The winds began to pick up, and she braced herself as the pilot wrestled with the treacherous up and down drafts created by the mountain range. Once Matt glanced to his left, watching her through narrowed eyes. She lowered her gaze, not wanting to make eye contact with him. Briefly a flicker of concern had crossed his features, but she forced herself to ignore it. The only thing the Marine respected was an ability to survive; there was no room in him for sympathy.

Chapter Two

𝒥t was noon when they finally landed at the base camp. Alanna swallowed hard, airsick from the jolting ride in the helicopter. Her stomach churned threateningly as she extricated herself from the tangle of boxes with help from a soldier. Without a word or much less a glance, Matt Breckenridge slid out of the chopper and was promptly met by his vanguard of aides, a mixture of Marine and Costa Rican police personnel. Alanna jumped to the ground behind him, her feet sinking into ankle-deep mud immediately. She groaned, watching as the red ooze claimed her expensive leather shoes. Rain slashed unrelentingly at her face, and she bowed her head, looking for the closest shelter.

The base camp consisted of ten or twelve sadly thatched huts; some made out of spare wood and rough-cut lumber, others out of grass and twigs and adobelike bricks. A feeling of despair began to shadow her as she continued to stand there. She hated the helpless feeling that came when a situation was controlled by someone other than herself. She had always been in control of her life . . . at least until she met Paul. Now, the bitterness she'd felt toward him welled up in her once more when she thought of the Colonel. He wanted to run her life, and she would never stand still for that again. Well, she would just have to take charge and go ask some questions. She muttered a curse at Colonel Breckenridge, blaming him for the discomfort brought on by this assignment. He wouldn't help a sick child, she thought, clumping slowly through the mud to a wooden structure that looked more substantial than the rest.

Alanna walked in, her hair hanging lifelessly about her pale oval face. Her raincoat was no longer shedding water, but soaking it up instead, and she felt damp and miserable. The flurry of Spanish was thick and fast as several enlisted men manned radios and a number of officers hovered above them. A contingent of six men left, and a few more straggled in, looking just as wet and exhausted as she felt. Finally, Alanna spied the commanding officer and made her way across the dirty floor to him.

After half an hour of haggling, showing him her papers and the necessary documents, Alanna made some progress. She managed to get hold of a soldier to show her where the supplies were being kept. The officer bent and kissed her hand twice, smiling provocatively, his brown, almond-shaped eyes alight with invitation. Alanna remembered the Colonel's warning and smiled politely in return, trying to maintain her dignity regardless of her muddied feet and ankles.

Following the soldier back out into the rain, she noticed more men standing around in huddled groups. There were two helicopters now, and they were both shut down. Looking to the north, she noted low-

hanging white clouds that probably signaled fog stealing in for the afternoon. That meant a delay, she
supposed, as they slogged through the mire to a series
of small shacks surrounded by a barbed wire fence. She
thanked him in Spanish as he unlocked and opened the
door.

The shack was damp-smelling, the odor of medicine
strong in the stale air. It was nearly dark, and Alanna
could barely make out the labels which announced the
contents of each crate. Taking out a pad and pencil
from her purse, she began to write down systematically
the necessary information. She lost track of time,
engrossed in her activity. Hearing the heavy thud of
booted feet, she snapped her head upward.

"You again," the Colonel growled, coming to a halt.
He was dressed in a rubber poncho, looking amazingly
dry despite the rain. For a moment, Alanna found
herself hating him for his apparent comfort. His gaze
roved from her feet up to her head, an unwilling smile
tugging at the corner of his mouth. "Well, I'll say this
for you, you don't quit regardless of difficulties."

Her mouth turned down. "I suppose that's a high
compliment coming from you."

"Yes, it is. You have spunk. I admire that in a
woman."

"Save your compliments for someone who will appreciate them, Colonel."

Matt walked slowly toward her, pushing the cap back
on his head. "I suppose a woman with your good looks
is used to getting compliments all the time."

She gritted her teeth and returned to her work,
trying to ignore him. But, God, he was impossible to
ignore! Just being around him made her feel edgy.
There was something dangerously, vitally male about
him. It was in his walk, his easy banter, the way he
looked at her. . . . Alanna felt herself melting inwardly

every time their eyes met. The senator had warned her about the Marine's ability to charm, and she redoubled her efforts to block him out.

He rested his arm against one of the crates above where she was working. "Well, is it true? You happily married to a man that appreciates your good looks and intelligence?"

Alanna pressed her lips together, aware of the pain in her heart. "That's none of your business," she hissed.

"I see. Sounds like either a divorce or you got jilted. Which was it?"

She rose from her crouched position after copying the numbers off the last crate. "Don't you have anything better to do than interrogate me? I thought you were so worried about getting supplies up to San Dolega."

He took off his hat and scratched his head. "I was until the fog socked us in. Not much we can do at the moment." His voice lost its mocking quality as he frowned, staring into the darkness above her. "We're reduced to three operating jeeps, and even those can't get through. The road is temporarily closed by a large avalanche of mud that occurred an hour ago. The only thing left is for the men to act like pack horses and carry these crates the last five miles on their backs." He sighed, focusing on her. "You're a sight for sore eyes, Miss McIntire. I needed a lift—this day started out rotten, and it's getting worse by the moment. I'm glad I stumbled onto you."

She shrugged off his banter. "What do you mean an avalanche? Aren't the people getting help now?"

"The rains are heavy this time of year, and the earthquake caused a loosening of the topsoil on the mountainsides. The result is an avalanche. The fog is due to cold air mixing with the higher coastal temperatures. This weather system is unusual, so we're more or less outflanked at the moment. And, to answer your question, no."

"I'm sure, with your brilliant tactical mind, you'll come up with something to save the day."

Matt shook his head, biting his lower lip. "Not always."

"Is this entire rescue mission run by the military?"

"Why? Do you think a civilian could come up with a better mousetrap under the present conditions?"

"Probably," she stated boldly. "You're so typical. If you can't blow it up, destroy it, or change it, you don't know how to deal with a problem."

He stared at her hard, some of the tenseness returning to his face. "I happen to have a degree in engineering, and I'm used to building things, Miss McIntire, not destroying them. You've sure got a hate for the military, don't you? But then, you're Thornton's assistant. Did he brainwash you, or did you come prepackaged to his office that way?"

Something snapped inside her, and she struck out at him. He caught her wrist easily, as if he were thwarting a child's paltry attempt at retaliation. "Let me go!"

Matt's eyes twinkled with irony. "My little dove is a hawk in disguise. You talk a good line of pacifism, but at the first provocation, you strike out like a cobra. Who's more aggressive here, lady?" And he suddenly let her go, grinning at her undisguised anger. "How did your boyfriend put up with that temper of yours?"

Alanna backed away from him, her eyes large and her breathing harsh. She rubbed her wrist tenderly, feeling the pain from his grip. "We never argued!" she admitted.

"No? Maybe you should have. A volatile argument every now and then is good for the soul. Now, don't you feel better?"

"No, but maybe I would if I could have hit you. You're such an—an arrogant bastard!"

He continued to smile, enjoying the moment. "And you're a vixen. But a very interesting, provocative one." He picked up the clipboard he had set on a crate. "I'm rather glad you came up. It certainly makes my life interesting."

"Do you always win, Colonel? I mean, does it make you feel good to know you're more powerful or stronger than someone else?"

"I don't always win. But I try my best, and that's all anyone can expect. And I don't normally go around exerting physical force on a woman unless she asks for it." His brows drew together in a downward arc as he watched her. "You don't look Irish, but you certainly have the Gaelic temper."

"My mother was from Hungary," she stated flatly. "They say we Hungarians are pretty volatile, too."

"That's okay. I enjoy a hot-blooded woman. Be seeing you around, Miss McIntire."

She stood there seething for five minutes before her flaring temper subsided back into glowing embers. She felt like a mouse caught between his paws. What was wrong? She had dealt with all kinds of men in her career and held a very prestigious job in political circles. How could a mere officer in the Marine Corps bring her so quickly to defeat? Where had her education failed her? She had always managed to deal with Paul and his intellectualism. But this man—he seemed to know everything about her! That was infuriating in itself, and it strengthened her resolve to prove that he was involved in the smuggling ring linked to Nicaragua.

Her feet were numb with cold as she snapped the padlock back on the door of the shed. The blanket of darkness had fallen quickly, and she turned, blinking as the rain stung her face. Had she ever been so utterly disconsolate? A thought crossed her mind in answer:

yes, living with Paul the last year of their torturous four-year relationship. Bowing her head, she slogged back through the mud toward the headquarters cum communications center.

Alanna shook the water off her raincoat after stepping inside. Her throat constricted as she looked up to see Colonel Breckenridge studying her from where he was standing. He tilted his chin, appraising her thoroughly. The radioman at the desk looked up, calling his name, and he turned away from Alanna's glare.

She waited until he was done and then walked over to him, gripping her briefcase tightly in her hand. "I hate to bother you, Colonel, but I need a place to get cleaned up and sleep tonight. Where are the facilities?"

"I'm sorry. Didn't your friend the commissioner tell you? There are none." He shook his head, amusement evident in his shadowy gray eyes. "I told you to stay in the capital. Up here it's blankets, sleeping bags, or just huddling up into a corner on the dirt floor of a thatched hut. Take your pick."

She gave him a stricken look. "No water? No bathing facilities?"

"No. I tried to tell you before, this is out in the middle of nowhere. We don't cater to civilians or anyone unessential to the rescue efforts. What little water we have is being chlorinated for use by the injured we're receiving off the mountain. Press people and other such personnel have to fend for themselves. There's a barrel of fresh rainwater right outside the door. You might get your hands and face washed there. . . ."

Alanna felt anger coiling inside her. "I'll bet you just love these conditions."

Matt shrugged, walking back to a makeshift desk composed of wood crates that had official-looking papers strewn around on the top of it. "I've had my share of sleeping in jungles," he agreed amiably, "but I prefer a bed when I can get one."

She stood helplessly in front of him. "When is the next flight back to San Jose then?"

"There isn't any. I told you earlier that we're socked in with unseasonable fog conditions. I can't lift a chopper to get to the village, much less to the capital. Everything is at a damn standstill at this moment."

She pursed her lips, the anger draining from her. She was so incredibly tired she felt dizzy. Her feet ached, and she could feel the grit of the soil between her foot and the sole of her ruined shoes. Six years at a university did not prepare one for this, and she felt bitterness toward Senator Thornton. He should have planned this expedition with less haste.

"Look," he said, more gently, "there's a side room over there where I sleep. It's a wood floor, and it will keep most of the insects from biting you. I'll give you half my blankets, and you can use my sleeping bag as a mattress. There's a basin of water in there and a towel."

It sounded heavenly, and Alanna raised her head, meeting his gaze. She felt an inexplicable warmth radiating from him, and she responded to his friendly overture. "You're serious?"

Matt smiled tiredly. "I told you before, I don't say or do anything I don't mean."

"Why are you doing this?" she asked, suddenly distrustful, remembering the senator's words of warning.

"Do you think the military is without a heart, Miss McIntire? That I can't take pity on people that are less well off than I am? You look bushed, and I have a weak spot in my heart for women anyway. So, if you want to share my room for tonight, you're welcome. Simple as that."

She gave him a measuring stare. There was nothing simple about this man, her instincts told her. She tried to probe beyond the honesty expressed in his face and voice. "What do you mean 'share' your bedroom?"

He shrugged lazily, picking up several papers and perusing them. "What do you want it to mean?" he retorted coolly.

"Damn you!" she hissed under her breath, her eyes blazing with the green fire of anger. "I have no intention of sleeping with you!"

"You could do a lot worse. Besides, with the temperature dropping like it is, it's going to get awfully cold before morning. Two bodies make more heat than one. It's simple logic."

"You're out of your mind, Colonel! I wouldn't sleep with you if hell froze over!"

He seemed to enjoy her explosive tirade, smiling as she stood there trembling visibly with fury. "Too bad," he murmured, putting the papers back down. "But since you can't stand the military and hate the sight of me, I don't think we'll have too much trouble sharing the same floor, Miss McIntire. I like to think that the women I sleep with look forward to the experience, and I don't feel like getting my throat slit by you. Rest assured, we'll have a line of demarcation between us tonight. Fair enough?"

Alanna drew in a deep breath, still distrusting that glint in his gray eyes. "Marines have a reputation as far as women go," she accused.

"That we enjoy them? I can't deny one word of it. Go get cleaned up, and quit looking like I'm going to pounce on you or something."

She felt human again after she got cleaned up with the aid of a small bar of soap and Colonel Breckenridge's olive green washcloth and towel. Taking her small suitcase, she pulled out a set of well-worn jeans and her only pair of socks and canvas shoes. The room was quiet except for the constant chatter of the radio transmissions drifting through the thin wooden door. She turned her back away from it, slipping off the damp blouse and bra, drawing a thin sweater over her head. It would be just like him to come in unannounced, she thought. God, how he provoked her! She hated his cool logic and his constant sniping at the political people she worked for.

His "bed" was a sad-looking affair. Alanna left him one green blanket and took the other one and the sleeping bag. She placed them strategically in the corner opposite his huge pack and the remaining rumpled blanket. Taking a mirror out of her purse, she tried to decide what to do with her drying hair.

She noticed dark circles beginning to appear beneath her large green eyes and touched one hesitantly. She was exhausted, although fighting with the Colonel seemed to increase her adrenaline, and the cold water had washed away some of her tiredness. Trying to make the best of the situation, she sat cross-legged on the floor and patiently parted her long hair, then wove the strands into two thick braids, tying the ends off with rubber bands she carried in her purse. Her stomach growled, and she looked up toward the door, frowning. Where could she get something to eat? Groaning, she got up, realizing she would have to talk to Colonel Breckenridge, *again*. Trying to put a choke chain on her temper, she slipped out the door and walked over to the desk where he sat.

For an instant, Alanna felt her heart tighten with compassion for him. He was resting his head in one hand, his brow furrowed in deep concentration as he studied a map in front of him. Gone was the mask that he seemed to hide beneath. Instead, the lines of weariness were accented at the corners of his narrowed eyes and around his mouth. He sat up, inhaling deeply as she quietly approached him. His eyes flared briefly with an unknown emotion as he took in her form.

"I didn't know you could work miracles," he murmured, putting the compass on the map.

"What do you mean?" She sounded defensive again. Damn. She was beginning to understand that if she lost her temper with him, it only made communicating more difficult. Alanna tried to compose herself and forced a smile she did not feel.

"You look like the girl back home," he commented, motioning toward her braids. "A farm girl from Iowa or some small Midwest town. None of that better-than-thou Washington stamp on you any longer."

"You mean less sophisticated?" she asked, restless beneath his hungry look.

"No, you still have class. That would show through no matter what you did or did not wear."

Alanna blushed scarlet, and she automatically touched her cheek, put off balance by his unexpected, brusque compliments. "Colonel—"

"You're very pretty when you blush, Alanna. Feel better now that you've got on some dry clothes?"

"Yes. Thank you." She cleared her throat, nervously shifting her feet. "I'm afraid to even ask if there's food available up here. Is there?"

"If you're a refugee from the village or part of the relief effort, yes. There's a small chow hall in operation at the end hut on the northern perimeter of the base."

"But I'm not a refugee, am I?" she growled back, understanding his faultless logic.

"In a sense you are. Thrown completely out of your element into a set of circumstances that you're unprepared for."

"I'm not some poor, lost waif! If you'll just tell me where I can buy some food . . ."

"Right now, with supplies running low, there isn't any amount of money that will buy food."

She raised her eyes skyward in reaction. "What do I have to do to get some food!" she asked tightly. "Would it go better if I begged?"

Matt shook his head. "You wouldn't make a very convincing beggar, lady." He slowly rose, as if stiff. He flexed his right shoulder in a rotating motion, frowning.

"Did you hurt yourself?" she blurted out, before she could stop her concern from expressing itself.

"Hmm? No. Old wound. It gets cranky when the weather is damp and cold." He studied her. "It's nice of you to care, though. That's a new twist for a political dove from D.C."

Alanna seethed inwardly, gritting her teeth. "God, you're so distrustful of my every action!"

Matt laughed, picking up his poncho and shrugging into it. "I have a hard time trusting any politician. Were you born a liberal, I wonder?"

"Don't make fun of what I believe in, Colonel. I won't change my views or ideas for food or shelter. Just because you're a born soldier, that doesn't give you the right to be rude to me."

"Maybe you're right. I owe you an apology. Why don't you go settle down, and I'll rummage around the chow hall and get something to eat for both of us. I'll be back in a few minutes. Anyway, we need to get some food into you so you won't look so damn skinny."

Alanna grudgingly admitted he was right on one point: she was skinny. It was a result of the long hours she put in at the senator's office. Trudging back to the small, barren room, she pulled the blanket over her shoulders and lay down on the inviting sleeping bag. Rolling the other blanket into a makeshift pillow, she closed her eyes for just a moment. Her thoughts spiraled around Matt Breckenridge. Despite their arguments, she found herself inexorably drawn to him. He was nothing like Paul. Just the opposite in fact. Paul was so distant, so detached that she doubted he knew what it was to lose his temper. And she had never lost hers in those years either. Now, with this Marine officer, it was like the Fourth of July every time they got within ten feet of one another. Paul had taught her to control her emotions. But Matt Breckenridge actually seemed to enjoy her outbursts. She sighed loudly, utterly confused and drained by the day's events. She didn't mean to, but she plunged into a deep, healing sleep almost immediately.

Chapter Three

*A*lanna moaned, partially aware of a hand on her shoulder, shaking her gently awake. She rolled over on her back, sleepily opening her eyes. Matt Breckenridge's concerned face came into view in the darkness. She frowned, almost frightened by the shadows that played across his strong, masculine face as he watched her.

"Uh," she groaned, slowly moving up into a sitting position, "what time is it?"

"Twenty-one hundred, or 9 P.M. to you civilians," he said with a half-smile. He rested back on his haunches, frowning. "You all right? You look pale as hell."

Alanna sleepily rubbed her eyes, pulling the blanket around her for warmth. The room seemed damper and colder as she looked around. A small kerosene lantern sat in the corner, giving off a weak semblance of light to the room and an odor that made her wrinkle her nose. "Yes—I'm fine. Just terribly tired."

"So it's true what they say about Senator Thornton, then. He works his people like slaves."

It was a statement. Not a question. Groggy and too weary to throw up her usual barriers of defense, she said, "I already put in seventy hours this week. Usually it's only sixty."

He shook his head slowly. "No wonder you're underweight. Don't you have anyone who takes care of you?"

A knot formed in her throat, and she closed her eyes for a moment. "I can take care of myself."

"Well, you need someone to help you expend all that energy you have," he answered gruffly, getting to his feet.

Alanna yawned, still wrapped in the euphoric embrace of awakening. The Colonel seemed infinitely more gentle now, and she felt herself relaxing for the first time since they had met. His booted feet sounded hollowly against the floor boards as he stopped and squatted back down in front of her. "Here's dinner," he said, handing her a Marine Corps issue mess kit. "When I got back, you were sleeping like there was no tomorrow. I decided that you needed sleep more than food. It's cold but palatable."

She took the lightweight metal plate, staring at the heaping amount of food piled on it. "There's so much!" she protested softly, giving him a stricken look. "I don't want to take food from the survivors."

He sat down by her, pulling up one leg and wrapping his arms about it, giving her an odd, searching look. "You're sincere, aren't you?"

She set the plate down on her lap. "Yes. Of course."

"Good. It becomes you. Maybe you're not the typical Hill politico after all. And don't worry, I didn't pull this food out of the starving mouth of some refugee. Now be quiet and eat."

Occasionally she glanced up at him as she wolfed down the food. It consisted of refried beans, corn mush, and a small piece of fried Spam, but it tasted delicious. To her own surprise, she ate every morsel. "I guess the mountain air improves the appetite," she offered sheepishly.

He took the plate, setting it by his side, and met her smile. In the gloom, he looked haggard and drawn, and Alanna wondered how long it had been since he had slept. "How are things going?" she inquired.

"Let's put it this way, Murphy's law hasn't got anything on us at the moment," he commented wryly.

Alanna laughed gently. "The axiom about 'if anything can go wrong it will'?"

"Yes. And there's an extension to that law: 'nothing is ever so bad that it can't get worse,' and that's exactly where we're at right now." He rubbed his forehead in consternation, staring off into the bleakness. "The fog is thickening, and the chief meteorologist in San Jose is projecting that it's going to hang around for two more days before we get some clearing."

Alanna crossed her legs, resting her arms on her thighs. "But you mentioned you were trucking up the supplies earlier."

"The trucks can only go so far and so fast. With choppers we can zip in and out, pick up the worst injuries, and have them down here for initial medical help in no time. I've got ten cases that require surgery, and now they're going to have to be carried over five miles on a stretcher to the jeeps, then bounced over these mountain roads to the hospital. Or, I can leave them up there waiting, and they might die during the night." He glanced over at her, his eyes broadcasting his undisguised concern. "Truck or auto is no way to transport people who need emergency medical treatment. They can die of shock in a matter of hours."

"You sound as if you know a great deal about it."

He shrugged, staring back into the darkness. "I'm a paramedic."

"I didn't know Marine officers practiced medicine," she commented, looking at him in a different light. The senator had always accused Breckenridge of being a bloody warmonger after a high body count. This was the second time that Alanna saw that claim refuted. He was an engineer who built structures and a paramedic who saved lives.

Matt shut his eyes, resting his head on his arm. "I was in a special contingent of the Marine Corps."

"What was that?"

"Recons."

Alanna felt genuine compassion flood her breast. He seemed so drained. In the pallid light, his skin looked taut and washed out. "I'm sorry, I'm not familiar with them."

"Most people aren't. It's a special branch of the Marine Corps that is molded into a crack surveillance unit to penetrate behind enemy lines. The reconnaissance information gained can be very important when our troops have to engage the enemy. We recorded troop movements for a period of five to ten days and then helicoptered out to the safety of our own lines. In a way, Recons save the lives of many men."

She shivered. "It sounds awfully dangerous."

"It can be."

"Is that why you became a paramedic, then?"

"Each member of the Recon team had to be a specialist in some field. I picked the medical end." He raised his head, rubbing his face slowly. "At least there was some honor in trying to save a life instead of having to take one."

She looked at him strangely, wondering at the softness in his voice. "I don't understand."

He smiled almost bashfully. "I delivered six babies while I was over in Nam. It sort of made up for the rest of it. . . . It gave me a clean feeling. Bringing life into the world instead of only watching it being taken."

"You delivered babies?"

"Sure. Why not?"

Alanna withheld her comment. It was a cruel one that he didn't deserve. He met her gaze fully, assessing her silently.

"You wonder how a trained soldier like me can revel in giving life rather than taking it, don't you?"

She trembled inwardly, suddenly tearing her gaze away from his weary features. How frighteningly honest he was. And how accepting he was of her less than compassionate view of him. It had to hurt him to see the way she stereotyped him because of the career he had chosen. Her brows drew downward, and she refused to answer, feeling the heat of a blush creeping up her neck and into her cheeks. The moments lengthened uncomfortably between them, and she licked her lips.

"Does—doesn't it bother you that people are repelled by your profession?"

"It used to when I was younger. It doesn't matter anymore. I've been through so much in such a short period of time, it's easy to separate what's really important in living and what is not."

"You make it sound as if you went through hell."

He managed a patient smile. "Everyone has his or her own conception of hell, Alanna. Take yourself: you view this experience as hell. There's no bed, no hot water, very little food. To me, this is luxury. I've spent too many years sleeping on the hard ground, in water-filled foxholes or in trees hiding from the enemy. A wood floor and a sleeping bag seems like heaven." His eyes crinkled as he smiled. "So you see, hell is a relative term, depending upon your past experiences."

"Obviously," she agreed quietly, gaining new and

increasing respect for him, regardless of what the senator had said. He wasn't trying to cajole her or twist her thinking. And she knew it. Alanna was almost positive he rarely talked this way to anyone, and that knowledge confused her. She was his enemy. She was out to ruin his military career by proving he was a smuggler. Guilt twinged at her conscience as she watched him. There was a quiet calmness that emanated from him as steadily as a beacon shining in the darkness. A depth of peace and a rock solidness that made her feel protected. And if something did go wrong, she knew Matt would do everything in his power to save her.

She jolted herself back to reality. What on earth was she doing? He was no knight in shining armor on a white steed. Alanna, you're too old to allow romantic thoughts to sway you from the position you've taken, she chided herself.

"Look," he said, interrupting her thoughts, "I'm going to try to catch a few hours' sleep. Are you warm enough with these?"

"Yes. Will you be warm enough? I mean, you've only got one—"

Matt rose, ambling over to the corner and shutting off the kerosene lamp. "I'll be fine," he assured her. "Good night."

She snuggled back down into the wiry wool blankets, pulling her legs up and curling into a kittenlike position. She heard him unlacing his boots and setting them on the floor. Soon, quietness pervaded the small room, and only muted voices in the next room and the constant sharp static of the radios interrupted the silence. Some time before she returned to sleep, she thought she heard the softened breathing of Matt Breckenridge and knew he had finally found an edge of peace in sleep.

* * *

Alanna awoke slowly, feeling drugged and groggy. Voices, low and urgent, became intelligible as she struggled out of the stupor. She forced her eyes open. A wedge of light slipped through the partially opened door, and she focused her attention on the whispered conversation.

"Matt, we've got to get up there. . . ."

"What are the weather conditions, Cauley?" he mumbled.

A sigh of exasperation broke from the other man. "The same. Dammit, we've got three children up there that were just found under a fallen structure. Two are seriously injured, and the third is close to death. If we can get a chopper up there and—"

"You're asking me to risk one of only three choppers, plus you, the pilot. I won't allow it, Cauley. It doesn't make any sense to lose one-third of our aircraft for an emergency flight in below-minimum conditions. Use your head."

"Matt . . . please . . . dammit, one of those kids is only four years old! I can fly it. God, how many times did I fly you and your team in and out of worse situations? At least we aren't getting shot at this time. I can do it. I know I can. Give me the chance!"

Alanna froze, holding her breath in anticipation of Matt's answer. She was wide awake now, tortured by the urgency of the pilot's plea.

"Cauley, this isn't war. And I know you're a crack pilot. What if I lose you? Do you know how long it will take to get a replacement? I don't have that kind of time. And what if you do crash? I'll have to take part of my men and search for you. I need every man I've got. We're short-handed and short on time. I can't afford to lose you, Cauley. If there wasn't this rotten weather, I'd okay it."

The pilot rose. "You owe me one, Matt," he growled

softly. "I'm collecting it now, buddy. I picked up your men against orders with Cong on both flanks and your backs to the river. You owe me. Six men were saved then. Let me try to save three lives now."

"You went against *my* orders," Matt gritted out, rising to his feet. "I don't owe you for that one, Cauley," he breathed harshly. Silence settled between them for tense moments. "Dammit," he said finally, "why is it always children? Look, you get Blake on the radio up there, and tell him we're going to try an emergency landing. Tell him to fire a green flare when he hears us and then ring the landing zone with red flares. Get Corporal Travis to alert the medical unit up there that we're coming in for those kids."

Alanna heard Cauley laugh softly. "Thanks, Matt. Just like old times, isn't it? Nothing in our favor and everything going against us."

"Yeah. Old times," he agreed flatly. "We'll try once, Cauley. And if we don't make it in, we're coming home . . . if we can get back."

Cauley slapped him on the shoulder. "You're a cold-hearted bastard, Breckenridge, but a hell of a Marine."

Alanna sat up, studying him as he entered the room, yanked on his boots, and picked up his jacket. "Are you going?" she breathed huskily.

His head jerked up, and he stared across the room at her. "You heard?"

"Sorry. I couldn't help it. Is—is there anything I can do?"

He laced the boots quickly. "Yeah, bring some sanity back into this whole goddamn situation." He moved fluidly to his feet, pulling on his heavy jacket and jamming the hat down on his head. Alanna stood, uncertainly clutching the blankets to her body.

"Then why are you doing it?" she demanded.

He halted abruptly in front of her, his eyes narrowed and intense. "For the kids. What else?"

"You could be killed."

He managed a cutting smile. "Would you miss me?"

She sobered, her throat aching with tension. "Yes," she admitted softly, avoiding his startled look.

He threw his hands on his hips. "I'll be damned," he muttered and suddenly reached out.

Alanna felt his hands upon her arms, gently drawing her against his hard, masculine body. It was so natural, so elemental. Her body rested against him fully, aware of his musky male odor. His mouth, strong and demanding, came down on her lips. He moved insistently against her, parting her lips with a ferocity that left her breathless and stunned in its wake. His hands tightened, pulling her suddenly closer. An explosion of fire seemed to go off in her spinning head. Her senses thrilled to his touch as his mouth softened against her pliant lips, becoming more gentle, coaxing. A small moan of pleasure sounded deep in her throat. She lost all sense of time and place, her fingers clutching at the fabric of his jacket, and her knees threatened to buckle beneath her.

She felt his mouth withdraw from her throbbing lips, and she leaned heavily against him, trying to reorient herself. Slowly, he lowered her to the floor. Her pulse raced as she gazed wide-eyed up at him, her heart contracting in her breast as she saw the hungry, undisguised desire ignited in his gray eyes. But there was a surprising look of tenderness there, too. He managed a small smile, reluctantly releasing her. "Lady, you are an incredible paradox," he whispered huskily, and then his eyes gleamed with amusement. "Don't go anywhere while I'm gone."

Alanna couldn't find her voice as he rose and spun around, heading for the door. She sat there, too shocked to move. What was happening to her? Why had she allowed him to kiss her? My God, what was wrong? Another, more frightening thought entered her spinning mind as she heard the helicopter blades whirring at a higher pitch somewhere outside in the blackness. What if something happened to Matt? Unsteadily, she got to her feet, walking out into the communications room, where the radioman stood at the window, watching.

He turned, glanced briefly at her, and then returned his attention to the unseen helicopter. Alanna stood beside him, listening to the rising crescendo of noise. The hut seemed to tremble as the helicopter lifted off into the impenetrable fog and darkness. She touched her lips, recalling his soul-branding kiss. My God, she had *never* been kissed like that before.

"Will they make it?" she asked after long, agonizing moments, her voice sounding strained.

"I don't know, ma'am." He scratched his head, turning away and going back to his assigned work. "Man, they've gotta be crazy, if you ask me. Choppers only fly by sight. Major Cauley had better have radar eyes, and the colonel better hope he still has the luck he had in Nam."

Alanna turned, stunned. "They really could crash?" she asked, her voice painfully hoarse.

"Sure. They're flying completely blind. I've ridden in enough choppers to know that it takes a crazy Marine pilot to go up in weather like this. They fly on gut instinct when all else fails."

Alanna felt dizzy, and she leaned against the wall. No, this couldn't be happening. Matt Breckenridge was too vital, too alive to die on some unknown jungle mountainside. Oh, God, she prayed, be with them. Guide them in. Don't let him die. Please, don't . . .

"Ma'am?" the radioman asked, coming back over to her. He touched her arm. "You look like you might faint. Come here, sit down for a moment." With concern in his voice, he continued, "I'm sorry, I spouted off about things I shouldn't have. They'll be all right. You wait and see. Can I get you some water?"

Alanna shut her eyes tightly for a moment. "No—no, I'm okay." She mustered a broken smile, looking up at his youthful features. "I'm—I'm not used to all this kind of excitement. A civilian," she explained lamely.

He shrugged and smiled. "Yeah, I guess you kinda have to get used to military operations. I'm not saying that what the major is doing is commonplace, but we're trained for emergency situations. And if anyone can pull it off, those two can. You know they did a lot of flying together in Nam?"

Alanna shook her head, only half-listening to the Marine corporal's conversation. Her thoughts revolved around the fact that military personnel were trained to accept sudden, unexpected situations as easily as breathing air. It was so different from her peaceful, neatly organized life. Until now. She wrapped her arms around herself, feeling suddenly chilled. Conflicting emotions raged within her. Matt's kiss . . . her body thrilled to that memory even now, and she felt giddy. Paul's kisses had never inflamed her as Matt's did. And to make it worse, Matt was the man who had caused Tim's death. She hung her head, utterly bewildered.

As the radio crackled to life, she jumped. It was Major Cauley's voice coming in loud and clear, reporting the spotting of the green flare. Alanna rose, giving the chair back to the Marine. She stood close, her hand covering her mouth in anticipation as she heard Matt's voice come over the airwaves. Her heart accelerated a beat, and she felt frozen to the spot. He was calling out the air speed and miles. He made a terse remark about how close the tall mahogany trees were to the helicopter as they slowly began their careful descent. She clutched her hands together as they moved below tree level. What if they had miscalculated the distance to the village? One rotor blade smashing into a tree would surely cause them to nose suddenly into the ground.

"I see it!" Cauley announced excitedly. "The red flares!"

Alanna took in a deep breath, grateful for Cauley's triumphant discovery. The radioman looked up, grinning happily.

"See, I told you so."

"Yes, you did, Corporal. I'm glad you were right. What about them getting back down here?"

"We'll follow the same procedure at this end."

The radio chatter ended, and Alanna hung around the radio, occasionally looking out in the darkness that was now turning gray with the promise of dawn. Finally, she heard Matt calling the radioman. In approximately twenty minutes, they would be landing. She closed her eyes, her heart and body responding to his husky voice. How could one man so completely disrupt her complacent life style?

She became aware of Marines and Costa Rican police gathering outside.

Several stretchers were stacked nearby, and the men waited in the thick fog like dark apparitions. Finally, the flares were lit, and then she heard the puncturing beat of rotor blades overhead. Cauley's happy voice exploded over the intercom.

"We've made it! We did it! Look out, here we come."

She felt a surge of joy rising in her breast as she returned to the window, watching the unwieldy helicopter slowly lower itself into the muddy area outside the hut. Tears crowded into her eyes as she saw the men running forward with the stretchers to be swallowed up by the wall of fog. Brushing the tears away, Alanna turned and walked back to the bedroom.

She tried desperately to sort out the turmoil of her

feelings. All too soon, she heard Cauley's jubilant words as he entered the hut and several other men's voices raised in laughter. She drew her knees up, resting her chin on them, and stared at the lone blanket in the opposite corner where Matt had slept briefly. The raucous joking and laughter continued for another ten minutes, and she managed a sliver of a smile as she heard Cauley telling his story.

The major's voice bubbled with excitement and relief. "As we dropped down the first time, I told Matt to be ready to kiss his rear good-bye if we hit anything."

"That ring of flares," Matt interrupted drily, "looked like a dull glow even ten feet up."

"Yeah," another voice interjected, "we noticed the left side of the chopper is smashed in. What'dja do, Major Cauley, try to land it on its nose?"

"Hell, no," Cauley chortled. "Things were so bad I set the girl to the left of the landing circle the first time. We found ourselves in the supply crates. If you think the nose looks bad, you should see the crates! Some new paint and it'll look like new, right Matt?" Cauley asked.

"It will, but I won't," he returned.

Alanna listened as the entire group exploded into laughter. She realized it was one way to relax after the harrowing event. From the sound of it, they were lucky they hadn't crashed. But her own tension was not so easily relieved. She was upset and unsure of herself due to his unexpected kiss. Humiliation flooded her at the thought of the way she'd allowed herself to be swept uncompromisingly into his arms. She had been frightened for him, and he had taken advantage of the situation!

Closing her eyes and rubbing her temples to ease the nagging headache, Alanna tried to find some acceptable excuse for her erratic behavior. She could hear

Paul's droning voice buzzing in her head: "Really, Alanna, logic should have told you the answer. Push aside your emotions and look at the black and white of the situation. If you do that, then answers become clear, and you don't knock yourself out with worry and anxiety. . . ."

Sighing, she opened her troubled eyes. Logic and emotion. Did they *ever* go together? Or were they like Matt Breckenridge and herself—too different to be combined? Alanna knew one thing: she would never allow the Marine colonel to touch her again. His kiss had evoked too many explosive emotions she thought finally controlled.

Chapter Four

She forced herself to go back to sleep, shutting out the noises from the other room. Her anger simmered just beneath the surface until utter exhaustion drew her back down into the folds of blackness.

It was daylight when she awoke the second time. Stretching stiffly, she sat up, feeling the chill of the room. Fog hovered around the small, paned windows, and she rubbed her hands briskly to get the circulation going. The door opened, and Matt smiled benignly, hesitating. "Just wake up?"

Ignoring his genial tone, Alanna frowned darkly and turned her back toward him. She heard him walking over to her and tensed as he halted at her side.

"I thought you might like to know we got the kids down off the mountain. They're probably in San Jose by now," he said, checking his watch. "It's nearly eleven o'clock."

"I'm surprised you're concerned about them at all,"

she stated icily, standing and folding the blankets. Fervently, she hoped her ruse would throw him off the track. She didn't want to discuss the kiss or invite further advances on his part. If she pretended not to understand their uneasy truce of the night before, it might keep him stymied so she could complete her investigation. He was much safer to deal with as an enemy. This morning, logic would dictate her decisions.

"What do you mean?"

Alanna stole a glance at him. He looked and sounded puzzled by her accusation. "That radioman was right, you're all crazy!" And she gave the last blanket a tight fold, throwing it on top of the sleeping bag. "You men remind me of boys who never grew up, Colonel. Little boys in uniform. Well, the uniform might fool some people, but not me."

He frowned, his gray eyes darkening with an indecipherable emotion. "Of course we cared about the kids," he snapped back. "What the hell do you think we made that trip up there for?"

She stuffed her feet into her shoes, pointedly remaining silent. Today she intended to count the rest of the supplies and then go up to San Dolega and find out if they were all arriving from the base camp. She heard him walking toward her, and Alanna spun around, cringing away from him, her back against the wall. "Don't touch me," she warned.

He halted, glowering down at her. "What's gotten into you, Alanna? One minute you're warm, responsive. The next—"

"A bitch," she finished, grabbing her coat and shrugging it on. "And you're going to find out the hard way, Colonel. I'm through with all your tricks. I'm only going to say this once—I want to go up to that village later today. You had better provide me with transportation."

"It's out of the question and you know it. You're stuck here whether you like it or not."

She felt her fury slipping as she watched the puzzlement grow in his eyes. Good, let him get into a quandary. It was his turn. "You're going to find out just how much political clout I've got behind me," she gritted coldly and walked quickly out of the room, wanting to be as far away from him as possible.

The rain began again at two o'clock, just as she finished counting the crates in the final building. Resting momentarily, she felt the weariness but ignored it. It was time to confront Colonel Breckenridge. In the makeshift building that housed Costa Rican police personnel, she was provided with dispatches she had been expecting from Washington. Armed with them, she went directly to the Colonel's quarters, feeling the tiredness slip from her shoulders to be replaced by a sense of power.

She found the Colonel back at his desk poring over several bills of lading and attempting to handle an argument between two Costa Ricans who were squabbling noisily. Alanna leaned back against the door momentarily, a grim smile on her face. He looked absolutely frustrated. Finally, he looked up, his eyes lighting with pleasure at the sight of her.

"I need your linguistic ability," he coaxed. "Come over here and interpret for me, will you? Either that, or I'm going to throw both of them out the front door."

She hesitated, thinking of the fiery kiss he had placed on her lips the day before. She hadn't forgotten it for one hour or one minute since then. "It will cost you, Colonel," she warned as she sauntered over.

"If you can get these two off my back," he answered grimly, "you can have the moon if you want."

"What I want will be close to that," she promised sweetly. Within a few minutes, the entire matter was set straight, and she had to smile to herself, watching Matt's face take on a look of relief. He looked harried, running his fingers through his hair more than once. After the pacified drivers left, he leaned back in the straight-backed wooden chair, sizing her up. He pointed at the yellow papers in front of him.

"You wonder why we have missing supplies? Here's part of the answer." He waved three sheets of official but tattered papers at her. "The truck driver receives a set of these when he picks up his load at the ship or airport. Then the warehouse provides another set which are invariably modified by the time the driver leaves the front gate." His voice tightened with frustration. "I guess it's too difficult to call a crate a crate instead of a carton, box, or container. When our men inventory the contents, we have four sets of numbers attempting to identify the same shipment." He shook his head, slowly getting to his feet and stretching.

"I have my own set of numbers, Colonel," she assured him briskly. "And I believe you owe me one."

He nodded, moving around the desk and pouring a cup of coffee into a tin mug. "You want some?" he asked. "It's instant, but it tastes a hell of a lot better than halizoned water."

"No, thank you."

"Oh, you like stronger stuff? Wine? Maybe Scotch. I understand that's the 'in' drink up on the Hill: Scotch on the rocks."

She put a chain on her temper. "I prefer a light claret, Colonel. As I'm sure you don't have any here, it's pointless to discuss the subject. Anyway, I want you to look at these orders." She stressed the word "orders," because that was exactly what they were. Orders from Marine Corps General Frederick to Colonel Breckenridge. She watched with satisfaction as he languidly unfolded the crisp white papers and sat back down at the desk. Taking a sip of his coffee, he frowned as he read through them. The skin across his cheek-bones tightened, and his mouth thinned into a single line. He looked up slowly.

"So, Senator Thornton got the brass over at the Pentagon to issue these orders. Your ability to manipulate impresses me," he said in a dangerously low whisper. "Do you realize what you've done?"

"I'm keenly aware of what I've done." Her heart skipped erratically, and it wasn't from anticipation. Her feelings bordered on fear as she saw the violent glint in his gray eyes.

"You didn't have to do this," he murmured. "Not this way and not now. I would have got one of the jeep drivers to take you up just as soon as the fog lifted. It wasn't necessary, Alanna."

She heard a note of hurt in his voice. Or was it disappointment? "The only thing you seem to understand and respect is power, Colonel. And that's exactly the game we're going to play here from now on. Politicians versus military. Dove versus hawk. Call it what you like. I want results. And I'm working for a senator who wants them now. You're ordered to personally take me up to San Dolega. *Right now.* I'm sure you have an aide who can take over here while you drop me off. It should only take an hour or two of your time."

Matt deliberately set the orders down, staring up at her. "I don't believe this is the real Alanna talking to me. What's happened? What's gone wrong? Did Senator Thornton call you and start screaming at you to get some results? What?"

She felt the blush sweeping over her cheeks and silently cursed the telltale sign. "If I told you, you wouldn't understand. You didn't this morning, and I don't think you ever will," she said defensively. "We're two different breeds of people. And all I want to do right now is finish this job and get as far away from you and this place as possible."

He studied her for a long time. Finally, he stared back down at the orders. "Are you sure this is what you want? If you can't wait twelve hours more until this fog lifts, I'm not going to be responsible for you or my actions."

Alanna's eyes widened at the softly spoken threat. He looked absolutely emotionless. His voice was as hard as tempered steel. A ribbon of fear jolted through her. What did he mean? Her throat ached with tension, but she forced the words out. "You're not making sense. You have your orders, now carry them out."

He stood, a hawk ready to make the kill, and she sensed the anger which up until now had been hidden. She took two steps back, stunned by his implacable determination. His hand shot out quickly, and she gasped as his fingers closed in a viselike grip around her upper arm. He guided her to the door, throwing it open and placing her outside it.

"You stay right there, Miss McIntire. I will be back in exactly five minutes, and then we'll leave for San Dolega," he snarled under his breath. "You want to play tough? We'll play it your way."

She stood there trembling, huddled against the hut, trying to keep out of the rain. She wasn't quite sure what was going to happen next, but she tried to convince herself that she could handle it. She closed her eyes, trying to take a steadying breath. She would *never* understand the military or the minds that ran it! Damn them all!

In exactly five minutes, Matt Breckenridge drove up in a military jeep. It had no protective covering over the top of it to keep the rain out. He was dressed in his poncho, his cap drawn down over his eyes so that she could not see his expression. Perhaps that was a blessing. In the rear was a huge pack with a small shovel attached to the back of it.

"Get in," he ordered tersely.

She slid onto the wet, slippery seat, gripping the metal siding as he yanked the jeep into gear. The vehicle slewed through the mud as he ground through a series of loud, noisy gears. The base camp disappeared behind them and was replaced with a rutted excuse for a single-lane road which wound beneath the tall tops of the mahogany forest that dominated the landscape. Rain slashed unrelentingly against her face, and she held up her hands to protect her eyes, compressing her lips in anger over his inconsiderate behavior.

It was a nightmarish ride. She had no idea how long they had driven; she was only aware of the continual bumping and jolting of the jeep as it roared through three inches of mud and the hardened ruts that had been created during the dry season. Her hips and thighs were bruised black and blue, and her back ached from the terrific strain placed upon it as the jeep leaped out of one rut and landed heavily in another. Fog swirled chokingly around them, and Alanna was grimly determined not to cry out. Not even once. She knew it would give him a measure of satisfaction. But he was going to get not one ounce of it from her.

Finally, they halted at the end of the road. Alanna's eyes widened as she saw at least two hundred crates of supplies stacked up before them and military and civilian men carrying them on their backs up a narrow mountain trail that seemed to disappear into the fog. Matt turned the key off, jammed it in his trouser pocket, and got out.

"All right, Miss McIntire, I suggest you roust yourself out of the jeep and hit the deck. We've got some walking to do."

Alanna stared stupidly at the line of porters slowly struggling up the steep grade and then swung her gaze to Matt, who was shrugging into the pack. "But," she stammered lamely, "you didn't say we had to walk."

"You didn't bother to ask before setting your plan into motion. I believe it was you who stressed the orders meant 'right now,'" he growled. "If you are really interested in reaching San Dolega, you have to walk, because the orders did not specify that I had to carry you. At your pleasure, Miss McIntire, the road to San Dolega," he added with a tight smile of triumph. "Come on, we've only got five miles and three thousand feet to go." He studied the thinning fog. "And maybe, if we're lucky, this fog will keep clearing as we get closer to the village."

She felt tears gathering in her eyes, a wave of humiliation sweeping across her. Why did she back herself into a corner with him every time? Five miles in her leather shoes? Alanna sighed, taking a grip on her briefcase, and walked carefully around the jeep. Without even a backward glance, he started off toward the mountain trail, and she silently followed, pushing to keep up with his long, fluid strides.

The jungle was forbidding, closing in on all sides as they walked beneath its canopy. Alanna heard him calling out to the porters, giving them words of encouragement as first he and then she passed them at a faster pace. She couldn't imagine carrying a thirty-pound crate on her shoulders for five miles in any circumstances. At one point, she caught up with him. Or did he slow down for her? She was gasping for air and vaguely remembered that the village was seventy-five hundred feet above sea level. Oxygen became sparse at that altitude. Her throat felt on fire, and she gulped down more air.

"Why are you carrying that pack?" she asked.

"Because it's a mobile home. It has everything I need to survive out here for seven days."

She eyed the canteen on the web belt around his

waist. "Please," she whispered, "I need a drink of water."

"Did you bring any?" he asked coolly, catching her startled look.

"Why—of course not. I thought . . . I thought you would share."

"Did you bother to inform me of your actions before you initiated them?" he demanded, slowing.

"I didn't have to!" she defended hotly, her voice becoming hoarse.

"It's called chain of command, lady. Something political people seem to ignore constantly. You reduce everything to trading so-called favors when, in essence, you're blackmailing."

"Damn jarhead," she hissed, jerking to a stop.

He turned, grinning. "Now where did you pick up that kind of language? I didn't think civilians knew any of the technical terms for a Marine."

"Technical term?" Alanna gasped. "That's an outright insult."

"If you had called me an Army dogface, then I might have gotten angry," he returned blandly. He reached down in his web belt, loosening the canteen and slowly unscrewing the cap before handing it to her. "Only drink a little," he warned. "At this altitude and with another four miles to go, you don't want it sloshing around in your stomach."

Her mouth felt as if it were full of cotton balls, and she eagerly reached for the canteen, putting it to her lips and swallowing a huge gulp. With a cry, she spit it out. "This is horrible," she wailed.

He gave her an impatient look. "Halizone has been put in it for your protection. If those tablets weren't dropped in there, you'd probably get dysentery. Now take a swallow and let's get going. And don't waste any more of my water."

She grudgingly took a small sip, wrinkling her nose in

utter distaste over the foul-tasting water. Matt, however, seemed hardly to notice the taste when he took a drink of it himself. Turning, he began to walk, only this time at an obviously slower pace for her benefit. Alanna cast a mournful look down at her pants. They were muddied up to her knees. Her feet were cold, and her toes felt numb as she forced herself to keep pace beside him. The jungle looked forbidding and threatening right now, and she felt anything but brave. In a way, she was thankful for his presence, even if it was an irritating one.

"What school did you graduate from?" he asked conversationally.

Alanna peered up at him, taken off guard by his friendly tone. For a moment she considered ignoring him but decided it was an unwise move. She might need to drink more water, and she wouldn't put it past him to refuse her if he felt so inclined. "Radcliffe."

"Did you major in political science?"

"Yes. How did you know?"

"A logical guess."

"I suppose I look like all those other politicos up there on the Hill. We all have black, beady, weasel eyes and are out to lie to the public and grovel for our power positions," she muttered.

He laughed. It was a full, resonant laugh that reverberated within the small cleared area of the jungle, and Alanna found herself warming to it.

"Hardly, lady. You're a sight for sore eyes under any circumstances, believe me. No, your problem is that you try to replace your intuition with rationalization and end up making the wrong decision. Such as this fiasco we're on now."

Alanna smirked. "Thanks for reminding me. But I still value my logic."

"Women were made to feel out situations," he commented seriously.

She laughed bitterly. "It goes without saying that you're a typical male chauvinist."

"No, you didn't hear what I said. Women think differently than men. For instance"—he pointed toward the jungle wall to their right—"most men would only see that as a barrier of trees and vines and a path in front of them. But a woman would take in much more—the odors, the sounds, the colors—utilizing all of her five senses to a greater degree than her male counterpart." He allowed a small grin, watching her closely. "I'm saying that you're cheating yourself by trying to rule your five senses with logic."

Alanna mulled it over. What he said did make sense. "How did you stumble onto this little gem of wisdom?"

"I found out the hard way," he offered. "Two years in a jungle getting hunted by the enemy and you become more aware of the five senses. You learn to depend on your intuition. Most men won't do that unless they're under severe stress. And even then, they may not. I've watched women react to other less dangerous circumstances and get a better overall impression of the situation. Men tend to take things at face value. The black and white of it. I think most women see *through* that and are aware of the shades of gray in life."

"And so you 'stretched' your intuitive abilities?"

"It's saved my life and the lives of others many times. You bet I did."

Alanna remembered Tim Thornton abruptly, wondering for an instant if the senator was wrong. She quickly dismissed that thought, unable to believe that the senator could feel so strongly about Colonel Breckenridge without due cause.

"So, who canned your five senses and forced you to make all your decisions on the basis of logic?" he asked.

She was beginning to breathe hard again, despite the

fact he was slowing down the pace. The trail twisted steeply, with roots and vines now crisscrossing the path. Her heart was pounding in her ears, and she felt a tension headache coming on. How far had they gone? How far was it to the village? The question caught her completely off guard, and she blurted out the answer without stopping first to analyze it. "The man I used to live with, Paul Ramsey. He is a political analyst for a powerful lobby in Washington. I'm afraid we were mismatched from the outset."

Matt stopped, pulling out the canteen and offering it to her as they rested at a small crest. His face had a sheen of sweat on it, but his eyes were hawklike in intensity, missing nothing. "A computer for a mind and no emotions?" he inquired.

Alanna gratefully drank the water down, the halizone taste seeming less potent this time around. She handed the canteen back to him. "Yes. You sure you aren't reading my mind?"

He lifted the canteen to his mouth, taking a small swallow and then replacing the cap and snapping it back into the belt. "No. It just comes from experience," he assured her.

"Look," she begged, "can we rest just a moment? My feet are killing me."

He checked his watch. "Five minutes."

Alanna collapsed on the spot, balancing her weight on a thick root that had been washed clean of the surrounding soil by the ferocity of the September rains. Her braids hung like thick ropes, tendrils of hair escaping around her temples, softening the angularity of her high cheekbones. Matt sat opposite her, digging out a candy bar from his pocket, breaking it in half, and offering it to her.

"It's high-energy. Go ahead, eat it."

She stared down at it. "Will it taste as bad as that water?"

He shook his head, a glint of laughter returning to his gray eyes. "No, I promise."

The seconds flew by in companionable silence, the only sound the plop, plop, plop of water drops falling from the higher reaches of the trees to the lower leaves surrounding them.

"How long did you live with him?" he asked quietly, breaking the pleasant tranquility.

"Four years."

"Meet him right after graduation or before?"

"I met him a year before he got his master's from Harvard."

He raised one eyebrow slightly. "Probably was the head of his class?"

She nodded, relishing the taste of the sweet chocolate. For some reason, it didn't hurt as much to talk about Paul. Before, whenever she thought of him, she could feel the ache begin in her heart, and it was too much for her to bear. At times like that she would throw herself into her work to forget the whole fiasco. "He's a brilliant man," she said earnestly. "A genius."

"Of ideology, no doubt."

Alanna gave a muffled laugh. "God, don't remind me!" She rolled her eyes upward. "I try to forget the hours we spent discussing economics, politics, and social issues. He always won out with his damn logic."

"How did he take that volatile temper of yours, Alanna?"

Some of the humor went out of her. "You can probably guess. It was simply a matter of control as far as he was concerned. Mind over matter or whatever." She gave a little shrug. "He had a minor in psychology, and he was convinced that my childhood was responsible for my reckless emotional state."

Matt tilted his head, watching her closely. "In what way?"

She finished her half of the candy bar, making a small

knot of the paper and slipping it into her drenched raincoat pocket. "Both my mom and dad died in a car crash when I was two. I—I don't really remember too much about it. My aunt told me I was in the hospital for almost six months recovering." She forced a smile. "In a way, I'm glad it didn't happen when I could recall it. It would be too painful . . . too horrible," she murmured, swallowing hard. She looked away from his compassionate gaze, feeling her eyes fill with tears. Why on earth was she letting him evoke all of these long-buried emotions? She had brought up the subject of her childhood only once with Paul, and he had never let her forget that it was responsible for her rash temper and explosive reactions. And if she cried, he would calmly tell her that it wasn't necessary, that her parents had been dead twenty-seven years and it was far past the time to bury that memory and go on living. She hugged her arms around her knees, drawing them close and shutting her eyes tightly, hating to hear those same sing-song words echoing in the corners of her mind. It had been a year since she'd left Paul, and she could still recall with absolute clarity his speech on the topic.

"Did your aunt and uncle raise you then?"

Alanna looked up, responding to the coaxing gentleness in his voice. "Yes. I know they loved me, but it just didn't turn out right. Both of them had their own careers, and they didn't have any children of their own." She shrugged. "I spent a lot of my time reading books, writing stories in my room. I learned how to keep myself entertained."

Matt nodded, rising. He held out his hand to her. "Personally, I like your unleashed emotions," he murmured.

Alanna's lips parted as she looked at his outstretched hand. Without thinking first, she placed her smaller one in it, feeling the warmth of his grip as his fingers closed around hers. He pulled her upward easily, as if she weighed nothing at all. Her heart was pounding erratically, and it wasn't from the altitude. It was from his touch.

Matt released her, a curious smile on his mouth as he reached out, lightly brushing her cheek with his fingers. "Alanna, don't ever apologize for who and what you are. The woman underneath is very warm and loving. Let her surface," he murmured. "Let yourself laugh and cry. Don't let someone tell you that it's right or wrong. And throw that damn logic of yours out the window. It's stifling the hell out of you. Come on, we've got some time to make up."

A tremor of longing coursed through her. For a split second, she thought he was going to lean over and kiss her, but then he turned and started up the trail. She wanted to feel his mouth upon hers once again, she admitted to herself. He was honest in a way she had never known a man to be. Woodenly, she followed him up the trail, so many sensations exploding within her that another mile fell away under her feet without notice.

He called a halt at the fourth mile, and Alanna leaned heavily against a tree, sliding down to the wet ground with a sigh. "Thank you," she murmured sincerely, removing her shoes and trying to shake the accumulated mud out of them. He smiled, squatting down in front of her.

"You have heart, I'll give you that. Maybe not a lot of common sense, but you're a stayer," he said, opening the canteen and offering it to her.

Alanna grinned recklessly, feeling vital even though she was on the brink of physical exhaustion. "Paul would have said not to let the heart rule the head. Causes stomach ulcers or some such thing."

"I'd rather have the ulcers," Matt commented, returning the grin.

She gave the canteen back to him, enjoying his closeness. "Why are you so easy to talk to?" she asked.

He shrugged. "It's the chemistry between us," he explained.

Alanna laughed lightly. "Oh sure, nitroglycerine and dynamite. A wonderful combination!"

"I'm not sorry about it. When I first saw you, I thought you were going to be one of those doves from the Hill who quotes economics."

"I am."

"No. Not really. Behind all that senatorial power you wield, there's another side to you." He pursed his lips. "Look at you now: you're in a foreign element, wet and probably hungry, and yet, you've come all this way without complaining. Think about it." He got up, and she automatically held out her hand to him.

This time, he did not let go of her hand; instead, he pulled her toward him. Alanna's breath caught in her throat as she looked up into his intent face, a shiver of expectancy racing through her trembling body. She felt his thumb lazily trace the outline of her jaw, trailing down the expanse of her slender neck. Her pulse accelerated wildly beneath his exploring touch.

"Such an incredible creature," he murmured in her ear, pulling her against him. His mouth brushed her forehead, eyes and cheeks and dormant emotions she had long thought dead stirred to life. She shivered helplessly at his whispered words, his breath warm and moist against her face. Artlessly responding to his touch, she slid her arms across his shoulders, her fingers entwining behind his neck. She was aware of his skin, a little rough like sandpaper, against her cheek, and of the male scent of him that made her heady with anticipation. His mouth claimed hers gently, parting her lips, grazing them tantalizingly with his tongue. Alanna moaned softly, resting against his hard, unyielding body, her knees weakening.

His mouth dominated hers as she responded to his urging. This kiss was so different from the first— tender, tentative, searching and asking her to participate fully in the exploration. Hungrily, she returned the pressure of his mouth, feeling him suddenly stiffen, a groan coming from deep inside him as his embrace tightened around her. His arms pinned her hips against him, and she was burningly aware of his straining body. His tongue probed her mouth, tasting the inner recesses, creating a vortex of fiery desire that uncoiled from the center of her body. His hands slid upward, cupping her face now, dragging her inexorably into the passion of the moment. She longed to continue this new, exciting experience. But slowly, reluctantly, he removed his mouth from her parted, wet lips. She could only stare childlike up into his undisguised features, into eyes flaring with a silver glint of desire for her alone. A shadow seemed to darken his gaze for an instant, and she felt a subtle change in the charged atmosphere surrounding them. Was it worry? Disappointment? Alanna couldn't be sure as she pulled herself from his embrace, feeling desire and rejection within the same moment.

But it was the rejection that finally won out. Alanna suddenly felt unsure of herself, and she took a few steps away from him, her fingertips touching her sensitized lips.

"Alanna?"

"Nothing," she whispered painfully. "We'd better get going," she said, feeling as if she were babbling like a child.

"Wait—"

She avoided his outstretched fingers, twisting away. "No," she cried.

"Dammit, don't run away from me. Come here." He put a restraining hand on her arm and she halted. "What's wrong?" he demanded.

She raised her hand, making a small gesture of irritation. "Nothing. Everything," she confessed.

"Look at me," he commanded. He cupped her chin, forcing her to meet his eyes. "Why are you behaving like this?"

She felt the hotness of tears gathering in her eyes. How could she tell him that she had never been kissed like that before? That Paul's kisses were drab in comparison? How could she, a twenty-nine-year-old woman, have been unaware of so much of life? Of feeling? A pang of regret went through her, and she lowered her lashes against her cheekbones. "Y–you frighten me, Matt," she whispered.

She felt his hands sliding down over her shoulders, holding her arms. "In what way, Babe?"

Oh, damn, she was going to cry! She pulled a hand free, dashing away the telltale dampness. Paul hated her tears, and he was a civilian. A military man would be sure to think them a sign of weakness.

"Alanna," he coaxed, "why are you scared? Tell me."

She looked up, the tears streaming unchecked now down her pale cheeks, the anguish she was feeling very evident in her green eyes. "I thought I knew who I was," she mumbled, "and—and, I don't. I mean, you seem to bring out a whole other side of me. Someone, something that was lost."

He gave her a gentle shake. "No, Babe, not lost, just hidden inside. Listen to me, Alanna. Your aunt and uncle started the process by giving you no outlet for your emotions, and then Paul reinforced your fear of expressing yourself. But don't be frightened." His words were spoken with a hushed urgency. "You're a giving, loving woman with so much warmth and sensitivity. Let your emotions surface and remain a part of you."

She choked back a sob. "You're a stranger I met two

days ago. How can you be right? Paul never made me feel like this. My aunt, my uncle . . . why now?" she whispered hoarsely. "And why you? Oh, God, this is such a mess." She freed herself of his grip, stumbling blindly back toward the tree to pick up the briefcase. Her heart ached with renewed anguish and pain. She touched her breast in reaction, doggedly walking along the trail, head bowed, bitter tears rolling down her face.

Her mind assailed her with facts and logical explanations. But the pain was real and so was the excitement coursing through her body. If Matt Breckenridge could cause this much emotion to surface in two short days, what would happen if she stayed around him longer? Suddenly, without reason, Alanna wanted to escape. He brought back ugly, half-forgotten memories and old hurts. She remembered times she had hidden in the bedroom closet as a child, sobbing her heart out for her unknown parents; and times when she had gone for long walks outside Paul's Georgetown apartment, hiding her tears from everyone until she could find an empty street devoid of staring eyes where the pent-up flood of emotion could be expressed.

They walked the last mile in gloomy silence. Matt trailed behind her, saying nothing, allowing her to pick her own pace. They arrived at the village near five o'clock in the afternoon, and the fog was again thickening like a wall of cotton around them. Alanna slowed as they neared the center of the village. The ruin and destruction were complete: homes had been torn apart like so many houses made of cards. Police and civilians covered with mud, their faces slack with exhaustion, moved among the rubble with shovels and pickaxes. Stretchers with bodies covered in plastic lay near the small medical facility housed beneath a large tent. Alanna looked away, unable to stand the sight of it. Matt took her arm, pulling her close.

"Look," he murmured, "you've been through enough today. I had hoped the fog would lift so that after you got your supply count, we could fly back to base. There's nothing up here, Alanna. No protection, no hut to sleep in, and no food."

The words sank into her exhausted mind. His fingers felt like a brand against her skin, and she longed to pull away, but she was too tired. She needed the strength that exuded from him. Wearily, she nodded. "What can we do?"

He pursed his mouth, looking around. "Let me take you over to our supply area to get your count. While you're doing that, I'm going to let Captain Jackson know I'm up here and try to smooth out any problems that have developed since we left base. I'll be back to get you later."

Chapter Five

Matt found her working between two walls of crates that were sheltered beneath a canvas covering. The glare of the flashlight hurt her eyes, and she turned her head away.

"It's quitting time," he noted, halting close to where she sat hunched over.

Alanna wearily reached out, using a crate to steady her as she stood. Matt's hand fitted firmly beneath her arm, helping her up. His touch sent a tingling sensation up her arm, and she pulled away. The humidity and fog had curled her hair so that long tendrils framed her face, softening the lines of tension that had accumulated there during the day.

"Quitting time means I can go home," she responded, her voice sounding a million miles away even to her.

Matt offered her a slight smile, his fingers closing around her upper arm as he led her from beneath the covering. "That's usually a logical assumption."

Alanna wanted to escape his presence, and at the same time, she yearned simply to rest against his lean, seemingly tireless body and collapse. To be in his arms. To be held by him. Yes, he would do that for her if she asked. At the thought a half-formed smile touched her lips. Already she had come to expect a unique kind of tenderness from him that she would never have expected in a man. Much less a Marine. But she couldn't allow that to occur. If it did, it would dredge up more unwanted emotions. As she worked, she had mulled over her response to Matt Breckenridge. It was nothing short of a miracle . . . but one that she could never allow to unfold and blossom within the warmth of his compassion or understanding. To do so would be to rock her carefully balanced world and to place her job in jeopardy. He represented the emotional freedom she longed for. Yet, at the same time, he was a threat to her sense of security. He was dangerous.

Alanna silently marveled at the changing pressure of his fingers against her arm as he guided her through the foggy darkness toward some unknown destination. The ground was a rutted, muddy quagmire from the recent rain. Matt seemed to have the eyes of a jungle jaguar as he continued out of the village, leaving the weeping sound of women and children in the distance.

"Where are we going?" she asked dully, not really caring because of utter exhaustion.

"Home," he murmured. "Sounds good, doesn't it?" he mused softly, almost to himself.

Alanna lifted her chin, trying to fathom the expression on his darkened features. There had been a momentary huskiness in his voice, almost a wistful note. "I thought you said we couldn't get off the mountain."

"We can't." He slowed, flashing the beam of light in front of them to reveal a small tent. "This is 'home' for tonight. Come on, get those ruined shoes off your feet

71

and take off the wet clothes you're wearing. I've got some dry utilities and an extra pair of socks and boots you can wear."

A gasp came from her lips as she turned, facing him. "I can't sleep here!"

Matt grinned, cocking his head to one side and studying her with interest. "Sure you can."

"But . . ." she sputtered. "I mean—it's too small for two people!"

He walked to the tent, throwing up the small flap. "While you're arguing the ethics of our situation, how about changing clothes? You're shivering. Come on," he coaxed.

Alanna remained frozen to the spot, her eyes wide. She simply couldn't sleep that close to him! The poignant memory of his kiss soared through her like a white-hot flame beckoning her to give in. Another equally panicky feeling replaced it. "Don't you have two tents?" she asked hoarsely.

Matt pulled out several utensils and cleared a small space for a fire. He squatted down, pushing the cap back off his head. Dark strands of hair dipped across his forehead as he concentrated his attention on the task of getting them some hot food. "Lady, you're lucky I have one tent. Are you going to stand there all night shivering, or do I have to drag you in there and undress you?"

Her heart leaped once at the velvet threat in his voice. Alanna had dealt with him long enough to know he meant it. Hastily she gathered up the briefcase and sloshed through the mud toward the tent. "I'll do it," she replied in a small voice.

He nodded. "Now you're being reasonable. By the time you're changed, we ought to have a meal."

Alanna watched him warily across the campfire as she dug hungrily into the food he had prepared. A light rain began to fall just as they finished. She dejectedly scratched the idea of sleeping outside and letting him have the tent. Her nerves fairly screamed with tension at the thought of being so close to him in such confining quarters.

"I'll clean up, Alanna. You take the sleeping bag on the right. I'd suggest you strip down to a shirt and socks for the night."

"What?"

Matt looked up, a wry smile pulling at the corner of his mouth. "I don't think you'll sleep comfortably in combat boots. Do you?"

She had the good grace to blush, scrambling awkwardly to her feet. The olive drab shirt and trousers were many sizes too large, and she looked like a lost waif within them. Clenching her hands at her sides, she had enough courage to blurt out, "Does our sleeping arrangement still stand?"

His gray eyes darkened slightly. "That's up to you," he answered, his voice a soft, rough whisper.

Pursing her lips, she muttered, "Separate corners. Just like base camp."

He shrugged, laughter in his tone. "Anything you want, Alanna. I don't need a sleepy, cranky woman on my hands tomorrow. So let's get a good night's sleep for both our sakes."

Once in the tent, she breathed a sigh of relief, and hurriedly slipped out of the trousers and boots. Snuggling down into the bag, her back toward his sleeping gear, she closed her eyes. Without meaning to, Alanna tumbled into a darkened abyss of dreamless sleep long before Matt ever entered the tent.

Shadowy shapes fled down the corridors of her mind, and Alanna moaned. Eventually, the shadows took the shape of one man: Matt Breckenridge. She watched in silent horror as he began unlocking first one door and then another. Alanna put her hands to her mouth, biting back a cry. Each door he opened held something from her unhappy childhood. When the final door was pulled open, she felt herself transported magically back into the arms of her mother. Tears spilled down her cheeks as she heard her mother cooing softly to her, pressing her tightly against her body. The sudden screech of brakes, of tires biting into the pavement, roared through her consciousness. Alanna heard her father shout a warning, and then blackness swiftly grappled at her, tearing her away from her mother. Everything began to tremble and shake beneath her feet. A roar surrounded her, and it sounded like a freight train was passing through the tight confines of the small tent. As the roaring reached a peak, Alanna screamed, fingers pressed against her mouth.

The blackness was terrifying. The earth shuddered convulsively beneath Alanna, and she inhaled sharply, realizing it wasn't all a nightmare. Matt had already sat up, reaching outward to pull her into his arms. With a small cry, Alanna groped blindly, falling against his warm, hard body. Burying her head against his shoulder, she let the sobs escape.

"It's all right," Matt soothed, his voice still husky with sleep. He stroked her hair, holding her tightly against him. "Just aftershocks, Babe. Shh, you're safe."

Alanna shut her eyes tightly, more tears escaping, to fall soundlessly against his naked shoulder. The roaring sound died away, and suddenly, the ground stilled beneath them. But the terror of the nightmare and the earthquake had totally shattered her fragile composure. She lay against Matt, arms entwined around his waist, frozen with fear.

"Expect a few more shocks after this one," he murmured, placing a kiss on her hair. "We'll be safe out here. There are no buildings to collapse around us.

Come on," he urged gently, "lie back down with me, there's nothing we can do."

Alanna remained within the asylum of his embrace, thankful for the protection it afforded her. His roughened fingers grazed her cheek.

"Tears?" he questioned. He forced himself up on one elbow, leaning over her in the darkness. "You woke up screaming, Babe. Bad dreams?"

Shakily, she brushed the wetness from her cheeks. "Yes," she answered thickly. "Oh, God. My life's such a mess. . . ."

He smiled tentatively, caressing her temple, pushing a strand of hair away and tucking it behind her ear. "No, it isn't. You're just starting another cycle of growing, that's all," he explained gently.

She made a wry face. She lay on her side, her body fitting snugly beside him. His quiet maleness seemed almost a palpable thing. How did he know she needed to be touched? To be caressed and calmed? Each grazing touch of his fingers against her face and neck sent little tingles of pleasure throughout her tense body. And each stroke relaxed her a bit more until, finally, she felt the fear slipping away. The tent was comfortable despite the damp coldness outside. Heat radiated from his body, his male scent a heady fragrance to her sensitive nostrils. Finally, as if sensing she was better, Matt lay back down, pulling the blanket over them.

It was good to be with a man again. There was a natural instinct to turn on her side, pressing against him, her head resting in the crook of his shoulder. Her arm slid across his chest in an unconscious gesture. Alanna felt him shift slightly, his hand gently caressing her back. "Go to sleep," he whispered huskily, his breath warm against her face.

Her thick lashes fell softly against her cheeks, and she sighed. With his arms about her, Alanna quickly fell back to sleep. For the first time in her life, she felt completely safe.

She awoke slowly. Beneath her ear, she could hear the steady, rock-solid beat of Matt's heart. It sounded like a strong drum beating within his chest, and she languished on the edge of slumber, content. The silken hair covering his broad chest tickled her nose. Reluctantly, Alanna pulled her hand from its resting place across his flat stomach, rubbing her nose. Opening her eyes, she realized with a shock that sometime during the night she had placed her slender leg over his. Violent emotions suddenly replaced her drowsy contentment. For an instant, she tensed. Matt stirred in his sleep, his hand moving across her hip and coming to rest at her waist.

Outside the tent, the tropical birds were beginning to awaken to an unseen sun, chirping in melodic patterns. Matt's heart beat changed, pulsing more strongly beneath her ear. His face was barely inches from her own, and Alanna's eyes widened as she watched him wake up. His features, usually imperturbable, were boyishly readable. The shadowed darkness of a day's growth of beard made his cheeks seem more gaunt. But the lines of tension around his generous mouth had disappeared, and so had the scowl that seemed to hover between his brows. Her lips parted as she gloried in the discovery of his vulnerability during those fleeting, precious seconds. Why did people have to hide their true selves? Matt looked approachable now and so very, very human. She frowned, thinking of herself. How much did she hide inside? He seemed to be able to lift the facade she had built around herself and see the real Alanna. The thought wasn't disturbing. She was safe with him.

Another more painful thought interrupted her musings. It would always be between them. The question had to be answered: Was he stealing medical supplies and selling them to the guerrillas?

Alanna gently extricated herself and found her ill-fitting trousers, squirming into them. What would the senator have to say about her sleeping with the man she was supposed to be investigating? She compressed her lips, struggling into the oversized combat boots. Part of her heart cried out at the unfairness of the situation. Alanna fought against her feelings for Matt. She couldn't get involved! Not now. Not until this whole investigation was over and his name was cleared. A feeling of panic shook her. What if Matt were guilty? Her heart was filled with pain. Despite the senator's inflammatory statements, Alanna had found nothing about Matt Breckenridge thus far that supported those accusations. Sighing heavily, she finished the last lace and turned, looking directly into Matt's gray eyes.

"Good morning," he murmured.

She sat very still, her heart hammering wildly in her breast. Awakened, he looked like that mountain jaguar her mind had so vividly created. He lay naked to the waist, the blanket covering his lower body. The play of muscles beneath his flesh was beautiful to watch. Nowhere on his magnificently sculpted body was there an ounce of fat. The dark hair on his arms and chest accentuated his maleness leaving Alanna helplessly ensnared by her attraction for him. Her own body traitorously responded to his nearness, and she quickly clamped down on her desires. This was no time or place to think of falling in love with a man. Especially Matt Breckenridge.

Alanna choked back a gasp: falling in love? Good God! Where had she concocted *that* nonsense? Panic overrode her coolly detached logic as the entire idea sank in. She avoided his gaze, pretending to busy herself with her long, braided hair.

"Did you sleep well after the ground settled down?" he asked.

"Yes." She turned, biting her lower lip, realizing her voice sounded strident and off-key. "I'm sorry. I just keep thinking of all that has to be done today," she offered, lying.

He seemed to accept her moodiness with good grace, sitting up and searching for a clean T-shirt. Shrugging it over his head, he pulled it down. "Then you didn't have any more nightmares?"

"No. . . ."

He gave her a disarming smile, slipping on the utility shirt. "I'm glad those earth tremors happened along."

Alanna's brows drew downward. "You would be."

Matt rested his arms against his blanketed knees. "You have to enjoy life one moment at a time," he reminded her. A slow grin pulled at his mouth. "And unless you want to stick around and see the rest of me, I have to get my trousers on. You're welcome to stay of course."

She blushed hotly. "I'm leaving," she muttered hastily, climbing out of the tent.

The chill of the early morning made her shiver. She wrapped her arms about her body, standing over the blackened area that had served as a fire the night before. Matt came out minutes later, fully dressed. He seemed buoyant this morning, and Alanna found herself responding to him despite the turmoil of her feelings.

Matt looked around, pursing his lips. "If I'm not imagining things, it looks like this fog is beginning to thin." He glanced over at her, beginning to build another fire. "Keep your fingers crossed that when the sun rises it will burn this stuff off."

She sat on one of the logs that Matt had found for her and watched him. "And if it does?"

"That means I can get those choppers up, supplies

moving, and, most importantly, the injured down off this mountain."

"Another sixteen-hour day for you?"

"Twenty-four to forty-eight will be more like it if the weather gods smile on us."

Alanna smiled wistfully, cradling her chin in her palms. Shortly, the fire was popping and crackling, and she edged closer, beginning to warm up. Matt came over, placing his large, bulky jacket across her shoulders.

"This ought to help. Now, what do you feel like for breakfast?"

She thought about it for a moment, dizzied by his closeness. How easy it would have been to make a half-turn and walk back into his arms. As easy as lying beside him last night in the tent. Alanna pushed those pleasant thoughts aside. "I'm really not hungry, Matt. . . ."

He frowned. "You're going to eat anyway. We've got a hard day in front of us if this fog lifts."

How could she eat? She was thinking of him, of her body's aching need for him and his electrifying touch. It was impossible to think when he was so near!

"I can't offer you eggs Benedict, but how about some scrambled eggs instead?"

"Y-yes, that would be fine."

"Coffee?"

Her lips parted. "Are you serious?"

Matt grinned, a twinkle in his gray eyes. "Have I ever lied to you yet?"

"That's one of your saving graces," she muttered. "Honesty at every turn."

He couldn't resist a retort. "Something that our great senators and representatives know little of up on the Hill."

"I suppose you include me in that generalization?" she asked, stung.

Matt rummaged through his pack, finding the necessary ingredients for their breakfast. "You couldn't lie if you tried," he returned equitably. "Your eyes give you away, you know."

Alanna felt heat creeping back into her face. My God, was he reading what she felt toward him? Nervously, she buried her hands in the huge pockets of the jacket, pretending not to hear his comment.

Over breakfast, Matt continued his pleasant banter. Alanna marveled at his ability to make small talk under such circumstances: they were out in the middle of a Costa Rican jungle, where disease was rampant and people's homes and very lives had been destroyed.

"So tell me, what is the apartment you live in like?" he asked, sipping the steaming coffee.

Alanna watched him warily. "Why would you want to know?"

Shrugging, he said, "Curiosity. To see if what I've imagined it's like is close to reality."

"You make a point of comparing furniture labels to the person?"

"Labels don't mean a thing to me. Usually you can visualize what people are like by the way they decorate their homes or apartments."

She moved uncomfortably on the log, not wanting him to ferret out any more information about her. "Why don't you tell me about your apartment instead," she challenged.

"Fair enough," he agreed, the smile reaching his eyes. "Actually, I don't rent an apartment. I live in McLean, Virginia, and own a house in a fairly wooded area."

"A home?" she echoed. "I didn't know Marines made enough money to buy houses over there in that posh section."

"I saved a lot of my pay by being overseas for so long."

"You don't like apartments?"

"No. I don't like being crowded in with other people."

"Antisocial?"

Matt grinned. "In a way, I suppose. I was born in Maine, and you know what people say about natives of that state."

"They mind their own business and maintain that cool New England veneer. You don't seem very cool, though."

He wrapped his strong, darkly brown fingers about the aluminum cup. "Only when I have to be. Being in the service forces you to become more of a social animal."

"Do your parents still live in Maine?"

"They did up until their death. I still own a cabin up there on the river."

Alanna took a sip of her coffee. "I'm sorry about your parents. . . ."

He shrugged, losing some of his natural warmth. "It happened a long time ago."

"I never thought you would own a home *and* a cabin. Even by Hill standards, you're quite well off," she commented.

"I do what I enjoy doing. How about you?"

She gave a slight shrug. "I earn a good living," she evaded.

"That's all?"

Her eyes darkened. "What else is there?"

Matt slowly rose, grinning. "Oh, a run in the morning with your dog when the grass still has dew on it, fishing on a bank getting warmed by the sun. Little things. Important things. Ever fished?"

She shook her head. "I'm a city girl through and through."

"That's a shame. Bet you've never been to Maine, have you?"

"Never."

"See what six or so years of college will get you?" he teased.

Grimacing, she stood. "Don't remind me. That and a relationship that made me feel like a prisoner." She handed him the cup.

Their fingers touched, and Alanna drew hers away first. Matt stood there, watching her with interest.

"Well, that's behind you now," he returned.

"Not quite in the past tense," she said unhappily. "As you can see, I'm still acting out of a lot of ingrained habits formed during those years."

"Oh, logic versus feelings."

"Yes."

"Well, in three days you've certainly made strides toward freeing up your emotions," he noted wryly.

Alanna grinned up at him. "You're enough to try anybody's logic."

He smiled fully. "I happen to like you this way. And if I've had a hand in unleashing the real Alanna, I'll take my due applause."

She moved away from his overpowering presence, sitting back down on the log. He washed the cups and plates, neatly repacking them. "Can I help you in some way?" she offered.

"No, just sit there looking beautiful while I break down the tent."

She blushed. Beautiful? Here in the mud, needing a bath, with her hair in two long braids? She watched him, curiosity overcoming her wariness. "Do you own a dog, Matt?"

He nodded. "Actually it's the other way around. Megan thinks she owns me."

"Megan, that's a lovely name. What is she?"

He looked up. "One of the biggest Irish wolfhounds you'll ever see."

She gave him a stricken look. "I've never seen one."

"They're somewhat rare."

"Like you," she added.

"Thank you, I'll take that as a compliment. When I'm home, I get up at six every morning and jog five miles with Megan before going in to work. She's one of the reasons I chose to buy a house with some acreage. You just can't pen a big dog like that up and expect it to be happy."

Alanna pulled up her legs, sliding her arms around them and resting her chin on her knees. He was so easy to listen to. She closed her eyes, content.

"You have to understand wolfhounds," he went on. "They think they're people and demand a large share of your attention when they can get it. Megan acts as my alarm clock and promptly leaps on the bed at six every morning."

Alanna suppressed her laughter, envisioning the episode. "Somehow," she said drolly, "I can't see you taking orders from anyone."

Matt pulled out the stakes that held the tent. "Under certain circumstances, I'm very docile and trainable."

"I find that hard to believe."

"You'll see."

Alanna's eyes flew open. "What?"

He straightened up. "I told you that after this mess is over down here I intend to see you on less businesslike terms."

Her heart beat wildly for a few seconds as she stared up at him. He seemed such a natural part of the jungle at that moment. A man completely in tune with nature. A frown formed on her brow.

"Aren't you worried that I might uncover some nasty facts in this investigation?"

"No. I told you before, I'm innocent, and so are my men."

"You could be wrong," she said stubbornly.

He turned, resting one hand loosely on his hip as he

stared across the distance between them. "You ought to know by now, Alanna, I don't lie. I've made my share of mistakes as a human being, but I don't actively go out to harm someone else."

In her mind she heard the senator's voice insisting that it was Matt Breckenridge's mistake that cost his only son his life in Vietnam. She inhaled deeply, genuinely confused. "Mistakes can get you into just as much trouble as a lie can," she whispered tautly, unable to maintain his even stare.

"Do you always form judgments based upon hearsay?"

"I didn't ask for this assignment, dammit!" she flared, leaping to her feet. She remained tense, fists clenched at her sides. "I didn't know a thing about you until I went to work for him, but then I heard plenty. I'll admit I came down here prejudiced against you. But now I just want to know the truth. Hate eats up a person, and the senator hates you. Right or wrong, he's after you."

Matt knelt over the tent halves, folding them precisely. "One of these days," he began softly, "I may tell you the truth of what happened out there."

She gave him a bewildered look. "If he is wrong, Matt, then why don't you just prove it to him? I don't understand!"

He finished the packing and rose, looking distant and withdrawn. "Looks like the fog is finally going to dissipate. Once the sun rises, we ought to be in good shape." He looked over at her, his face unreadable once again. "Come on, let's get you situated at the main loading area. I want to meet with Captain Jackson and get those choppers warmed up."

Frustrated by his sudden change of mood, Alanna walked awkwardly toward the village with him. Twice within half an hour she had seen him withdraw into a shell. Once when she mentioned his parents and the other time over the incident in Vietnam. Stumbling, she nearly fell into a large rut. Matt's hand shot out, quickly catching her. Alanna rested momentarily within his arms, and she looked up to see him smiling faintly, the warmth returning to his veiled gray eyes.

"Want to learn how to fish someday soon?" he asked, retaining his hold on her.

Her eyes widened. "Fish?" she echoed, maddeningly aware of his body and his fingers against her flesh.

"Sure. It will be a beautiful time of the year up at the cabin. The leaves will be turning, and the flounder will be biting. How about it?"

"I—"

"Remember, use your gut instincts, not logic," he chided, his smile increasing.

Alanna trembled inwardly. Every time he dropped that cool facade, she melted like snow on a warm March day. "Oh—all right, I'll think about it," she muttered, pulling free of his hold.

His laughter was rich and free, and she found herself turning and fighting back a smile. "What's so funny?"

Trying to suppress his grin he said, "You look like a duck with big, black feet. I wish I had a camera."

"I'm glad you don't!"

His parting comment at the supply tent was, "I think Megan will like you a lot." She had turned to ask him what that remark meant, but he had disappeared. Alanna struggled to contain the joyous feelings that he inevitably brought to life in her and returned to the work at hand.

Chapter Six

The sun rapidly burned off the fog, leaving blue sky above the suffering village of San Dolega. Alanna was amazed at the pace of activity as the helicopters buzzed up and down the mountain like angry hornets. The temperature rose quickly, and the humidity dropped to a tolerable degree. Volunteer police and villagers were constantly stowing more and more supplies at the main staging area. Alanna sidestepped their bustling activity and calmly checked each set of numbers against her own copies.

By late afternoon, she was beginning to doubt the possibility that precious medical supplies were being stolen. In a corner of her mind, she felt Matt would never be involved in something like that. There was a ribbon of integrity that ran through him like a vein of gold in quartz. She was kneeling down in front of a new load of crates when someone came up behind her. Hoping it was Matt, she felt her heart beat slightly faster in anticipation. Alanna turned.

An unknown Marine in flight uniform smiled down at her. "Miss McIntire? I'm Major Jim Cauley, one of the chopper pilots. Matt sent me up here to find you. He said to drag you down off the mountain so he can feed you. How about it?"

Alanna slowly got to her feet, returning the carefree smile of the pilot. She had not had a chance to see Cauley before. Judging from his sparkling blue eyes, square jaw, and lean body, he was the type to hunt up trouble if it didn't find him first. She smiled, putting the last of the papers into her muddied briefcase.

"I don't think you'll have to drag me, Major Cauley. I'm starved."

Jim nodded, motioning her to follow him. "He said I could go as far as hog-tying you if necessary."

She was grateful that he slowed his pace for her as they entered the bright, sunlit area from beneath the tent. "He did?"

"Yeah. Said you had a real hair-trigger temper." He glanced down at her. "Red hair and green eyes. I'll bet you give everybody hell when you're mad."

"I rarely get angry, Major."

"Call me Jim. Don't worry about it. Matt tends to overexaggerate on occasion."

"If I remember correctly, you two go back quite a ways together?"

"Yeah, we got into a lot of hot water together."

"It's nice to have friends like that," she commented.

"Matt is that kind of person, you know? I always said I'd go to hell and back for him, and damned if he didn't ask me to do just that."

Alanna laughed with the pilot. They approached the dull green chopper, and Jim opened the door, helping her into the copilot's seat. "Be sure to strap in," he ordered.

She watched his economical movements as he guided the helicopter away from the landing area. He glanced over at her, motioning for her to put the headset on. Alanna fumbled with it, finally fitting it over the top of her head. Cauley winked at her.

"That's better," he said. "Never did like to try to outshout a chopper engine. Good way to get hoarse."

She nodded. "I'm sure it is."

"Hey, on the serious side, Miss McIntire—"

"Call me Alanna, please," she interrupted—

"Pretty name." He hesitated and then continued. "Is it true? Are you here to investigate Matt?"

She squirmed inwardly, aware of the worry in the pilot's expression. "I'm afraid so, Jim."

"Did Thornton put you up to it?"

"I get paid by the senator, if that's what you mean," she answered coolly.

"Then you've got to know that Thornton would like to see Matt's name and career smeared. Right?"

"I think that's a bit overstated," she said, hedging.

Cauley's features darkened. "Look, Alanna, you're barking up the wrong tree. Can't you see Matt wouldn't steal supplies? God, he puts in forty-eight hours at a crack making sure this whole relief plan works properly. He's a damn fine career officer, and he's got more decorations than nearly any man that came out of Nam. I don't see how you could do this to him."

She colored under his misguided attack. She was sure Matt had not put his friend up to this. He would handle his own problems personally. Cauley struck her as a man who was loyal beyond the point of reason. "Jim . . . I'm sure you mean well by all of this. I don't have a choice in this matter. It's part of my job to investigate. I didn't come down here prejudiced against Matt. Well, . . . maybe just a little," she added. "But that's all changed," she added hastily. "I see him as someone who has a great deal of integrity and a strong sense of responsibility. I'm not out to smear his name for the senator, believe me."

Cauley pursed his lips, glancing at her for a few seconds before returning his attention to the helicopter. "You aren't some undercover agent from the Defense Department?"

"What?"

"This isn't the first time Thornton has tried to undermine Matt, you know. He's sent men from two government agencies at different times since Matt's return from Nam to try to slander his name. I figured this time Thornton was getting smart by hiring a damn good-looking dame to do the job."

She sat there dumbfounded. "Of all the—"

"Maybe Thornton finally figured out that a woman would be able to take Matt in easier than a man. I don't know. Let's keep this straight—as long as you're nosing around, I'm going to be watching you, too."

Perspiration broke out on the palms of her tightly clenched hands. "I'm not some femme fatale out to frame Matt!" she shot back, anger evident in her tone.

Cauley brought the chopper into a wide banking turn, the verdant green of the jungle thousands of feet below them. "I felt Thornton would jump on this sooner or later," he muttered. "Don't tell me you weren't aware that Matt lost his wife and baby as well as his parents in a car crash?"

Alanna inhaled sharply, her eyes widening. "Oh—no . . ."

Cauley's blue eyes narrowed. "That's right, all four of 'em were killed in a head-on crash up in Maine." His mouth thinned, and he watched her intently, trying to plumb the depth of her horrified reaction. "Matt was out on Recon patrol and didn't know of their deaths until a week after the crash. Can you imagine what he went through? They were already dead and buried by the time he set foot back on friendly soil. And to make matters worse, he and his team got ordered back into the bush for an extended patrol that lasted damn near a month when he got back from the States." He stopped, gauging her reactions. "Most men would have cracked up, but Matt didn't. He was responsible for six other Recons, and he carried off that mission. No one but a few people up in the Pentagon knew how important that one mission was. I can't even talk about it because it's still top secret."

She swallowed hard, her throat dry and constricted. My God, he had lost his entire family. . . . Anguish slashed across her heart. And Alanna thought she had suffered emotional pain. How had he coped with such agony so successfully? It made her feel terribly small, her own problems insignificant in retrospect. Tears swam in her eyes, blurring her vision. "Jim, I would never intentionally hurt Matt. Please, believe me. I didn't know about his family. My God . . ."

"I hope for your sake you're exactly what you claim to be," he said grimly, easing the chopper down toward the landing area near the base camp. "Matt swears you're innocent. But after those two other attacks on him, I'm not so easily convinced."

She didn't know what to make of the picture Cauley was painting. But she felt dirty and less than honorable for undertaking the task that Thornton had assigned to her. "I'm not out to damage Matt's career," she repeated stubbornly.

Cauley's blue eyes seemed to bore right through her. "He likes you, you know?"

Alanna looked up, startled. "What?"

"I said Matt likes you. Maybe a little too much." He set the chopper down, shutting off the engine and watching the rotor blades slowing to a halt. "I wish like hell he'd fallen for anyone but you. I don't mean to hurt your feelings, Alanna. Maybe you are innocent. Judging by your outward appearance, I'd say you look vulnerable as hell. But women can look that way and kill. When this is all over, I may end up owing you an apology. But for right now, I'm going to be shadowing your every footstep where Matt is concerned. We've saved each other's lives too often. Now it's my turn to protect him against you. He's gone through so much hell that I just don't want him to go through any more unhappiness because of that bastard Thornton."

She sat perfectly still for a long time, hands clasped in her lap. "I never realized all of this," she confessed quietly. "I can't even be angry that you're defending him. I wish I had friends of your caliber who would come to my aid when I was in trouble."

Cauley managed a smile, unstrapping the safety harness and pulling the white helmet off his head. He placed it on the seat, studying her. "Matt has earned friends like myself. Friendship like ours is a rarity in this world nowadays, and I think you know that. If that impresses you a little, then maybe you'll quit trying to frame him in this investigation." He sighed heavily, slouching back against the seat. "You're bright and beautiful, and you have that volatile temperament he's always been drawn to. Rachel was like you in some ways. . . ." He shook his head, opening the door. "Come on. I talk too much. I'll walk you over to the chow hall."

Having lost her appetite, Alanna sat morosely beneath the tin-roofed shack that served as a makeshift chow hall. Cauley had grabbed a couple of sandwiches and stuffed them into his pockets, walking back to his chopper. Within minutes, he was airborne, heading back toward San Dolega.

Alanna pushed the rice around on the paper plate, oblivious to the chatter of Spanish and the men coming in to eat. Ignoring the Costa Ricans' curious stares, she trained her eyes on the table.

Now she knew why Matt had grown suddenly serious when he mentioned his parents earlier that morning.

She tried to imagine what it would be like to lose four people whom she loved intensely all at once. Finding it impossible, she dejectedly placed her plastic fork down by the plate. Funny, she mused, that we've both lost our parents in car accidents. Had their lives paralleled one another at other points? She doubted that. How would she feel if Paul had suddenly been ripped out of her life? She found it was hard to imagine that too. From its outset their love had been fault-ridden, like a rock with fissures beneath the surface. Alanna was sure that Matt had loved his wife and child with a fierceness rarely matched in other men.

She herself had felt that same concern in him on a number of occasions. It was as if he held himself in tight check so as not to smother her with that fierce protectiveness. He managed a nice balance between the two extremes; caring enough to allow her room to make mistakes. But if she did make them, he would be there to support her afterward. The more she stayed around him, the more impressed by his wisdom she became. Perhaps it was a wisdom forged out of suffering and pain. That sort of insight carried a heavy price.

"Don't tell me you're not hungry?" Matt demanded, sliding in across from her and putting down his heavily laden tray.

Alanna jerked her head up, startled and suddenly speechless. He smiled warmly, taking off his cap and stuffing it into his back pocket.

"Or did Cauley scare the hell out of you with a wild ride down the mountainside?"

She swallowed hard, frantically trying to gather her wits. "No—I—"

Matt stopped eating momentarily, a frown forming on his forehead. "Are you all right?"

"I—I guess it's just the change in weather." She offered a weak smile of apology. "D.C. weather isn't like this, you know. Maybe I'm just a little tired."

He seemed satisfied with her stammered answers and returned to eating. Alanna toyed with the aluminum cup containing the strong, thick coffee. Her gloomy spirits were lifting, and she enjoyed watching him as he ate. A soft smile played on her lips: he reminded her of a precocious ten-year-old boy gobbling down a hurried meal in order to rush off to Little League practice.

"You must be awfully busy to be gulping food down at that rate. Don't you know that's bad for your digestion?"

"Second nature," he explained between bites. "In the service you learn to inhale food like air."

"If you don't have stomach ulcers after eighteen years, you won't get them now," she agreed.

"As some rich millionaire once said, I don't get ulcers, I give them."

She managed a laugh. "I doubt that! Not with your insight into people and their problems. I can't see you yelling at someone unless it was a last resort."

Matt grinned. "Guess I've come up against a lot of last resorts, then."

Alanna laughed with him, momentarily freed from all her anxiety and confusion. "Do you always keep your sense of humor?" she asked.

"I've been very close to losing it in the last two days."

"Because of me."

"No, the weather situation." His gray eyes twinkled. "You have been a slight pain, but not much of one. Getting to see your pretty face every once in a while is all I need. In a way, I'm glad Thornton sent you down here. How else could we have met?"

She felt her cheeks grow warm and avoided his gaze. She envied his honesty. "I can still turn out to be a pain," she reminded him tartly. "The investigation isn't over yet."

He set the coffee cup on the table, leaning forward

on his elbows. "By the way, how's it going? Any numbers not jibing with one another?"

"No. It's perfect so far."

Matt nodded. "Good."

"I'm glad, too," she confided.

"If you're going to wire your senator of your progress, I'd suggest you do it soon. I've got my ace radioman down here now, and he's going to be busy tinkering with some channels late this afternoon."

Alanna nodded, slowly getting to her feet. "Thanks for the tip. Right now, I think I'll waddle over to your sumptuous suite and change into some of my own clothes."

Matt rose and escorted her out of the mess hall. "You mean you don't like wearing Marine utilities? Afraid that a little gung-ho attitude is going to rub off and tarnish your dove image?" he teased.

She smiled, loving his closeness. She enjoyed watching his loose, fluid walk and the grace of his well-muscled body. "If Senator Thornton ever finds out I spent a night in the same tent with you and wore your clothes, I'll probably get handed my head the moment I step off the plane," she laughed.

He grew serious, pulling his utility cap from his pocket and throwing it back on his head. "That isn't funny. I'm sure you have enough common sense to keep him from finding out."

"I do," she promised fervently. But what about Cauley? For an instant, she wanted to confide the conversation she had had with the chopper pilot. Then, thinking better of it, she decided to say nothing. There was no sense in causing trouble between the two men, and Cauley hadn't been vicious in his criticism of her investigation. He possessed an honesty similar to Matt's, and she couldn't hold that against him.

Matt halted at the door, opening it for her. He

pushed the cap back on his head, studying her frankly. "Care to dine with me tonight, Miss McIntire? Or are you getting your fill of the Marine Corps?"

She smiled. "No, I'd like that."

He scratched his head. "Maybe you ought to keep wearing those utilities, lady. I think I'm making a friend out of a former enemy."

"I was never your enemy, Matt," she answered, her eyes darkening.

He reached out, his fingers brushing her cheek. "I knew that, but I don't think you did. Anyway, we've got a truce right now, let's keep it that way. I'll have Captain Jackson make sure you get down off that mountain by nightfall. Be careful around those crates. Some of these laborers aren't stacking them carefully, and I've already had a couple of injuries.

She nodded, secretly thrilled by his touch. "I'll be careful," she promised huskily.

Later Alanna was standing near some newly delivered crates when a violent aftershock occurred. Panic-stricken Costa Ricans could be seen scrambling out from under the tent as crates tottered and began to fall from their poorly stacked positions. Alanna froze, unacquainted with safety procedures during a tremor. Screams and cries sounded nearby. Another shock jolted the village, and one wall of supply boxes tumbled downward, smashing apart.

She was knocked to the floor of the collapsing tent as a crate grazed her shoulder. Blackness edged her vision as she lay helplessly trapped beneath several crates, her legs feeling numb from the weight. Vaguely, Alanna was aware of quickened Spanish voices. She gave up trying to pull her legs free and yelled for help instead. A trickle of blood flowed down her right temple. She raised her hand to check the bleeding and succeeded in only smearing it across her cheek in the effort.

If she hadn't been trapped, Alanna might have found the whole rescue effort laughable. The police were highly excited, gesticulating wildly, their voices reaching an octave higher when they discovered Alanna. She lay on her back, calmly answering them in Spanish, trying without success to reassure them she was all right. It seemed like hours before they removed the last of the offending crates and she was able to sit up. A porter handed Alanna a dirty cloth, and she pressed it against the cut on her temple.

Her feet were throbbing, and she took off her shoes, rubbing the toes tenderly. Matt suddenly appeared at the end of the hall of scattered crates, striding quickly toward her. His narrowed gray eyes were black with an intensity that frightened her. The Costa Ricans quickly retreated as he knelt by her side.

"What happened?" he demanded huskily.

She made a weak gesture. "I was stupid enough to stay in the tent when the tremor began. They told me afterward I should have run for an open area. I'm sorry, Matt, I didn't mean to cause such a fuss."

His eyes lost their hardness as he anxiously searched her features. He removed the cloth from her bloodied fingers. "Head wounds always bleed heavily," he offered. He pulled out his own clean handkerchief and pressed it against the injury. "Are you sure you're all right? You're pale as hell."

She felt incredibly stupid and embarrassed. "Just get me out of here. I can't stand all these men staring at me."

The corner of his mouth tugged into a semblance of a smile. "Want me to carry you, or can you walk out under your own power?"

"I'll walk," she promised hastily, gripping his hand and standing.

As Matt escorted her out into the dusk, Alanna

heard one of the policemen yelling excitedly in his native tongue. She halted, twisting around.

"What is it?" Matt demanded, frowning.

"Something . . . wait. He's saying that some medical supplies in at least a half a dozen boxes are missing. Oh, my God," she said, automatically walking quickly toward the raised voice.

Matt remained at her side, saying nothing, a scowl deepening on his unreadable features. Alanna hurriedly entered the conversation as Matt prowled around the broken crates, sifting through the contents. He looked over at her.

"Ask him to get me the sheets on this shipment, will you?"

Hastily, Alanna translated. She bit her lower lip, watching Matt with building dread. Did he know about this? If he did, he was certainly masking it effectively. He looked upset, despite his ability to control his emotions in a tense situation. The policeman returned, giving him the documents. He got up, moving back to where she stood.

"They're in Spanish," he growled.

She wrote down the products and quantities that should have been in each crate. Matt personally counted each of the items against the bills of lading. It was growing dark when he finally called a halt to their investigation.

"Let's get down the mountain," he ordered. "We'll complete the search tomorrow morning."

Alanna agreed, aware of how taut his facial muscles had become. There was an air of tightly checked anger about him as he slowly escorted her to the awaiting chopper. To her relief, Jim Cauley wasn't the pilot. Right now, she didn't need his accusing stare or outspoken opinions to drive a wedge between them. She climbed in, her head aching dully where she was cut.

Silence hovered between them as they ate their dinner on the floor of the makeshift quarters. Outside the room, the squawk and chatter of the radios provided some relief from the brittle tension building in their room. She picked absently at the refried beans, wrinkling her nose.

"You'd better eat," Matt suggested, setting his plate aside and leaning back against the wall. He closed his eyes for a moment, exhaling softly.

Her heart wrenched as she watched his features grow haggard. She swallowed hard. "I'm sorry, Matt. I didn't want this to happen," she whispered. She took one last look at the food and laid it aside.

He managed a half-hearted smile meant to convince her that everything would be fine. But her instincts told her differently.

"It's not your fault, Babe." He opened his eyes and leaned forward, wrapping his arms around his drawn-up legs. "I've been running it over and over in my mind, trying to figure out how the theft could have happened and where it was occurring. Who might be heading up the scam."

"Any ideas?" she asked, barely choking out the words.

He ran his fingers distractedly through his dark hair. "It probably occurred at the depot where supplies are taken off the ships or the cargo planes."

"But the bills of lading aren't typed up until the contents are checked."

He gave a shrug. "Who says the foreman at the dock can count right when he's getting money on the side?"

"Could they be stopping the truck en route and taking part of the supplies off?" she asked, hope in her voice.

"That's a strong possibility," he agreed.

"Could it be done here at the base camp?"

Matt got up, hands behind his back, pacing the length of the room slowly. "It would be much harder to do, and the risk of discovery is high. I have guards posted here and up at the supply depot in the village. Of course, who's to say the guards can't be bought? Damn." He rubbed his jaw absently, halting at the window, staring into nothingness for at least a minute.

Alanna felt his mounting frustration. "It looks as if the guerrillas are after the drugs for the most part," she provided.

He snorted softly. "I would be too if I were running a jungle campaign. Morphine can mean the difference between heaven and hell."

She lowered her gaze, responding to the undercurrent of pain in his husky voice. "Did it happen to you once?" she ventured unsurely.

He said nothing for a long time, his shoulders slumped downward, head bent as if in prayer. Finally, with an effort he said, "More than once."

She regarded him intently, trying to understand the anguish behind the spoken words. "This is going to sound stupid," she began tentatively, "but I sometimes feel that we're aliens, Matt. I mean," she groped, "you've seen such violence and death that I don't know how to respond to you. I can't understand how you can walk around in the world I know as a functioning human being after what you've gone through." She avoided his gaze as he turned, studying her in the light of the sputtering kerosene lamp.

Alanna tensed inwardly as she heard him move across to her. He crouched down, his gray eyes a curious slate color. "I know what you're saying, Alanna," he said, his voice strained. "Sometimes it isn't easy. I'm lucky to be alive, and I always hold onto that thought no matter how bad the nightmares become."

She met his gaze. "Despite your military background

you seem to be able to cross over into my world. Why can't I do the same?"

He picked up her hand, turned it over and thoughtfully traced the outline of her slender fingers. "You're idealistic and innocent—that gives you a different perception of life and a unique ability to care." A sad smile touched his mouth. "Those are two qualities that I find so terribly important. So you see, you have abilities that I don't."

Her hand tingled fiercely as he gently massaged the palm with his thumb. "I can't believe that you don't care," she murmured.

Reluctantly, he placed her hand back into her lap and rose slowly. "I had to retrain myself to care. You come by it naturally."

"Yet you cared about me," she protested.

He smiled tiredly. "That's because you're special. Come on, let's get some sleep. Tomorrow we'll devise a plan to track down the missing drugs."

She acquiesced without another word, huddling on the sleeping bag with the blankets drawn securely about her shoulders, missing Matt's warmth and strong, protective body. Sleep came slowly because her mind dwelled on the events of the day. Tomorrow she would have to wire Senator Thornton and tell him that his suspicions about supplies being stolen were correct. She was going to make sure that Matt was not implicated. Not unless solid proof was found to condemn him. Shutting her eyes tightly, Alanna prayed that would never happen.

Alanna stood pondering over each carefully worded sentence of her message to the senator. Could any of it hint that Matt was guilty? Her stomach knotted, and she fought down a rising tide of panic. The paper trembled in her fingers, and she exhaled softly. When had she ever had such a problem making a decision? As Paul had said, make it black and white. Simplify. Yet how could she simplify this situation? She knew Thornton would leap at any suggestion of Matt's guilt like a wolf leaping at the jugular of his enemy's throat. And what about her unstable, growing relationship with Matt? God, she groaned inwardly, shutting her eyes. Realistically . . . no, pure logic told her she ought not to be involved with the Marine colonel.

She opened her eyes, their greenness darkening to jade with pain. The pain of truth: she was falling helplessly in love with Matt Breckenridge, against all her better judgment and reason. Alanna gently laid the message on the stained desk beside the radio operator. And what had Matt always told her? There were times to forget logic and go on gut instinct alone. What did her instincts tell her to do now? Alanna shook her head in despair, pushing the paper in front of the radioman.

"Can you send this, please?" she asked in a small, barely audible voice.

"Yes, ma'am."

Her stomach tightened nervously as she watched the man send it out over the airwaves. Dread enveloped her, and she took a step away, feeling as if she were a traitor. There was a bitter taste in her mouth, and she swallowed, blindly turning away.

Strong, warm hands closed around her arms, bringing her to an abrupt halt. Alanna's eyes flew open.

"Matt—" she gasped.

He managed a quick smile. "Ready to hop a chopper to the mountain?" he asked.

A tumult of unleashed emotions roared through her as she stood within his grip. If he had seen her send the message, there was no hint of chastisement or bitterness in his eyes or the husky tenor of his voice. The knife of guilt sliced across her heart. He doesn't deserve this! a small voice screamed inside her. Looking up into his drawn features, she saw for the first time the amount of pain and suffering he had managed to hide from the world at large. A tenuous thread of unspoken need flowed between them, and she responded.

"It's going to be all right," she murmured. "I know it is."

The smile deepened slightly as he reached out, sliding his fingers down the clean line of her jaw. "Is that logic or instinct talking?"

Alanna smiled grimly, touching her breast. "I feel it here."

He guided her out the door into the pale light of early morning. "It's just another skirmish," he returned.

"And you're tired of fighting."

Matt drew his cap down, shading his dark gray eyes. "Have you ever gotten up in the morning and felt fragile? So damn fragile you're afraid that if one thing goes wrong during the whole day you're going to snap in two?"

Alanna cast a sharp glance over at him, her heart thudding heavily in her breast. She licked her dry lips, slowing as they neared the awaiting chopper. "Yes. Several times when I was breaking up with Paul. Why? Is that how you feel today?"

Matt opened the sliding door of the chopper, helping her into the cargo area. "I'd like to deny it, but I can't." He made sure she was belted into the seat and then moved forward to the copilot's position.

A new, desperate longing filled her: to reach out to protect him. How many times had he protected her in the last four days? She studied his grim, stony profile with compassion. She had never realized that perhaps a soldier got tired of fighting, got tired of death and destruction. In some unexplained way, she knew that Matt Breckenridge had reached that point.

At San Dolega, Alanna followed him silently to the supply depot area. The police commissioner met them, resplendent in his khaki uniform and newly polished brass. She suppressed a desire to giggle over the man's overbearing manner. Matt, however, patiently stroked the man's incredible ego as they outlined a plan to discover where the supplies might have been stolen. With Alanna acting as interpreter, Matt's plan was finally approved after an hour of haggling.

As they walked back toward the medical dispensary set up inside another tent, Alanna said, "What a pompous bastard!"

Matt grinned. "What's this? My dove from the Hill resorting to foul language unbecoming to a lady?"

She grinned. "I'm sorry. I just don't see how you could stand there and take his bluster and bluffing. He didn't know a thing about the job he's charged with. I'll bet he never gets out of his air-conditioned office."

"Very perceptive on your part. Say, you're becoming indispensable to me."

"I'm not sure whether that's a compliment or an insult," she returned, matching his smile. Her heart soared as she saw some of the exhaustion and depression lifting from his taut features. His gray eyes lightened, and that familiar spark of laughter reappeared within their depths. For the moment, even the shadow of Senator Thornton dissipated.

Matt lifted the heavy mosquito netting for her, and they ducked inside the medical facility. "Believe me, that's a compliment. You're very good at interpreting."

"Except for understanding my own actions," she put in dryly.

"You just needed a few things pointed out to you."

"I owe you for a lot of those discoveries," Alanna said, becoming serious.

Matt took off his cap, stuffing it in his back pocket. A new glitter came to his eyes. "And I intend to collect, believe me," he promised, the velvet threat sending shivers through her body.

Chapter Seven

At noon, Alanna was famished. She tried to forget that, by the time they came down off the mountain that evening, there might be a message from Senator Thornton. The thought sent a chill of fear through her. She ignored that, relishing each new job that Matt showed her during his appointed rounds. There was little more she could do now since all the supplies had been duly entered on the log sheet. And until the police commissioner and his roving teams of men found some evidence, she would have to wait it out just like Matt.

Finding two empty petrol cans, they made themselves comfortable while they ate. With the blazing sun high overhead, the insects buzzed annoyingly around them. Alanna took another swipe at one, muttering a curse under her breath. She looked up to see Matt grinning.

"You don't like jungle living?" he taunted.

"No! How did you ever stand living over in Vietnam?"

"It was an adjustment," he agreed congenially.

"You probably used up mosquito repellent by the canful."

"No. The enemy would smell us coming three miles away if we wore that stuff."

She stopped eating. "You simply amaze me, Matt. I had no idea of what kind of things you or any of those men had to go through over there."

"Few people do," he agreed. "But don't feel bad, it's not your fault. It didn't make interesting news or good material for the ratings war carried on by the evening news programs."

"I never realized the extent of a serviceman's commitment, that's all," she answered lamely. "I feel more than a little guilty over giving you such a tough time about the military when we first met."

"The last few days have softened your view?"

She nodded, a note of awe in her tone. "More than just a little. Paul used to put down the military, and I guess I allowed his attitude to rub off on me. All my friends went to college and avoided the draft. And when I started to work for Senator Thornton, I really got brainwashed on militarism."

He set the plate down at his feet. "You should never feel ashamed of being ignorant about something, Alanna. Unfortunately, that's the way we all learn, blundering into new areas, stumbling, maybe falling." He offered her a smile of encouragement. "I figured if I gave you half a chance, you might change your mind about us."

"You looked like you were ready to murder me that first day," she confided.

"It was a damn good thing you were a woman. Two hours earlier I had had a confrontation with a group of television reporters who bumped some medical personnel off another C-130. When Haskell didn't show, it was the perfect end to a very bad day."

She grinned. "Then I'm glad I *am* a woman. If looks could kill, I'd be dead. You scared the hell out of me."

Matt laughed. "You've seen me at my worst. Now we have no place to go but up."

Caution replaced her ebullient mood. "Maybe . . ." she whispered. She saw his eyes widen with a brief startled expression. "Matt . . . this investigation, I have to finish it. I worry what the senator will do with the message I had to send this morning. I don't even want to go into the radio shack to find out." She rubbed her arms, suddenly chilled by the prospect.

"Alanna." His tone was steadying. "You do the job you were assigned. Report the facts and stand your ground. He may try to railroad you with his political razzle-dazzle. I know Thornton too well. He's known on the Hill to blow things out of proportion on just a few thin threads of circumstantial evidence. You know he'll do the same no matter how you worded that message. I worry more about you in this situation than I do about myself."

Her brows drew down in puzzlement. "Why? I mean, aren't you afraid of what he might do to your career?"

Matt rested his arms against his thighs, watching several workmen begin to haul away rubble from a destroyed hut. "He's tried this twice before, Alanna, and I know his strategy and tactics by heart." He turned, looking down into her upturned face. "I worry because you've never seen him in action before. He can twist things, Babe, and perhaps make you believe them. You're at a vulnerable stage in your life, and he might try to manipulate you in these circumstances."

"That's impossible! I'd never do anything under-handed, Matt!" Her nostrils flared with indignation at his accusations.

"Not knowingly," he soothed. He looked down at his dusty boots. "Damn," he swore softly.

She tilted her head. "What?"

Matt rose, picking up his aluminum plate. "I have the poorest timing in the world," he muttered.

Perplexed, she fell into step with him. "On what?"

"Nothing. Come on, let's drop these off at the chow hall and go over to see our zealous police commandant."

Alanna's spirits rose even more when she excitedly reported to Matt that the commissioner had discovered some partially dismantled crates out in the jungle. Matt had spread a map out on an excuse of a table in the bright sunlight and was hunkered over it with the Costa Rican official. Painstakingly, he forced the policeman to pinpoint the spot. Just as Matt was going to say something, the radio he carried on his belt blared to life. She stood to one side, listening intently to the conversation. It was Captain Jackson asking Matt to meet him at the base camp immediately. Matt pursed his mouth, signing off.

"Ask the commissioner to send his best men out to that spot and get photographs for me, Alanna. Tell him I'll be back in about four hours." His voice deepened with authority, and he gave her a measuring glance. "In the meantime, you stay put, understand?"

"Of course," she answered, stung by the accusing tone in his voice. She relayed the information to the commissioner, and Matt seemed satisfied.

"I'll see you in a while," he promised, and then turned, jogging back down toward the center of the village to the chopper landing area.

Alanna waited until the helicopter disappeared down the side of the mountain and turned to the commissioner. She smiled disarmingly, pulling her official papers from Washington out of her briefcase.

"Por favor," she began, watching his dark brown eyes light up with instant interest. "I would like to go

with your men to this site. I also need photographs for my boss, the exambassador, Senator Thornton."

"*Sí, sí, señorita.* I personally know your illustrious ambassador to our great country. I would be honored." He bowed his head, giving her an oily smile.

Alanna cringed inwardly, hoping that the trio she was to travel with wouldn't be so unctuous. "*Gracias,*" she murmured, demurely lowering her lashes and avoiding his openly hungry expression.

Within half an hour, they had begun their trek to the east of San Dolega. Almost immediately they were swallowed up in the dense forest of towering mahogany trees. Alanna doggedly carried her briefcase, trying to keep up the pace that the policemen had set. Each man wore a heavy pack resembling the one she had seen Matt carry. A stray thought hit her as they struggled over another steep hill which led into a ravine on the other side. How far away was this place where the crates had been found? She pushed a stray tendril of hair away from her eyes, perspiration running down her temples. Well, it was too late now. More than anything, she wanted photos of the area. She didn't trust the Costa Ricans' ability to take the shots that might end up extricating Matt from this whole messy affair. Luckily, she always carried her own pocket camera in her briefcase and a few rolls of extra film.

The sun's light dimmed as they progressed toward their destination and evening approached. The thick jungle foliage and ever-present vines forced them to use their machetes. In those moments Alanna was able to stop and catch her breath as they hacked a narrow trail through the undergrowth. She noted that each man carried a side arm, but no rifle.

As the cape of darkness slid across the jungle, Alanna drew to a halt. The team leader motioned his men to put down their packs and make camp for the night. She found a clear spot and put her briefcase down, sitting on top of it. Pulling off the ruined shoes, Alanna tenderly rubbed her aching feet. A sense of despair fell over her. Memories of sharing Matt's small shelter surfaced in her mind. She had felt safe with him. As she looked at each of the men with her, she felt no sense of safety. The team leader had, on more than one occasion, tried to strike up a conversation with her. She had politely dismissed his attempts. But now his almond eyes expressed a more direct interest in her. Where would she sleep tonight?

Unhappily, she reviewed the choices, and none were pleasant. She remembered what Matt had said about a lone woman out in the jungle. Goosepimples rose on her arms, and she rubbed them briskly. It can't be helped, she thought. I've got to get good photos. How do we know they'll take the proper shot or the right angle? What if they miss something that I might find? But knowing she had made the right decision in coming didn't help her to cope with the niggling fear she felt.

The team leader, Juan, offered to share his food with her. Starving, Alanna had no choice but to accept the tidbits. Morosely, she huddled near the open fire, trying to stay warm in her jeans and blouse. Why hadn't she brought a coat? It always grew chilly and damp here at nightfall. What had she been thinking of?

After dinner, the policemen huddled around a well-worn map, consulting it and then checking their compass reading. Finally, after two of the three crawled into their small tents, Alanna talked with Juan.

"How far must we go to reach the crates?"

He shrugged dramatically. "Far, *señorita*, very far. You must be very tired, no? You must sleep so that you can make the trip tomorrow, eh?"

"How far is far?" she demanded, her voice hardening.

Juan scratched his stubbled jaw. "Another five kilometers, perhaps. But it is over the roughest terrain, *señorita*. I think you should use my tent." He grinned, the gap in his front teeth showing. "It will be cold tonight, and you cannot stay out here alone." He bowed elegantly. "We are honored to be of service to Ambassador Thornton. I would not want to bring shame on our country by allowing his lovely assistant to be mauled by jaguars."

Alanna gasped. "Jaguars?"

"Sí, señorita, they roam only at night. That is why we keep a fire going, to scare them away. They fear only fire, not us. You will be safer in the tent tonight, no?"

Suddenly, the night vibrated with a piercing, almost human cry that seemed to echo throughout the blackened forest. Alanna whirled around toward the sound, hands against her mouth.

"Jaguar!" Juan whispered hoarsely.

Immediately, the other policemen tumbled out of their tents, their pistols in hand. Excitedly, they talked for a few moments in Spanish, casting uneasy glances around the forest. Alanna realized they were just as frightened as she was. The fire threw a small ring of light around the camp; shadows like writhing ghosts waited at the edge of darkness to haunt them all.

Alanna had turned toward the jungle, the policemen and tents behind her. She blinked, her heart pounding in her chest and her throat constricted with fear.

Without warning, Alanna sensed rather than heard something coming out of the jungle to her left. Half turning, her eyes widened. Matt Breckenridge seemed to materialize out of the jungle like a silent ghost with another Marine close behind him. One of the policemen gave a cry of fear, and the others whirled around. Matt's angry gaze swung to her.

"Tell them to put those damn pistols down before they kill me or themselves with them," he barked at her.

Alanna stumbled over the order. She watched as the

Costa Ricans took a deep breath of relief as the Marine colonel and a tall corporal entered the circle of light, shrugging off their field packs near the fire. Matt's upper body was bathed in a fine sheen of sweat, his shirt darkened beneath the armpits and down the front of his chest. Giving orders to the corporal to set up the tent he carried, Matt swung toward her and in two swift strides gripped her arm.

"Just what the hell do you think you're doing?" he snarled, giving her a small shake and then leading her away from the main group.

She opened her mouth to speak, stunned, the anger in his eyes incredibly frightening.

"I told you to stay at the village. Instead you run off with these idiots. Dammit, Alanna, sometimes you don't have a brain in your head! Do you realize that there might be guerrillas in the area where those crates were discovered? Did you ever think that you might get killed in a firefight?" He released her, his teeth clenched. "I suppose you had to go," he ground out, "to get proof for your dear senator."

Her eyes stung with tears. "No! I mean—" she choked.

"Weren't their photos good enough for you?" he growled.

Anger finally overcame her initial shock. "Don't yell at me, Matt. Yes, I did come along to get pictures. I—I didn't want them taking just a few photos and maybe taking the wrong angle. Or—or maybe missing something that I might see . . . anything to keep Senator Thornton from accusing you."

He put his hands on his hips, disbelief etched in his fiery, silver eyes. "Tell these men to go to bed, will you?" he ordered tightly. "You and I have a few more things to discuss without them gaping at us like idiots."

Quickly, she conveyed his orders, watching them retreat gratefully back into their individual tents. The corporal who had come with Matt crawled into his own tent, pulling down the flap. Hesitantly, she returned her attention to Matt. He had opened the pack and was setting up his tent opposite those of the Costa Ricans. Chewing on her lower lip, she shuffled over to where he knelt.

"I asked the police commissioner to tell you where I had gone. He said he would do it."

He glared up at her. "That bastard didn't say a thing. I sent Cauley all over the damn place trying to find you. Your dear commissioner left hours earlier without so much as a good-bye."

She rubbed her forehead in consternation. "I didn't know—"

He jerked the shelter halves upright, tying the last rope, making it taut. "You drive me crazy, Alanna. One minute you're a mature woman and the next you're a thoughtless child."

"I am not a child!" she cried, stamping her foot.

He jerked the sleeping bag out of the pack and the blanket. "Your actions prove that, lady. For two cents I'd take you over my knee and paddle your rear."

"I said I was sorry! I can't help it if the commissioner didn't convey the message to you. Why are you so angry at me?" she rattled, tears blurring her vision. Her voice trembled. "All I wanted to do was to make sure that we had good photos. I didn't think any of these policemen were trustworthy photographers."

He dragged the pack alongside the tent and un-snapped the webb belt around his waist which carried a .45 pistol. "Yeah, and you can get killed just as easily for all your good intentions," he snarled, placing it on the blanket inside the tent.

Alanna choked back a sob, clenching her fists. "At least I'd die doing something right for a change!"

He turned like a lithe jungle cat, gripping her arms, his face inches from her own, his breath hot. "Dammit,

I won't allow you to put your life in danger!" he rasped. "You silly little fool!" He released her just as suddenly, and Alanna stumbled backward, hand against her mouth, tears streaming down her cheeks.

Shadows danced over the planes of his face as he glared across the short distance between them. "Heroics are for fools," he breathed harshly. "Your life is worth more than any damn picture you might take, even if it is the one that could save my career."

Her emotions were in utter chaos. She felt naked before him, a naughty child caught doing something wrong. Anger mixed with her confusion, and she knew she had to defend herself.

"You think all of the people who work on the Hill are cheats and liars. Well, they're not! I'm after the truth in this mess, Matt. And if it means I go out tramping around in a jungle to get the evidence, then I'll do it. I'm no heroine, believe me. I don't want to die. But I also believe that you are innocent, and I want to prove Senator Thornton wrong. How can I do that by sitting back in San Dolega? What if these policemen accidentally destroyed some evidence that might help vindicate you?"

He shook his head, running his fingers through his damp hair. "You don't understand, do you? God, you're like so many of those young men who went over to Nam, volunteering out of some idealistic sense of right and wrong. . . . This world doesn't give a damn if you ride a white horse and fight on the side of justice, Alanna. That doesn't mean a thing anymore! And if you went to that site and got killed, do you think Thornton would drop one crocodile tear over your death?"

She stood frozen, her chin high, eyes blazing with a sense of righteous wrath. "Of course he would!" she defended.

Matt swore vehemently. "Quit being so naive! He

doesn't care if you get hurt, maimed, or tortured as long as he gets evidence against me! And I refuse to have you hurt because the bastard wants my head on a platter!"

"I'm not being naive. And you're wrong about justice being nonexistent in this world. My God, has the military destroyed that much of your faith and trust in people?"

He stood there, silent and brooding. "The military didn't do it, war did."

"Well, I can't understand that, can I?" she hurled back bitterly. "War is foreign to me. I can only work from my reality and what I know to be true. I think war has warped your whole view of human beings, Matt. You're distrustful and jaded."

His mouth compressed into a single, thin line as he looked past her into the darkness, the silence icy and brittle between them. "That's how you see me?" he inquired softly, a razor edge to his voice. "A warped, emotionally crippled human being who views the world through jaded eyes?"

Alanna realized the dangerous ground she was treading on. Oh, God, why had she flung words at him without thinking first? Paul's dreary advice came back to her: Bridle your temper just long enough to think before you act, Alanna. That way, you won't be misunderstood. She spread her hands out before her in a gesture of apology. "Please," she whispered, "I'm tired and—and I got angry. I spoke before I thought out what I wanted to say."

His eyes glittered with animal ferocity. "Sometimes the truth comes out in anger."

Her shoulders, stiff with tension, slumped in exhaustion. "I told you once before, we're aliens to one another. You're from a different world. I'm trying hard to understand, Matt, but you put up so many walls between us. You talk in riddles."

His eyes lost their harshness, but he maintained his tense stance. "Such as?"

Alanna shrugged tiredly, hanging her head. "Like the statement you made about the soldiers going over to Vietnam thinking of themselves as knights rescuing someone in distress. I don't think it's fair of you to say that. Sure, I know a lot of soldiers probably see themselves that way. But what's wrong with fighting for something that you believe in?" She met his unreadable gaze. "Why did you go over?" she whispered.

He exhaled harshly, allowing his hands to drop to his side. His face lost its hardness, and there was raw emotion in the depths of his gray eyes. "I was one of them," he began, strain evident in his voice. "I made every mistake in the book when I arrived over there. You're right, you know, about the white knight on the charger. Hell," he rasped, shaking his head, "we were all nothing but a bunch of Don Quixotes tilting at windmills."

"So?" Alanna cried. "Why do you have such contempt for yourself for being that way?"

"I was one of the few with that attitude who survived. It took one tour to change my mind, and all my friends were dead by that time."

Alanna moved within a foot of where he stood, unsure, but sensing the importance of the moment. "You said you were there for two tours?"

He frowned, avoiding her gaze. "That's right," he repeated without emotion.

She was bewildered. "But why? If you were disillusioned, Matt . . . oh, God, I feel so helpless when I talk to you," she admitted, unable to bear his closeness for one more second. She started to turn away and felt a restraining hand on her arm.

"Stay," he commanded softly, pulling her back toward him.

Alanna felt the heat of his body. So close . . . so vital

and strong. She swayed back against him, vaguely aware of his arm sliding around her waist. "Oh, Matt," she whispered brokenly.

He held her tightly, his head resting against her own. They stood there for a long time, and she felt the ragged beat of his heart. Closing her eyes, she was aware of the anguish within him.

Finally, he forced the words out, low and tortured. "I was married once, Alanna. I came home after the first tour and married Rachel. I guess I don't do things on the spur of the moment because I had known her for five years before I asked her to marry me. Now . . ." his voice faded. "Well," he began heavily, "it's too late now. She became pregnant, and I was on top of the world. I had finally found a woman whom I could love just as fiercely as she loved me. Then, because of my previous military record and my training as a Recon, I got ordered back to Nam for a second tour." He halted, resting his head against her shoulder in the gloomy darkness. "I was out on a mission when—when I got word that Rachel, our child, and my parents had died in a car crash." His embrace tightened. "I couldn't even fly home to see them buried, it was too late. I never got to see our baby daughter . . . just photos of her that Rachel had sent right after she was born. I took my leave right away, and all I could do was place flowers on their graves."

Tears flowed freely down her face as she turned around in his embrace. Slipping her arms about his waist she murmured, "I'm sorry, Matt, so very sorry. No one . . . no one deserves that kind of agony. Not you, not any human being."

A grimace tugged at the corner of his mouth. He absently brushed her cheek dry of the tears. "There's more," he warned her briefly.

She swallowed the lump in her throat. "I want to hear it."

His eyes were dark as he studied her in the gathering silence. "I've never talked to anyone about all of this," he admitted. "Funny," he mused. "You have a lot of strength to stand here and listen. Either that or—"

"I care enough to listen, Matt," she returned, her voice firm. "What happened next?"

He rested his hands on her shoulders, gazing back into the darkness. "I lost it, in three simple words. After their deaths I went back into the bush and turned all my grief into hate for the enemy. I damn near lost my men near the end of the tour. Fortunately, Cauley rescued us against my orders." He sighed heavily, returning his gaze back to her upturned face. "I was a madman of sorts over there. I volunteered for every mission that had a high probability of enemy contact. I wanted to die myself."

"But it never happened, thank God," she whispered fervently.

He shrugged. "With time I've worked out most of the grief. I stayed over there too long. My commander should have rotated me. But during that period we were pulling out, and it was every man for himself."

"Did you eventually get help?"

"No. I just lived through it." He gave a sad smile. "Just like thousands of other men, Alanna. I was no different from them. And my problems were small compared to some of theirs."

She bit down on her lip. "Is—is that why Tim Thornton got killed?"

He caressed her neck, taking one braid and bringing it across her shoulder. "Tim was transferred into my company just before we pulled out," he acknowledged.

Her heart began beating faster as his fingers sent small tingling shivers up and down the slender column of her neck. He leaned down, his breath moist against her cheek.

"Sometime, Babe, if things go as I want them to, I

may tell you what actually happened to Tim. I promised never to divulge the truth to anyone."

She pulled away, yet remained within the circle of his arms. "The truth?" she echoed, puzzled. "I thought the truth was already known from the way the senator always talked."

"Not all of it," he admitted reluctantly.

"Who will the truth serve, then?" she wanted to know.

"No one, in the end."

She shook her head. "My God, I would have spilled it a long time ago if I were you!" she exclaimed.

Matt smiled patiently. "At whose expense? It would mean Senate hearings and public embarrassment for several prominent people. Hell, if it was just Thornton, I wouldn't care. But it involves good military officers who would be hung out to dry if the truth were known. I've seen it happen too many other times. Washington needs a scapegoat when there's a public embarrassment, so they chop heads in the military. I've seen brilliant officers who were outstanding leaders get canned. I'd rather keep my mouth shut over the incident and take the heat from Thornton occasionally than let this mess ruin good men's careers." He gazed down at her. "Does that make sense to you, my dove who doesn't understand war?"

She shivered as he caressed her cheek with his roughened fingers. "I understand the principle, Matt." A soft smile curved her lips. "And you know something else?"

He leaned down, his mouth brushing hers with a tentative, feathery kiss. "What?"

His maleness was overpowering, and she fought to maintain the thread of thought. "I—I think you're a gallant knight on a white horse who believes in justice and fairness after all. Despite your contemptuous words, Matt, you're a knight. Perhaps your armor is tarnished and badly dented, but you continue to be gallant and honorable, even in dishonorable circumstances."

He laughed softly, nuzzling her ear with delicious slowness. "Like I said, Babe, we're all Don Quixotes tilting at windmills."

Her eyes sparkled with unshed tears as she met his tender gaze. "By standing for what you believe in," she whispered, "you are a giant among men."

"I'll settle for just being special in your eyes," he returned huskily.

His mouth descended upon her parted lips, the salty wetness of her tears giving a bittersweet taste to the kiss. She sighed rapturously, leaning fully against his hard male body, delighting in the feel of his warmth and strength. In her mind and her heart, she welcomed this man who made no excuses for his weaknesses or his strength. He was vitally human in a heady, exciting way, and she treasured each moment spent with him.

His mouth fit perfectly against her lips, parting them with gentle, exploratory pressure. A moan of pleasure slipped from her throat as he tasted her mouth thoroughly, his tongue igniting a burning heat in the center of her trembling body. Entwining his fingers through her thick hair, he imprisoned her face, drawing her more deeply into the fiery kiss.

An uncontrollable heat swept through her, and she returned the ardor of his kiss. A groan vibrated through his body, and he pinned her tightly against him, his hand sweeping down her spine to capture her hips and mold them against his own. Her heart pounded wildly; her breath was stolen from her. Slowly, ever so slowly, he released her. Alanna met his hooded, intense eyes, shivering with need for more of his knowing touch. Her lips parted, wet and throbbing from the force of his mouth as it had plundered hers. No man had ever evoked such violent desires in her.

He leaned forward, kissing her forehead, cheeks, and eyes. "I want you," he breathed thickly. "God how I need you, Alanna. You affect me like no other woman I've ever known. . . ."

Her mind rebelled for an instant only. Then her instincts and emotions overruled logic, and she willingly melted back into his awaiting arms. "Matt," she whispered, slipping her arms around his neck, "Hold me, just hold me. . . ."

The night was shattered by the throaty scream of a jaguar. Alanna gasped, clinging to Matt. The cry of the jungle cat was much closer this time. She felt him tense, his arm moving protectively around her body as he looked out into the night. Alanna heard the Costa Ricans stirring, stumbling out of their tents, mumbling in Spanish. Again the jaguar screamed. It sent a shiver of pure fear down her spine, and she cringed against Matt's shoulder.

"He's close," he muttered. "Get over by the fire and start throwing more wood on it," he ordered quietly. Matt released her, giving her a gentle shove in that direction. "Go on," he urged, moving to the tent and drawing out his .45.

Fearfully, Alanna did as she was ordered, trying to penetrate the darkness for a sign of the cat. The Costa Rican policemen followed her example, quickly scrambling for other pieces of wood. She stood tensely, watching Matt. He walked outside the circle of protection, and she held her breath. An excited jumble of Spanish fell against her ears, but her attention was riveted upon Matt. He seemed to become a cat himself as he melted into the shadows, his feet landing on the earth without a sound. She lost sight of him, her heart beating painfully as she waited an eternity until he came back.

His features were black with anger when he returned. He had something in his hand and threw it down at Juan's feet. "Ask him what the hell he's doing throwing C-ration cans out there. Doesn't he know the cat will be drawn by the smell of meat? He should have buried the garbage."

Alanna translated haltingly, and Juan's face turned a deep plum color. Refusing to meet Matt's demanding glare, the policeman shrugged.

"Tell him we're going to have to stand watch tonight. No one's going to get much sleep because of this. Someone will have to stay awake and keep the fire high. I tried to find the rest of the garbage they threw away after their meal, but it's useless."

Alanna slept off and on throughout the rest of the night. Matt had taken the first watch, much to her relief—he was the only one she trusted to be able to cope with the threat of the jaguar. When he slid in beside her much later, she awoke groggily.

"Matt?" she mumbled.

"It's all right," he murmured. "You're shivering."

Sleepily, she turned on her back, barely awake. "I'm cold."

He smiled patiently, putting the pistol back into the holster and placing it nearby. "I can see that. Come here, sleepyhead." He pulled her into his arms, tucking the blanket around her shoulders. Then he lay down, bringing her against him. "Better?" he inquired softly, touching her hair.

Alanna nodded, slipping back into sleep, feeling warm and protected within his arms.

Chapter Eight

Alanna sighed languorously, unconsciously snuggling more deeply into Matt's arms. The vague, comforting feeling of someone stroking her unbraided hair brought her half awake. The coarse weave of Matt's shirt, the solid beat of his heart reassured her as she remembered the screaming jaguar of the night before. That thought made her stiffen, and she immediately felt his arms tighten in response.

"Go back to sleep," he coaxed huskily against her ear.

The first rays of light trickled through the flaps of the tent as she opened her eyes. She was lying in his arms, her body pressed against him. She felt a sense of peace, a rightness in being there that she could not explain. She rubbed her eyes.

"I can't sleep," she whispered, resting her hand against his chest. "The jaguar . . ."

"He's gone. Cats only prowl at night. Probably home

with his missus up in some tree right now." There was a hint of humor in his low voice.

She knew she should move, but Alanna craved his closeness. He was unlike any other man she had known. The men she had dated after leaving Paul had had one thing in mind: getting her into bed at any cost. She had grown tired of their pawing and sloppy, hurried kisses. She thought of Matt's kisses, of his tender hands, and she closed her eyes, happy simply to share this quiet time near him.

"You aren't like the rest," she said, her voice barely audible.

His fingers trailed down the velvet slope of her cheek.

"Rest of what?" he teased.

"The men I've dated."

"In what way?"

She shrugged, embarrassed over her slip. "Don't mind me, I'm just waking up."

"I love it when you wake up. Your voice is throaty . . . very sexy," he murmured. He gently dislodged her head from his shoulder and raised himself up on one elbow. There was a tender flame of warmth lingering in his eyes as he studied her. "You're beautiful when you sleep. Do you know that?"

Alanna's lips parted in response. "Do you always say the right thing?" she accused.

He smiled, reaching out and smoothing a rebellious strand of hair away from her forehead. "I don't know. Do I?"

She smiled with him. "Either you're awfully sly, or you're being honest."

Matt ran his thumb across the smoothness of her forehead as he traced the varying planes of her face. "You have a funny way of affecting me, Alanna McIntire. Maybe it's your Hungarian heritage. Or your stubbornness. Do you realize how close I came to turning you over my knee last night?"

"Matt, I didn't come out here to make you worry. I want to clear your name and—"

His fingers descended upon her lips. "Sshh," he whispered. "I don't want to argue with you first thing in the morning." A smile tugged at the corner of his generous mouth. "You know, this is getting to be a pleasant habit. Sleeping with you, that is."

She colored prettily. "Believe me, I don't make a habit of sleeping around," she said defensively, starting to rise.

"Wait." Matt placed his hand on her shoulder. "Don't look at me like a frightened rabbit."

"I'm not frightened!" she gulped.

"Yes, you are," he taunted softly. Leaning over, he nuzzled her ear.

Little shivers raced up and down her neck as he nibbled at her earlobe. Breathlessly, she closed her eyes, unable to ask him to stop. Not wanting him to stop. Never had any man had the capacity to arouse her so fully with the mere touch of his mouth. Paul's attempts at lovemaking seemed cold and remote compared to Matt's masterful caresses.

Alanna sighed as she felt his hand cupping her chin, drawing her face upward. His mouth pressed gently against her lips in a breath-stealing kiss. Fire surged upward through her as she strained to meet his body. He tore down every barrier that she had erected against his advances. There was something clean and good in his touch, and she yearned to be a willing partner. Ever so reluctantly, he disengaged himself from her.

"You could drive a man crazy," he said thickly. "I want you, Alanna, but not here and not now."

He must have seen the confusion in her widened eyes. He bent down, capturing her lips in a light kiss.

"I'll be damned if we're going to be interrupted by a jaguar or our friendly policemen across the way," he explained, mirth in his expression.

She should have felt embarrassed, but she didn't. Not in his arms. She managed a grimace.

"Some of the men I've dated would have tried it anyway," she confessed.

"Are you disappointed?"

Surprise showed in her eyes. "No. . . . I've never met a man like you, Matt. You keep me off guard. Your life style, the way you think is so different."

He nodded. "It's not wrong to want to love you, Alanna. And when I do love you, it will be the right way, at the right time."

"That's what I mean," she murmured. "You're willing to wait. I've never met a man who could wait."

He laughed softly, kissing her cheek and brow. "Lady, you have no idea how difficult it is. Especially with someone like you."

She slowly sat up, crossing her legs beneath her, taming her unruly long hair with one hand. A new sense of elation swirled around her and she reveled in his closeness. Almost immediately, that fragile, budding feeling withered as she remembered the investigation. She had to try to stay uninvolved. At least until he had been vindicated! The "what ifs" were too threatening to contemplate. What if he were indicted? What would that do to her, their relationship? Alanna stole a look at him as he knelt over the blankets, rolling them up. What about her job? Pursing her lips, she tried to quell the smoldering desire Matt had brought to life within her dormant body. How could she have fallen so helplessly in love with a man whom her boss was out to destroy?

Resolution surged within Alanna. That couldn't happen. Somehow, some way, she would have to gather evidence to clear his name.

As Alanna and Matt ate their C-rations breakfast, the Costa Rican policemen stumbled out of their tents. The Marine corporal emerged a moment later, setting about making breakfast for himself. None of them looked as if they had slept particularly well. The vines and leaves shimmered with dew as the sun slanted through the dark jungle. Birds were calling melodically, and Alanna spied a small four-legged creature moving through the dense underbrush.

"Juan said it was about five kilometers to where they had found those crates," she mentioned.

Matt looked over at her. "That's not too far."

She stretched, getting to her feet. "I'm glad. I don't think I could keep on walking for another day."

"What gives you the idea you're going any further than this camp?" he demanded.

She stared down at him. "I'm going with you," she answered tightly.

"Like hell you are." His mouth thinned. "Didn't anything I said last night sink in?"

Anger fanned through her. "Don't try and tell me what to do, Matt! I haven't come this far not to get those photos."

He rose slowly, the muscles in his jaw clenched. His gray eyes were like dark thunderclouds. "What if we ran into guerrillas out there? Do you know what they'd do to us? To you? Alanna, this is not some kid's game we're playing. They have semi-automatic and automatic weapons. They'd cut us to shreds that fast." He snapped his fingers.

She shrugged, agitated. "Don't try to scare me, Matt."

He threw the remains of his coffee out of his cup. "I'm calling base to have a chopper pick you up."

Alanna stood tensely in front of him. "You can't have it land here—that would alert the guerrillas that you're coming," she tried to reason. "It's also not safe to leave me behind because I'll try to follow you . . . even though I'll probably get lost.''

His gray eyes burned with unshielded anger. They stood like poised adversaries for almost thirty seconds before she finally dropped her gaze from his.

"No doubt all this concern is in behalf of your beloved senator. All right, Alanna, have it your way."

She was miserable throughout the two-hour journey. He had ordered her to remain close behind him as they found a small, well-beaten trail through the jungle leading to the site. More than once, Alanna had acted as interpreter for Matt as he ordered the policemen to maintain at least fifteen yards between each man. Matt behaved differently under these circumstances, she noted. His expression was intense, his gaze restless and observant. More than once, he halted to listen, or to study what seemed nothing more than shadows created by the shifting sunlight.

Perspiration soaked her blouse and her hair as the humidity rose around them. Finally, they broke into a small clearing ringed by huge mahogany trees. The policemen grew excited, trotting toward several broken crates out in the middle of the cleared area. Matt halted on the perimeter, remaining within the tree line. He put his arm out, stopping her forward progress. "Stay here," he growled. Wiping the sweat off his face with the back of his sleeve, he ordered the corporal to scout around the area.

It seemed obvious even to her that if they were in potentially unfriendly territory it would be unwise to rush out in broad daylight where the enemy could see them. Alanna appreciated his caution and contented herself with digging her camera out of her dirtied briefcase. "By the time I get back to Washington, Senator Thornton is going to owe me a new briefcase," she muttered.

He glanced coldly down at her as she knelt over it. "Don't take any bets on it. He's known to be a real penny pincher."

She tried to ease the tension between them and offered a smile. "You don't have to tell me. I got a cost-of-living raise in January and that was it."

"For all the sixty-hour weeks you put in?"

"I guess he figures that's part of the glamor of working for a senator," she answered brightly, standing up. "Oh, damn," she muttered, "I've only got four pictures on this roll." Worriedly, she reopened the case, finding a second canister of film. Stuffing it in her pocket, she shrugged. "I've got exactly sixteen pictures. I'd better make every one count."

He gave her a neutral look. "Sixteen ought to be more than enough. Come on, Corporal Huffman is signaling that it's safe. It looks as though our guerrilla friends aren't around today."

"Maybe the jaguar scared them."

"Could be," he agreed.

What little was left of the smashed crates was carelessly thrown about the small field. Alanna stayed close to Matt as he carefully inspected each piece. She leaned down to read the black stenciled numbers on the crates.

"This isn't even from one of our shipments," Matt growled. "It's a different number code."

Alanna gasped involuntarily. "You're right!" Hope rose in her heart. "Maybe these crates held stolen supplies that the guerrillas took from someone else." Hurriedly she brought up her camera and clicked the shutter. It wouldn't budge. She gave the camera an aggravated look, and realized that she had run out of film. Quickly changing rolls, she took two photos of the crate lettering. She looked over at Matt. "Am I right?"

"Beginning to look that way. Come on, let's comb this place for more evidence."

They spent another half-hour finding more broken

slats that had been tossed here and there. One police-man cried out, motioning for them to come where he was standing. Alanna saw tire tracks imprinted on the muddy surface of the jungle floor. Matt knelt down, studying them intently. Finally, he looked over at her. "Looks like heavy transport vehicles." He grimly added, "The kind that are used by the police."

"What? Why, that's impossible. Why would the police be hauling supplies out here?"

Matt slowly rose, wiping his muddy fingers on the thigh of his utilities. "Simple, a black market scam."

"Then we've stumbled onto a smuggling ring?"

He nodded, following the grooved tracks back into the jungle. He knelt down over another spot, motion-ing her to join him. "Look here. Our truck has a slashed tire."

Alanna took several photos of the odd tire configura-tion. It appeared to have been cut by something, but not cut deeply enough to have caused a flat.

Finally, Matt said, "We've wasted enough time here. I'm going to radio Cauley to pick us up. I've got to get back to base anyway. Ready?"

She nodded. "Right now, the base sounds wonder-ful. Just think, a board floor to sleep on tonight." She gave him a warm smile, remembering his own words on the subject.

Matt returned it, digging the radio out of his pack. "Now you can begin to appreciate what I meant when I told you earlier that a floor was a luxury in some cases."

It seemed only a short time before a helicopter hovered over the clearing to pick them up. Alanna marveled at the time it had taken them to hike in on foot, appreciating the helicopter's usefulness. She sat against the fuselage, watching as Matt and Jim Cauley talked on the microphone to one another. She felt a surge of warmth whenever Matt smiled or laughed. If only she could share that kind of laughter with him one day. She clutched her briefcase as they landed, relieved that the crates they had discovered did not belong to San Dolega.

Alanna would choose another time to approach Matt on the remaining problem of the half-empty medical crates found up at the village. He was swamped by half the base personnel the minute he stepped off the chopper. Cauley gave her a distrusting look but said nothing directly to her as she left the confines of the helicopter.

It was near evening and they were sitting on the floor, eating their barely warm food when she finally brought up the subject.

"What are you going to do?"

Matt gave her an intent look. "Fly into San Jose tomorrow morning and start an investigation dock-side."

"Mind if I tag along?"

"Is that a proposition?"

She smiled, responding to the teasing warmth in his husky voice. "Want it to be?"

"Absolutely."

She felt a rush of excitement at the thought of finally being alone with him. There would be no interruptions, no phone calls. . . . Her heart sank. The investigation. What if Senator Thornton found out? He would tear the report up if he knew how she felt about Matt.

"Why the long face?" Matt asked.

Alanna placed her half-empty plate on the floor beside her. "I'm worrying about a lot of little things."

"That if Thornton finds out you're consorting with his arch enemy your job will be on the line?"

She avoided his gaze, his honesty jarring her. Alanna felt small and guilty. "That's part of it. But more importantly, if he finds out about how I feel it will discredit the report I have to do on you. If I turn up nothing conclusive, he's going to badger me for some silly detail. And if I provide none and it gets back to him we were sleeping in a tent together, he may think I'm covering up something, trying to protect you." She gave a helpless shrug. "I'm sorry."

He finished his coffee. "There's nothing for you to be sorry about, and your worry is understandable under the circumstances."

She entwined her fingers in her lap, twisting them. "You seem to take such gigantic hurdles with such ease, Matt. Most men would be angry or upset. There seems to be no way I can help; a good report can be as damaging as a bad one."

He got up, gathered the plates, and took them out to the radio room. The hollow sound of his boots striking the wooden floor was somehow soothing. He sat down close to her, his hands closed around his drawn-up legs. "Look, I've been dogged by the senator before, but this is the first time I stood to gain something from it. I met you." He grinned. "I don't feel angry or upset, lady, I feel impatient waiting for you. But where I come from, they believe in old-fashioned ways, such as long court-ships."

She gave a laugh. "So you're used to waiting?"

He grinned. "Not often, but when something's worth waiting for, I have all the patience in the world."

Alanna suddenly felt panicky. "Matt, I'm afraid. . . ."

He untangled her fingers, holding her right hand firmly within his own. "Why?"

"I'm afraid," she blurted out unsteadily, "of myself . . . of you. If you acted like those guys up on the Hill, I'd probably feel more secure about you and myself. But I don't," she added unhappily.

He didn't say anything for a long time, simply tracing the outline of her fingers. "Perhaps the men you've been meeting lately are out for a few nights of entertainment, Alanna. When I meet a woman who interests me, I like to take the time to get to know her. One of the many things I learned coming out of that war was to live each day like it was my last. That doesn't mean compressing a lifetime into twenty-four hours. It means capturing each nuance." He turned his head, studying her openly. "Like you, for instance. I love watching the color of your eyes change with your moods. Or those strands of hair at your temples that curl in the humidity. I like to hear you laugh. It's like listening to the bells at an old California mission, so clear and pure." He gave her fingers a squeeze, then released them.

"I understand the predicament you're in, and I don't want you to lose your job. I think I know what it means to you. So no more worry in those lovely eyes of yours. Let's get your investigation completed and sent off to Thornton and then pick up where we left off. Fair enough?"

Alanna packed her meager belongings, anxious to board the helicopter. She stood behind Matt, out of the way of the hustle and bustle as he gave last-minute instructions to the men in his command. With the advent of good weather, the airlift of supplies, and the hospitalization of most of the injured completed, the pressure had eased off.

Matt finally turned to her, walking over to lead her out the door.

"Ready?" he asked, smiling.

She detected a subtle warmth and excitement in his eyes. Returning the smile she whispered, "Yes."

Her spiraling mood of happiness quickly disappeared as her glance met Jim Cauley's suspicious look. Pursing her lips, she strapped herself into the seat behind the pilot's and said little else. As always, he and Matt donned the headset and conversed with one another freely. Alanna concentrated on the scenery, noting the various shades of green in the jungle far below them. The mountains were clean looking from the recent rain, and the sun was brilliant and hot. With a wry smile, she looked down at her feet. Her shoes were ruined, and her slacks were stained and muddied. What would the people at the hotel think? How would her colleagues react if they ever saw her in this disheveled state? She longed to bathe and wash her hair, to don a feminine dress, anxious to show Matt that she could be beautiful.

A small voice whispered to her, But he finds you beautiful anyway. She leaned her head against the fuselage, closing her eyes, contented.

The hotel clerk's pencil-thin eyebrows rose in horror as Matt walked into the plushly carpeted lobby in his field boots and well-worn utilities. The clerk's eyes traveled to Alanna, and the brows fell into an angle of suspicion. She saw several American hotel guests studying them with frank surprise. Their looks had not gone unnoticed by Matt, and he leaned over, his voice a confidential whisper.

"You sure you don't want to give a fictitious name? We're getting a lot of stares."

She grinned. "What, and ruin my image?"

"If this ever gets back to the Hill, you'll be a fallen woman among your friends," he suggested mockingly.

Her eyes gleamed. "You know, for the first time in my life, I don't care."

Matt squeezed her elbow reassuringly. "That's my gal. Do you want to do the honors of getting us rooms? I'm afraid this guy might lapse back into Spanish from sheer shock."

Alanna suppressed a giggle. "Well, you have to admit, we wouldn't make the best-dressed list."

He shrugged his broad shoulders. "Lady, you would

look beautiful no matter what you did or didn't wear, take my word for it."

She blushed becomingly as they halted at the desk. Gathering her scattered thoughts, Alanna requested two rooms next to one another.

The clerk's darting brown gaze traveled to each of them. *"Dos?"* he repeated disbelievingly.

Matt leaned over. *"Sí, dos."*

"And all along you said you didn't know Spanish," she accused.

"I understand it sometimes," he admitted. "In this case, I can count to two in Spanish and get the point across to him before he faints."

She swallowed a smile, unable to keep the merriment from her green eyes. The clerk meekly handed them keys, refusing to meet their eyes.

She padded down the carpeted expanse of the fourth floor hallway. "Matt, I feel like I'm in a dream. Carpeting. My God, this is an unheard of luxury!"

He stopped at her door, unlocking it and pushing it open. "Now you know how I felt when I returned from Nam. I was used to mud, water, and the sky for a ceiling."

She shook her head in amazement, stepping into the large, sunny room. "Two different worlds," she murmured.

"Look, take your time getting cleaned up. I'm going to take a quick shower, change, and make a few phone calls." He looked at his watch. "How about lunch at one o'clock?"

That would give her two hours. "Sounds good."

He placed her small suitcase beside the bed. "I'll knock on your door," he said, and then disappeared down the hall.

Alanna stripped off her smelly jungle clothes and dropped the shoes in the waste basket, mourning their loss. For the next half-hour, she stood beneath the hot, pummeling shower and scrubbed her hair until it was squeaky clean. Then she lathered herself with an apricot-scented soap. As she stepped from the bathroom wrapped in a large lemon yellow towel, she halted at the end of the bed. Should she lie down? Picking up her wrist watch, she noted that she had an hour and a half left. It looked so inviting. . . . Towel-drying her hair until it was only damp, Alanna slipped into her light blue robe and sank down onto the bed. Oh, what extravagance. Closing her eyes briefly, she dropped off into a deep, badly needed sleep.

Chapter Nine

An insistent knock at the door pulled her unwillingly out of the healing slumber. Groggily, Alanna stumbled off the bed, hands outstretched, vaguely aware that it was dark in her room. Groping for the knob, she fumbled with the lock and pulled the door open. The light was blinding, and she put up her hand, shielding her eyes momentarily.

Matt stood there in his khaki summer uniform, a slight smile on his mouth.

"Feel better?" he inquired.

She pushed several strands of hair away from her face. "What? Come in," she mumbled. Turning, she went to sit on the bed, still fighting the stupor of sleep. Alanna heard the door being closed quietly and the sound of Matt walking over to the sliding glass doors and opening them. A fresh, cooling breeze entered the stuffy room.

"How long did I sleep?" she muttered, rubbing her eyes.

He ambled over, taking his garrison cap off and tossing it on the bedstand. "It's eight-thirty. Probably close to ten hours."

She gasped. "No!"

He stood there, seemingly enjoying her drowsy state. "Hungry?"

Alanna suddenly became aware that she was wearing a very revealing robe. She felt her heart begin to beat faster. There was a curious gray flame within his eyes, a half-smile pulling at one corner of his mouth. A shiver coursed through her, and she felt both desirable and slightly frightened. The silken material of her robe outlined the curve of her rounded breasts, slender waist, and hips. Everything she wanted to say seemed to freeze on the tip of her tongue.

"I just got back from the Department of Transportation," he began, moving to the balcony area. "I thought we might discuss what I discovered over dinner tonight."

Whether he had understood her sudden discomfort and embarrassment or not, Alanna was thankful that he had turned away to give her time to scoop up her only set of clean clothes.

"I'd like that. Give me a minute, and I'll join you."

When she assessed herself in the bathroom mirror, Alanna wrinkled her nose. Somehow, she didn't feel special or magical in a plain cotton blouse of mint green and a pair of blue jeans. Matt was still resting against the balcony, gazing out into the night, when she walked softly out onto the small terrace area to join him.

"You look terribly handsome in dress uniform," she said, turning and catching his gray gaze.

"You mean you aren't going to be embarrassed by eating dinner with a military man tonight?"

She gave a low laugh. "If you had asked me that question five days ago, I would have said yes."

"Five days," he reminisced. "It seems like years ago, doesn't it?"

Alanna sobered, enjoying his closeness. "Yes, yes it does, Matt. Are you sure you won't be embarrassed having dinner with someone from the Hill?" she teased. "This is probably a first."

Matt smiled. "It is."

"I suppose you stick to the Pentagon people for your friends and entertainment," she prodded.

"And you stick to the Hill circuit and make all the parties," he finished.

"Mmm, sometimes," she hedged. "But with my busy schedule parties never have drawn me."

"Oh? Why?" He was resting his elbows on the railing. But even when he was relaxed, there was something exciting about the way his body moved.

"I'm not a crowd person," she explained. "I like to talk with one or two people instead of milling around like some cow in a herd."

Matt smiled and ran his fingers through her loose, silken hair. "See, you have more country in your soul than you first thought."

She shivered inwardly at his caressing, fleeting touch. "You don't strike me as a man who enjoys parties either."

"Never have. I'm like you in that respect, I enjoy a one-to-one relationship. See, we do have something in common."

Alanna laughed with him, a new sense of joy bubbling up in her. She had caught up on her sleep and felt refreshed, and there was a delicious wave of excitement swirling between them.

"We have something else in common. I'm starved."

He nodded, moving fluidly upright. "Let's go then."

"I'm just worried that they won't let us in to eat dinner the way I'm dressed."

His fingers closed around her elbow as he escorted

her down the hall to the elevator. "We'll eat here in the hotel. I don't think anyone will say anything, so relax," he soothed.

Alanna leaned forward and rested her elbows on the cleared table. The meal had been delicious. Matt was watching her through half-closed eyes.

"Penny for your thoughts?" he inquired.

"You probably already know."

"That you're happy? And sharing a meal makes you think of old times at the base camp or up at San Dolega?"

Alanna returned his smile. "You'd better be careful, Matt, or I'll think you're a mind reader."

He slid his hand across her fingers, picking them up and squeezing them. "I only read the minds of people who give away every emotion in their eyes and faces."

She wrinkled her nose, acutely aware of the pressure of his strong fingers. "I just can't believe I'm that readable. My God, how many times must Senator Thornton have seen what I was really thinking!"

He turned her hand over, lightly stroking her palm in an unhurried fashion. "Remember, not everyone has trained themselves in our nonverbal language," he reminded her.

Alanna felt her pulse quicken at his knowing touch. Reluctantly, she drew her hand back. "What did you learn while I was out like a light?" she asked.

If Matt was disappointed by her gesture, he didn't show it. Instead, he rested his jaw against his hands, appraising her in an intense, disturbing way.

"I managed to threaten the police commandant enough to find out that there is a renegade band of guerrillas in the area where we found those crates. Also, they have stolen some transportation trucks and used them to take their heisted supplies close to the border of Nicaragua."

"And our missing medical supplies?" she asked, her voice betraying her panic.

"I've got Captain Jackson investigating it right now. I coaxed the police to check all the names of the men working for us during this effort. I have a hunch that at least one or two of them will be connected with the guerrilla force."

She chewed on her lower lip. "I hope so."

Matt smiled. "Don't sound so worried, Babe. It will all come out in the wash."

Shrugging in an almost painful gesture, Alanna murmured, "I want it to . . . for your sake, Matt. I really do."

His eyes darkened. "Our sake," he corrected gently.

Something blossomed within her injured heart. There was such a confidence and sureness about him and the belief he held in their future together.

"I know so little about you," she whispered.

"What do you want to know?"

"Everything."

He smiled. "I was born in Kittery, Maine, and grew up there."

"Any brothers or sisters?"

"One brother, John. He's a lobster man at a place called York Harbor."

Alanna smiled. "I would never have thought you a fisherman."

He poured them both more coffee. "I've never outgrown the love of fishing. As a matter of fact, that cabin I told you about is a little ways inland of Kittery on the Piscataquis River. I usually take two weeks in the fall to go up there and fish my fill of black-backed flounder." He looked up. "I still want you to join me after this tempest in a teapot is over with."

Her green eyes crinkled with humor. "I've never picked up a fishing pole in my life, and I refuse to bait a hook with a poor, defenseless worm."

"We don't use worms to catch flounder. I'm afraid if I tell you what we do use, you'll turn my invitation down."

She grinned carelessly, thinking of what a joy it would be to share that time with him. No military or Hill politics to interfere. "Where is Kittery?"

"Just above Portsmouth, New Hampshire. I suppose you don't travel too far from D.C.?" he asked, teasing.

Alanna gave him a scowl. "I may be a city girl, Colonel, but that doesn't mean I haven't traveled a little."

"I see. That means within the state of Maryland and Virginia?"

"I've gotten as far as New York City and points west."

"Well, that's a start."

"To you it probably seems like a drop in the bucket. Traveling all over the world like a cosmopolitan jet setter."

Matt grinned. "Hardly in jet-setting style, believe me. More like the ride you took on that C-130 Hercules to get down here, packed between sweaty bodies and cargo crates for sixteen hours."

She joined his laughter. "So much for the image, then," she said.

Sipping her coffee, she studied him in the muted light surrounding them. Despite the outer garb and his military bearing, Matt's face was devoid of its usual stoniness. Instead, his gray eyes were lively with a silver sparkle in their depths. He smiled readily and often, the laugh lines at the corners of his eyes deepening, the harshness gone from his features. Across the table sat a man whom she felt herself responding to with effortless ease. The aura of sensitivity and gentleness around him left her breathless and wanting to explore more of this hidden side to him. When he talked of Maine his eyes lit up and his voice took on a wistful note.

142

"Did you mean it?" she asked suddenly.

Matt studied her. "About what?"

"Going fishing?"

"Of course. The best time is in mid-October, when the leaves are turning. There's no place like it, Alanna. I think you'll fall in love with Maine."

She shivered inwardly at the huskiness in his voice. "I want to see it because it's a part of you," she explained.

"Ahh, explore the lion's den."

"Carefully," she assured him, watching his eyes widen with silent laughter.

"I don't bite."

"Ohh, is that an understatement!"

"Only when I get my tail stepped on," he amended. "Like that first time we met."

Alanna tilted her head. "You had me so scared I was ready to fly back to D.C. under my own power."

Matt reached out, recapturing her hand and holding it gently in his own. "Do you have any idea of how beautiful you are?" he asked softly. "For two days before you arrived we had fought the Costa Ricans on the proper way to set up the relief plan, and I was ready to rip anyone's head off. And then, out of this C-130 comes the most beautiful woman I had ever seen. I didn't know what to do: whether to kiss you or turn you over my knee for bumping my radioman."

Her heart was pounding furiously, and she felt heat rising into her face. She frowned, unable to meet his tender gaze. "Please . . ." she whispered tightly, "don't, Matt, I—"

He raised her hand to his lips, kissing it gently. "Why not? You deserve to be flattered."

A lump grew in her throat until it squelched any words that she might have thought of. But under the circumstances, she couldn't think coherently anyway.

Living with Paul for four years had effectively numbed her sense of her own attractiveness.

Matt rose after he released her hand and moved around to her side, slipping his hand beneath her arm. "Come on, it's time to turn in," he urged gently.

As she walked silently at his side, Alanna tried to understand the varied emotions Matt Breckenridge had released in her. They halted at her room, and he captured her shoulders, turning her to face him. Lips parting, Alanna moved her gaze upward, meeting the silver flame smoldering within his hooded eyes.

"Lady, you're very special to me," he whispered huskily as his head descended.

Her breath caught in her throat, and she automatically closed her eyes, hungering for his nearness. His mouth brushed her lips in an earth-tilting caress. Alanna leaned forward, wanting, needing further contact with his mouth. A low groan came from him as he pulled her hard against his straining body, his mouth fitting perfectly against her awaiting lips. A soft cry echoed in her throat: one of pleasure, one of surrender to his masterful, guiding touch. He moved his hand down her spine, pinning her hips against him. Fire caught and exploded violently within her aching body, and she moaned, returning the heated kiss with unleashed intensity.

Gradually, ever so gradually, Alanna became aware of Matt gently pulling her away from him. Her eyes must have betrayed her disappointment because he slid his fingers through her hair in a caressing motion.

"You'd better get inside, or I won't keep my promise to you," he growled thickly. "Go on. I'll see you in the morning."

Alanna lay awake for a long time afterward. No matter how she tried to ignore the awakened desires of her hungry body, she could not sleep. Finally, she slipped into her blue robe and walked out to the patio, staring up at the stars overhead. A slight breeze ruffled her hair, and the scent of citrus wafted on the air. She inhaled unsteadily, gripping the railing. Suddenly, her well-ordered life was crumbling before her very eyes. It was a continual agony to be with Matt. The hotness of tears scalded her eyes, and she shut them tightly, her fingers whitening against the wrought iron. She loved him. God, she loved him so much it hurt! And never in her life had she felt the anguish of awakening love like this.

Finally, she opened her eyes, the tears streaming down her cheeks making silvery paths in the moonlight. Was it love or just a strong sexual attraction between them? When had any man made her body feel as though it were a singing, throbbing instrument to be played? She released her grip on the railing, trying to stem the flood of tears without success. She wanted to trust Matt . . . her heart did. But her head was more cautious. If Matt were brought up on charges and she let it be known she loved him, Thornton would have her fired in an instant. Matt had never said he loved her. But she sensed that the trembling huskiness of his voice had betrayed his feelings when he'd told her she was special only hours ago. . . .

It was his utter honesty that totally unstrung her. She was used to the games that the men around her played. Was Matt's honesty a game in itself? No, her heart whispered. If it were, why hasn't he gone against his word to keep the relationship neutral until the outcome of the investigation is known? Alanna knew he was restraining himself for her sake.

Matt could have taken her to bed tonight, and she would have gone willingly. She recalled with poignant sweetness the trembling of his hard, lean body against her own. It had been only his iron-willed control that had finally separated them. In his arms, she was clay to be molded to his desires. Turning, she stared in at the darkened bedroom, her lashes wet with tears. What heaven it would be if Matt were in there, waiting for her to return to his arms. . . .

Alanna awoke early the next morning. After a quick shower and a change of clothes, she was ready when Matt knocked on the door. Opening it, she gave him a smile.

"Come on in, I'm almost ready."

He stepped inside. "I probably should have warned you last night, Alanna, where we're going today, you'll want to wear some clothes you can afford to get dirty."

She made a half-turn, disappointment written on her face. Well, so much for looking feminine. She noticed he was in a pair of well-worn jeans and a short-sleeved shirt of light blue. "I was wondering why you weren't in uniform."

He grinned. "Only wear that thing when I have to, lady. You have one of those pairs of jeans you used up at the base camp?"

She made a wry face. "Okay, I get the drift. Can you wait five minutes?"

He nodded, amusement in his gray eyes. "You're worth waiting for," he returned.

She glanced up sharply, a slight blush tinging her cheeks at the compliment. He looked terribly handsome standing there, his weight shifted to one foot, his hands resting against his hips. This time, Alanna didn't try to fight the fluttery feeling in her stomach. "Thanks," she whispered, and then disappeared into the bathroom to change.

Matt led her downstairs to a small cafe for a quick breakfast. Alanna sat opposite him, giving him a questioning look.

"What are we up to today?" she asked.

Matt poured coffee, handing her a cup. "We're going down to the docks to do a little searching for a certain truck that's got a slash mark on its left rear wheel. Sounds exciting, doesn't it?"

Alanna lifted the cup, sipping the fragrant, strong coffee. "Somehow, Matt Breckenridge, anywhere with you is exciting."

He returned her smile. "Hasn't been dull since we met, has it? Back on the Hill you probably cause just as much commotion."

"Not really. I sit quietly in my office with stacks of information piled all over my desk doing statistics and surveys for the senator."

"That sounds positively boring."

"Compared to your life style, I'm sure it does."

"Didn't that set of papers you showed me the first day mention you were his South American specialist?"

She shrugged. "Supposedly. I haven't really had a chance to stretch into that area as I thought I would. The senator keeps an iron-clad grip on everything that involves South America."

Matt gave her a strange, unsettling look. "So he doesn't trust anyone with his former territory? I'm surprised he didn't come down here himself to investigate me."

"He would have if he hadn't had a filibuster the following Monday," she assured him.

Alanna detected a certain uneasiness about him and remained silent. She was amazed at the sharpness of expression that appeared in his gray eyes. One moment he was human; the next, a predatory hawk circling his prey. She shivered, setting down the cup. "I'll be so glad when this is all over," she muttered fervently. "I feel like I'm walking on thin ice with no hope of rescue."

Some of the hardness went out of his eyes at the frustration in her voice. "I'll always be there to rescue you, no matter what the circumstances. Just remember that."

She felt buoyed up by his huskily spoken promise. Hesitantly, she moved her hand forward. Immediately, his warm strong fingers clasped her hand, and she felt her pulse pounding in response.

As if he were reading her mind, or perhaps the strain on her features, he said, "This will be over very shortly, Alanna."

Compressing her lips, she avoided his gentle gaze. "I-I don't know Matt. I keep getting a horrible feeling here, in my heart. Call it instinct or whatever, I just know this isn't as simple as it all looks."

He released her hand, sitting back as the waiter brought them a breakfast of eggs and toast. "Thornton may try something, but as usual, it will be a bluff. Remember, he's tried it twice before on me." He scowled, studying her face. "I worry more about you in this mess than anyone. You're the one who is open to hurt, Alanna. I've seen Thornton put the screws to people before, and I don't think he's above doing it to you if push comes to shove. Just make damn sure that you log in your reports and keep a copy of them under lock and key somewhere other than your office."

She picked at the eggs, upset. She no longer believed Matt would lie about his skirmishes with the senator. But she had never seen that side of Senator Thornton . . . only his ready smile, his sometimes raucous, off-color office jokes and his ability to manipulate lobbyists for what he believed was right. Putting down the fork, she rested her hand in her lap, looking up to meet Matt's eyes.

"I'm frightened, Matt," she admitted. "I-I don't

know who to believe anymore. You've had terrible experiences with politicians. I work for one, and he seems so friendly, extroverted, and sincere in his desire to help the American people." She gave a little shrug. "God, I'm scared for both of us. . . ."

Chapter Ten

*H*aving no more than landed at Washington International Airport, Alanna received a call from Peggy as she entered her apartment. The senator's secretary began a point-by-point discussion of Alanna's report, which was expected on Senator Thornton's desk within twenty-four hours. Tiredly, Alanna agreed and hung up the phone. She gazed around her cheerful Georgetown apartment. Walking over to her spider plant, she caressed one long green and white leaf. It needed water, she decided, trying to shrug off the irritation of the phone call.

Her heart wasn't in her work. Saying good-bye to Matt had been more wrenching than she cared to admit. After snooping in and out of warehouses for nearly two days and finally discovering what had become of the missing medical supplies, she was exhausted. But that hadn't made their parting any less agonizing. Matt had insisted on maintaining his military bearing and demeanor. He didn't trust Thornton not to have a spy following Alanna's every move. And because of that, he never touched or even kissed her when they said good-bye.

Sighing softly, Alanna determinedly set to work on the report. It was nearly two in the morning when she completed the first draft. Well, she thought dully, the senator is going to be disappointed. Matt was clear of any scandal, thank God. Putting both canisters of film, the report, and a report filed by the police department in her attache case, Alanna went to bed. She slept poorly, nightmares lurking in the recesses of her mind. Despite Matt's vindication, she sensed that the situation had not yet been fully resolved. She awoke the next morning groggy and ill-tempered.

Her colleagues welcomed her back to work as she entered the spacious office complex. Peggy was waiting with her usual primness, hand outstretched for the report. Alanna clamped down the urge to make a few catty remarks to the blond-haired woman but decided against it, silently handing her the packet. Peggy gave her the standard cardboard smile.

"The senator gave orders to send you in to see him the moment you arrived back, Alanna. Let me tell him you're here."

Alanna pushed her fingers through her hair in an aggravated motion, then dutifully went to sit in the outer office. It was almost ten minutes before Peggy reappeared.

"He'll see you now."

Alanna rose from the chair, walking briskly into his office. The senator looked up from the desk, a smile on his lips.

"Welcome home, traveler!"

She returned the smile wearily, suddenly feeling all her apprehensions vanishing beneath his beaming appraisal. "Thanks, Senator."

He cocked his head, studying her. "You still look bushed. Rough down there?"

Alanna stood uncomfortably. "Very rough," she agreed. She noted the opened packet beneath his right hand. "I wasn't prepared for the kind of living they have to endure down there."

"If we had had more time, we could have briefed you more carefully, Alanna. I'm sorry if you were caused any undue discomfort. Please, sit down, you look terribly nervous."

She gave him a quick smile. "Just incredibly tired. Remember, Senator, I'm a city girl. That was pure country living at its worst down there. Not to mention the hiking around I did all over that jungle looking for evidence."

Thornton patted the packet gently. "I briefly scanned your report, Alanna. And it seems that Colonel Breckenridge is cleared of any wrongdoing. Is that true?" His eyes bored into hers, and his voice took on a razor edge.

A warning bell went off deep within her. Only a few seconds flew by, but Alanna remembered Matt's description of that intuitive alarm that always sounded when there was danger. She scrutinized the smiling, relaxed senator. Where was the danger? Her stomach was tied into knots for no apparent reason. It would be so easy to shift back to her logic . . . but she cared deeply for Matt and couldn't afford to ignore the advice he had given her. Licking her dry lips, she sat up straighter in the chair.

"I had to work at Colonel Breckenridge's side almost all the time, Senator. We discovered parts of some crates deep in the jungle south of San Dolega. They ended up being supplies that had been stolen off the dock, but they were not bound for the relief effort. At the docks we found the truck that had moved them."

Thornton nodded his massive head. "And the crates at San Dolega? You said five of them were only partially filled with medicine. What happened to them?"

"The colonel had the police commissioner looking into it, checking the names of the Costa Rican personnel who were ferrying those supplies up to the base camp. We found two men who were responsible for the disappearance of the medical supplies. Both are in custody now and awaiting trial in the capital city."

Thornton compressed his lips momentarily in thought. "I see. . . ." Finally, he looked back up at her. "So, in your opinion, Colonel Breckenridge is innocent?"

Alanna squirmed inwardly. Why did she feel close to panic? Swallowing hard, she nodded. "Innocent, Senator."

"The two incidents were entirely separate and unconnected, then?"

"It appears that way. But I really can't say much on that right now because the prisoners hadn't been interrogated before I left. Colonel Breckenridge felt that the San Dolega supplies may have been stolen by a local black market ring. The other supplies were probably taken by Nicaraguan guerrillas."

If he was disappointed, it did not show. He politely excused Alanna, telling her to take two days off and catch up on her rest. Alanna left the Hill feeling strangely unsettled by her meeting with the senator.

She counted the days until Matt would return. It had been nearly a week since she'd returned to Washington, and it was Friday evening. The weather was pleasantly warm and dry for mid-September, and it seemed as if she had never been to Costa Rica. Since returning to work, she had put in several twelve-hour days already.

Puttering in her kitchen, she made herself a salad,

took it into the living room, and turned on the television. Just as she sat down, the phone rang. Alanna placed her bowl on the glass coffee table to answer it.

"Hello?"

"Did anyone ever tell you how sensual your voice sounds over the phone?"

"Matt! You're back." Her heart rose in her throat, and she curled up at the end of the couch, cradling the receiver against her ear.

He laughed softly. "I got back last night as a matter of fact."

"You've got to be exhausted."

"A little. I spent today trying to knock down the piles of reports on my desk and didn't get anywhere."

"You ought to take a few days off and recover. I'm still suffering from jet lag."

"Mmm, that's not a bad idea. But I'd have to insist that my time off would include you."

She colored prettily. "As much as I want to say yes, I can't. Not just yet, Matt."

"Your senator?" he queried.

"Yes."

"What did he make of your report?"

She frowned. "He didn't seem disappointed but . . ." she searched for words to describe her feelings at that meeting.

"What was your gut reaction?" he coaxed.

Alanna squirmed on the couch. "God, I would much rather go with what I saw and my logic!" she breathed.

"Can't always trust those two together, Babe. You're hedging. I can feel it in your voice."

"I just got an unsettled feeling, Matt. I—I can't explain it. And Peggy, his secretary, has been acting awfully cold toward me ever since I've returned. I don't know why."

There were a few moments of silence on the other end of the phone. Finally, Matt spoke, his voice more serious. "This isn't over yet, but I figured as much. He's going to try to find a way to pin it on me anyway."

Alanna gripped the phone convulsively. "No!" she whispered tautly. "He can't!"

"He'll try it."

"I hope you're wrong. I just want this to blow over so that we can see each other."

"Makes two of us, Babe." He exhaled. "Look, under the present circumstances, let's take a raincheck on that weekend until I'm sure he's going to let bygones be bygones. If his secretary is not treating you like she usually does, it could mean that he had you followed down there. Your job might be in jeopardy."

She got up, suddenly unable to sit still, and paced back and forth, carrying the phone. "And I thought I had an active imagination," she accused him.

"Secretaries know everything, Alanna. I haven't met one yet who didn't know the most intimate secrets about her boss."

"But the senator seemed so friendly to me. How could he hide his anger if he knew that I—we—"

"I told you before, politicians are the ultimate gamespeople of the world. They'll smile one minute and stab you in the back the next. What's your schedule look like for the next few weeks?"

Alanna sat down on the couch. "He's sending me to California for almost three weeks."

"Well, I figure if he doesn't spill something on this in about a month, it will be safe to see one another."

"I feel like we're acting out a scene from *Romeo and Juliet!*" she complained. "This is so silly! Instead of the Capulets and Montagues feuding, it's Thornton and Breckenridge."

"That's right, honey, and you're standing right in the middle of the game. Look," he soothed, "no one wants to see you more than I do. I can hardly stand to wait, knowing we're in the same city. It would be so simple to drive over or to have you come to my home. But Thornton might still be having you tailed until he's sure which way to swing with your report. If he suspects you're an ally of mine, then what good are you to him in an investigation hearing against me? Do you see my point?"

Morosely, she agreed. "Just call me Juliet until this stupid tempest in a teapot is over," she griped unhappily. She heard him laugh, and that raised her spirits. It was the kind of laughter that was full and resonant, and it sent shivers through her body. "It's good to hear your voice, Matt. I—I missed you. I never thought I'd ever say that to another man."

"You just keep the first weekend in October open, Babe. By then, the leaves will be turning, and I'll fly us up to Kittery. Do you like kids?"

Alanna smiled, beginning to relax beneath the caress of his husky, warm voice. "Love them. Why?"

"I haven't seen my brother John or his wife Ev for nearly a year, and I wondered if you might want to stop in and see them Friday night. They have three lovely daughters that range in age from five through eleven."

"It sounds wonderful. That's one thing I miss around here; there are so few children. Where I grew up, the block was always filled with them."

"Like kids, huh?" he teased.

"Always."

"You'd make a good mother," he said huskily. "I'm sure Ev will let you try your hand at it. Just remember, I warned you beforehand. The girls will mob you at the door."

"Like they do you?" she laughed. Somehow, she had never envisioned Matt in that role. Yet, recalling his tenderness and sensitivity with her, it was easy to imagine him dealing with children of all ages.

"Yes, I get mobbed. But that's because they only see their Uncle Matt once a year."

"I'll bet. You probably spoil them rotten," she accused gently, smiling.

"Me? Nah. I'm the tough Marine colonel, remember?"

"You're a raging lion with a heart of gold, Matt Breckenridge, so don't try to fool me, too!"

"Promise not to tell anyone? It wouldn't help the image I've carefully nurtured over at the Pentagon."

Alanna laughed joyfully. He had such an incredible knack for releasing her inhibitions and fears, melting them with his humor and wit. "Your image here in Washington is of a man who has a courageous heart and a backbone of steel."

"You believe everything you read in the papers?" he asked blandly. "Old war records and medals are always good fodder for the starving press."

"How many people know the real you?" she wondered idly.

"Not many."

"I feel privileged in knowing the other side of you. Well, at least a little bit of you. Oh, Matt, we have so much to talk about and—"

"Very soon, Babe, we'll have the time to explore each other thoroughly," he promised. "But until then, be a good Juliet and stay in your office. Listen, let me give you my office and home number. Never call me from your office. Wait until you get home."

Alanna scribbled down the numbers. "Another four weeks, huh?"

"You want to keep your job, don't you?"

At that instant, she wasn't sure. "I feel like a prisoner of fate," she groused.

"Fate brought us together," he agreed amicably, "but you're *my* captive."

Alanna shivered at the velvet promise in his tone. "Why do I have the feeling you're a lion stalking his next victim?"

"You're worth stalking, lady, believe me. Look, I'll give you a call in a few days before you leave for California."

Reluctantly, she set the receiver back down on the cradle, staring at it. Finally, she raised her chin, staring at the gathering darkness outside the apartment. Everything felt right since Matt's phone call. He gave her so much!

The clear, cobalt, October skies beckoned to Alanna. She threw her briefcase into the back of her Mustang and said a silent good-bye to the Hill. Three weeks out in California had left her with a golden tan, making her eyes seem greener and her hair redder. As usual, Washington traffic was a snarl, and it was nearly six-thirty before she finally reached her apartment.

She had no more than stepped inside the door when the phone rang. Throwing her briefcase on the couch, she picked it up.

"Hello?"

"Well, are you ready to be stolen away for the weekend?"

Alanna breathed in deeply, lingering over the huskiness in Matt's voice. "Oh, yes!"

"How about if I pick you up in an hour? I've got a few last-minute things to attend to here at the office, and then we'll fly on up."

"Fly?"

"Sure. Don't you trust me?"

"Always," she murmured fervently. "I've never flown in a small plane before. This ought to be quite an experience."

"Well, hurry and pack a few things for living at a rustic cabin. We'll stay with John and Ev tonight and go up to the cabin Saturday morning."

Alanna had hurriedly packed jeans, T-shirts, and one good dress when a knock sounded at the apartment door. She skipped through the living room, turned the lock, and pulled the door open. Matt stood there in his dark green wool uniform, a smile in his dark gray eyes.

"Come here," he whispered, holding out his arms.

Alanna flew into his embrace, pressing the length of her willowy body against the hard oak of his. "Oh, Matt . . ." she whispered, nuzzling against the side of his cheek and neck.

She heard him growl and felt the steel grip of his arms wrapping about her. Instinctively, she turned her head, meeting his descending mouth eagerly. Her heart surged with joy, beating wildly against her breast as his mouth came savagely down against her awaiting lips. A wave of heat curled upward through her, leaving her weak and breathless within his powerful, demanding grip. He touched her eyes and lips, trailing a series of kisses down the slender expanse of her neck. Raising his head, he stared at her, his eyes turbulent with barely contained passion. Alanna languished within his embrace, longing to feel the taut hardness of his male body against her. He ran his fingers through her long hair with a wistful look on his face.

"You've grown more beautiful," he whispered, leaning down and kissing her one more time. "God, how I've missed you, Babe," he said thickly.

"I've missed you even more," she whispered breathlessly.

Matt gently released her, unwilling to allow her to leave the shelter of his arms. "A lot of the officers over at the Pentagon think I've turned into a daydreamer," he said, a wry smile on his mouth.

"Why?"

"I keep thinking of you instead of doing my work. If I look out my office window and see the trees, I think of your lovely green eyes. And if I stare at my book cabinet, I'm reminded of the walnut color of your hair and running my fingers through it."

She sighed, reaching up and kissing him lightly on the mouth. "You're a hopeless romantic," she accused gently. "But don't stop, I love it."

Matt removed his hat and pulled her inside the apartment. "I'm not a romantic, I just know what I want. Look, let me take five minutes to change into some civilian clothes, and then we'll get going." He pulled her against him, giving her a final, earth-shattering kiss that left her feeling weak with need. "I'm going to have a hell of a time keeping my hands off you," he warned, a dark growl in his voice.

Matt handled the twin-engine Aztec with the sureness of experience as he nosed the plane skyward. Once out of the busy traffic centers around Washington D.C., he glanced over at her.

"Nervous?"

She shook her head. "How can I be? I'm in your hands."

He winked, motioning to a small compartment situated on her side of the cockpit. "Dinner is in there. It will be about two hours before we land at York. There's coffee and some roast beef sandwiches."

Alanna busied herself with the preparation of their meal, awed by the beauty of the view at eight thousand feet. The night sky scintillated with a myriad of twinkling stars that looked close enough to reach out and touch. Below, the lights of city after city fled beneath them. They reminded her of jewels set in the velvet blackness of the earth's crust. The red, green, and white lights became rubies, emeralds, and diamonds, while sulphur lights were transformed into amber gems.

Drawing up one knee, Alanna rested her coffee against it, finally asking the nagging question that had been lurking in the back of her mind.

"Matt, do you think the senator has given up trying to implicate you?"

He sipped his coffee. "It appears that way. You said that Peggy is acting more friendly?"

"Yes, she's all smiles now. I have to admit, though, I did do a good job of working with those lobby groups while I was out in California."

"Naturally. You're good with people, Alanna." He grinned. "Look how well you've handled me."

She joined his laughter, and the cabin was filled with the rich sound. "That's a lie! No one handles you, Matt Breckenridge."

"Only when I want to be handled," he agreed. "Well, in another hour we'll be down, and the girls can mob you this time instead of me," he commented good-naturedly.

John and Evelyn Breckenridge met them at the York airport and Alanna suddenly felt shy. She hung back until Matt put his arm around her waist and brought her forward. John was tall, like Matt. He had dark brown eyes, black hair, and a ready smile. Evelyn was petite standing beside the brothers, smiling warmly as she took Alanna's hands and gripped them with friendly strength.

"It's so nice to meet you, Alanna," she said enthusiastically. And then she raised one eyebrow, giving Matt a scolding look. "It's about time Matt brought you home! Goodness, he called John right after he got back from that relief mission in Costa Rica and told us all about you." She gave Alanna a quick hug. "You've got to be very special," she whispered, "very special."

Alanna thought she saw the glitter of tears in the other woman's hazel eyes but said nothing. Sitting in the back seat with Matt, she was content to listen to the brothers talk. Their conversation centered around John's trawler, the lobster pots, the change in temperature occurring along the Atlantic seaboard which was forcing the lobster to move in a more southerly direction. Closing her eyes, she was content to feel the warmth of Matt's family around her. It was a new, wonderful feeling. She hadn't realized how much she had missed being part of a family. Not until now.

At the door of the Cape Cod house, high above the beach outside York, three girls anxiously waited for the car door to open. Matt helped Alanna out, matching his stride to her own, his arm possessively about her shoulders. He leaned over, looking boyishly delighted. "I'll bet that Susanah takes a shine to you right off," he whispered, kissing her brow.

Alanna didn't have time to respond. The girls squealed with delight, tumbling like playful puppies off the porch and running down the sidewalk.

"Uncle Matt! Uncle Matt!" they shrilled.

Alanna laughed and stood back, watching all three girls attack Matt in unison. Even in the darkness, the porch light revealed that two of the girls were towheads and the third a brunette like her parents. Matt knelt down, laughing and hugging all three of them simultaneously. Squeals of delight, cries of "We missed you!" and "Gimme another kiss!" filled the night. John walked by, grinning. Evelyn simply shook her head and followed her husband into the house.

"Come on in as soon as you can get Matt loose," Evelyn called laughingly over her shoulder.

The night was chilly, but Alanna was too interested to notice. Inside, a new kind of warmth was glowing within her heart. The little girls loved Matt. She was mesmerized by the boyish quality of his face, the fullness of his laughter, and his ability to hug and kiss them without reserve. Thoughts of her aunt and uncle and of what she had missed struck her. And suddenly, without warning, tears filled her eyes.

Matt gently extricated himself, reaching out and drawing Alanna back into the circle of his arm. "Girls,

I want each of you to politely introduce yourselves. Let's start with the smallest here."

The five-year-old, a child with large gray eyes and dark hair, came forward, awed by Alanna. Alanna knelt down, giving her a tender smile. The little girl put her fingers in her mouth, regarding her shyly.

"You Aunt 'lanna?" she wanted to know.

Alanna glanced over at Matt who had knelt beside her. Matt laughed, drawing the child into his arms and giving her a quick hug.

"Not yet, Susanah, you little imp. Now be a good girl and give Alanna a welcome home hug."

Susanah giggled and shyly went to Alanna. She had expected a hug, but instead, the little girl suddenly reached up, her tiny arms encircling Alanna's neck, and placed a wet kiss on her cheek.

Shaken, Alanna felt tears rolling down her face. She returned Susanah's gesture, kissing her brow and then touching her silky dark hair.

"You look so much like your father, Susanah," she whispered.

"She's the spitting image of John," Matt agreed. He leaned over, brushing the tears from her cheeks. "Welcome home, Babe," he whispered.

Something broke loose deep inside her. It took every ounce of control to stop the tears while Matt introduced Libby and Sarah, the blond-headed girls.

"Go on in, girls, we'll be along in a minute," Matt ordered.

Susanah was the last to go, still staring wide-eyed up at Alanna. Finally, Alanna leaned down, giving the child a long embrace. "We'll be right in, honey," she promised.

Matt watched as the door closed quietly and then put his arm around Alanna. He walked her out beyond the small concrete sidewalk and led her down between the dunes to the darker sand where the waves were crashing inland.

He halted, taking her into his arms, holding her silently. He brushed his cheek against her hair. "You all right?" he asked gently.

"I—no. . . ." Her voice wavered with tears.

"You can cry," he urged, tilting her face up to meet his gaze. "You've been too long without a family, Babe. Consider our family yours."

She sniffed, the tears making hot trails down her face. Matt provided her with a white handkerchief. "You were right," she said finally.

"About what?"

"Susanah liking me. She's so pretty, Matt. I feel my heart expanding like a flower when I think of how she came up and kissed me."

"She's exactly like you, guileless and innocent." He caressed her shoulders. "You have so much natural love and affection stored up in you."

"It's news to me," she protested, drying her eyes.

"How could you know? You've been holding your emotions in since you were a tiny child."

Alanna shook her head. "I've missed so much," she whispered tightly.

Matt leaned down, his mouth pressed caressingly against her lips. "Until now, honey," he said huskily.

She trembled within his embrace, the chill of the night seeping into her light jacket. He held her more closely, his hand pressing her head against his shoulder. "I think this is going to be the most beautiful weekend I've ever had," she murmured, nuzzling against him.

"It will be," he promised her. "A new chapter in the book of our lives, honey. Come on, I know Ev probably has a late dinner warming up for us. Hungry?"

Alanna looked up into his strong, open face. "Not anymore," she murmured.

Evelyn had just set two large bowls of steaming clam chowder on the table when they sauntered into the house. The girls, all three of them, greeted them with a chorus of giggles and crowded around them as they sat down.

"John," Evelyn said, a hint of warning in her voice, "I think it's well past the girls' bedtime."

"Ohh, Mom!" Libby, the ten-year-old, exclaimed, crestfallen.

Alanna turned, smiling at the precocious youngster. "They aren't bothering us," she protested.

John halted at the door, grinning. "See, I told you she'd like kids."

Little Susanah climbed into Alanna's lap, smiling shyly up at her and then burrowing into her arms, content. Ev rolled her eyes upward.

"Oh, all right!"

A cry of victory went up, and everyone sat down at the table. John brought two more chairs in, pouring coffee for the adults and allowing the girls a small glass of orange juice each. The kitchen was small and crowded, but it glowed with a happiness that Alanna had never encountered. She ate the chowder with relish, not realizing how hungry she had been. Occasionally, she caught Matt watching her out of the corner of his eye. Then he would quirk one corner of his mouth upward, his gray eyes shooting her a look of reassurance. The chatter was nonstop, and Alanna found herself laughing more than she had in years. Susanah loyally remained ensconced in her lap while Alanna finished off the soup.

It was nearly eleven o'clock when Evelyn noted, "I think all the excitement has worn her out." Susanah had fallen asleep in Alanna's arms.

"She's so beautiful," Alanna whispered, exchanging an intimate glance with Matt.

John rose, stretching his tall, lean body. "The girls have been talking for two weeks of Matt and you coming up. Here, I'll take her and tuck her into bed."

Ev smiled warmly. "After all, we didn't invite you here to play babysitter."

Reluctantly, Alanna gave up the warm little bundle. "I don't mind, Evelyn. Believe me, this is exactly what I need after working on the Hill like a slave for the past couple of years." She winked over at Matt. "Right now I feel like I've been rescued by a knight in shining armor and taken away to his castle."

Evelyn rose, smiling. "Our home isn't exactly grand by most people's standards, but do consider it your home, too, Alanna. And as for Matt, he *is* a knight as far as we're concerned." The pride in her voice was unmistakable. "Five years ago we lost almost everything we had in a hurricane, Alanna. If it hadn't been for Matt, John would never have gotten the loan he needed to buy another lobster trawler." She gave a slight shrug of her shoulders, her eyes bright with unshed tears. "Raising three girls and trying to make ends meet up here forced John to put less insurance on his boat than what was necessary. The hurricane wiped us out." Ev walked over to Matt, resting her hands against his broad shoulders. "Then this guy comes up on thirty days' leave and helps us find another house, salvage what little we could, and put a down payment on a new boat." She leaned over, pressing a kiss to Matt's brow. "You're very fortunate to know him, Alanna. Take our word for it."

Alanna watched Matt, a serious expression on her features. He had the good grace to flush slightly from Evelyn's praise. Reaching up, he gripped Ev's hand, squeezing it.

"For someone born in Maine, Ev, you sure get sentimental," he teased.

Ev gave him one more hug and walked toward the

door to the living room. "He'll never tell you this, Alanna, but Matt has been the mainstay of the Breckenridge family since their parents died. We wouldn't know what to do without him."

Matt rose, stretching to his full height. "Being godfather to their three girls hasn't left me much time *not* to be interested in family concerns," he drawled.

"And you love every minute of it," Alanna responded softly.

Evelyn nodded. "He's a natural. Well, listen you two, let me show you our makeshift bedding arrangements, and then we'll let you stay up as long as you like."

Alanna followed Evelyn into the living room, thinking of how nice it was to see the lived-in look of their home. Her apartment always looked so immaculate—almost as if no one lived there. A soft smile crossed her lips as she drank in the homey atmosphere.

"I'm truly sorry," Evelyn said, touching her arm. "But as you can see, the house is small. We have only three bedrooms, and I thought, if you don't mind, Alanna, that I'd let you share Susanah's room with her. Matt, as usual, you get the couch, and you know where the blankets and pillows are kept."

Matt nodded. "Second closet on the right. I'll get them."

Evelyn glanced up at her. "Do you mind sharing a room?" There was hesitancy in her voice. "Susanah has been looking forward to sleeping on the cot we keep for just such occasions. She sleeps soundly through the night and probably won't wake up until nine tomorrow morning since she went to sleep so late."

Alanna shook her head, a full smile on her lips. "No, I'd love it. To tell you the truth, I've missed family life. This will be like making up for it."

Evelyn stopped at Susanah's room and pointed to the bed. "The bed is full-sized. We just couldn't afford to buy the girls shorter ones. Figured they would grow into them, anyway."

Alanna laughed, noting that Susanah was happily tucked away in the cot opposite the bed. The furniture was pale blue with white trim, and the wallpaper was covered with tiny pink roses. A sharp ache intensified in her heart. She recalled too poignantly her own childhood room: it had been an antiseptic white and spare in comparison. Here and there in Susanah's room were little feminine touches, her favorite dolls and stuffed animals, a coloring book open on the antique dresser with crayons spread across the top of it. "I'm going to enjoy this," she promised Evelyn, a slight tremble in her voice.

It was almost midnight before the household settled in for sleep. Matt had boiled water and made tea for them. Alanna sat across the table from him, idly stirring the contents of her cup. She looked up, meeting his gray gaze. "I feel like I'm in heaven," she confided, her voice barely above a whisper.

He returned her smile, removing the tea bag from his cup. "Would you think I was lying if I told you that you look like a different woman?"

She tilted her head, mystified. "In what way?"

He poured a teaspoon of sugar into the china cup. "The tension is gone around your mouth, and your eyes are bright. It's funny how a high-pressure job will make you tense and nervous. I've never heard you laugh before as much as tonight. I love watching your face, it's so mobile and expressive."

She warmed beneath his husky voice and slid her fingers around the base of her cup. "That makes us even, then. I didn't realize just how much of a natural father you really are. You were right, the girls did mob you." She toyed with her cup for a moment. "It seems like I've always known you, Matt," she confessed uncertainly. "There is a—" She groped for the right words. Paul had taught her to be specific about her emotions, and now she tried desperately to find words to describe the new feelings growing within her heart. "When you walked into my life, I felt we could get along despite our differences." She shook her head. "That's a new one for me."

He reached across the table, capturing her fingers. "Hand in glove," he provided softly.

"I see I'm not the only one who depends on your strength. Not every family would pull together in a crisis like John and Evelyn experienced. She idolizes you, Matt." She smiled. "You're easy to idolize."

"Careful, lady, don't be putting me up on any pedestals. I fall off pretty quickly, and I have feet of clay just like everyone else," he warned.

"Knights in shining armor never tarnish or go out of style."

Matt grinned, releasing her fingers. "Now who's the romantic?" he teased, taking a sip of the tea.

Alanna wanted to say that every hour spent with him was like a fairy tale come true. But she remained silent. After four years of hearing that harsh reality was the stuff life was made of, she was afraid to fully enjoy this mini-vacation. When would the bubble burst? How much of this was just a figment of her imagination? She tried to analyze her feelings but soon gave up, overwhelmed by a feeling of euphoria that could only be love. A love that was new and breathtakingly fresh. And it was all due to the man who now sat quietly opposite her at the table.

"Look," Matt began huskily, "let's get to bed. We'll be getting up early tomorrow, and I want you well rested, lady."

Alanna stood, taking the teacups and placing them in the sink. She felt his presence behind her and stood very still.

He slid his arms around her waist, drawing her back

against him. Matt rested his head against hers, his breath warm against her cheek. "You know, lady, if you keep looking this content, I'm going to have to do something about it," he whispered.

Alanna willingly leaned against his hard, warm body, languishing against his shoulder. She closed her eyes, sighing softly within his embrace. "If I get any happier, I think I'll explode," she admitted.

"You deserve some happiness," he returned, kissing her cheek. "Come on, let's get to bed," he coaxed.

She turned, remaining within the security of his embrace as he walked her through the dark, silent house. At the door, he leaned down, kissing her lightly on the lips. "I'll see you tomorrow," he whispered.

Alanna caught the gleam of humor in the depths of his gray eyes. "I have a feeling I won't be safe from you after tonight," she said.

He kissed her lingeringly. Raising his head, he murmured, "You won't be. Good night, Babe."

Chapter Eleven

Alanna awoke groggily the next morning, aware of a small body snuggled up beside her. She heard the door open, and was vaguely aware that someone was walking quietly around the bed. Barely opening her eyes, she looked up to see Matt standing above her, a careless grin on his face. He sat down on the edge of the bed.

"What's this?" he teased, reaching out and ruffling Susanah's dark hair.

Susanah giggled, her small body squirming with laughter. Automatically, Alanna's arm tightened around the girl.

"Uncle Matt, I couldn't sleep in the cot," she began dolefully, stealing a glance up at Alanna.

Matt raised one eyebrow, catching Alanna's sleepy gaze. "And here I was going to come in and wake up my fairy-tale princess with a kiss," he said, pretending to be miffed with the child.

Alanna turned carefully on her side. "You still can," she murmured huskily.

Susanah curled up tightly, laughing as Matt tickled her. He leaned across, touching Alanna's lips, his mouth strong and warm. Then he scowled darkly at the girl.

"Looks like I'll have to kiss you too, or you'll turn into a frog, young lady."

Delighted, Susanah reached out and Matt embraced her, planting a kiss on her small brow.

"No frogs now, Uncle Matt?"

He got to his feet. "Nope. The prince just kissed his two ladies, so everyone's safe now. And, if you two can force yourselves to get up, I think Evelyn has breakfast waiting."

The morning was clear and crisp, a light glaze of white, shimmering frost coating the landscape. Alanna sat contentedly near Matt as he drove the last few miles to the cabin. The sky was a deep cobalt blue, and seagulls and terns wheeled far above them like milky white opals against the fabric of the sky. The white bark of the birch trees, the yellows, reds, and oranges of the maple and oak mingled against the dark background of the evergreens. Inhaling deeply, Alanna drank in the sweet odor of decaying leaves and the tangy salt of the sea. She leaned against Matt, their shoulders touching. He captured her hand and rested it upon the hardness of his thigh. She could feel the steel strength of his muscles beneath the rough texture of the jeans he wore.

"Happy?" he asked.

"Mmm, incredibly happy. I keep thinking that this is a beautiful dream and I'm going to wake up soon and find myself back on the Hill."

He squeezed her hand reassuringly. "We both needed a break from our jobs."

"Now I see why you love to come up here."

He nodded. "When I got back from Nam, this place helped to put me back together again. I wouldn't have made it without John and Ev's support."

Alanna detected raw pain in his voice, yet he wasn't asking for pity. Somewhere, deep within her, she knew Matt wanted to reveal other sides of himself to her. And she was eager to understand what made him the man she was so completely in love with. She looked to her left, studying his strong, clean profile. She saw the military bearing, the years of hardship he'd suffered. At the same time, the slight upward curve of his mouth softened the lines of his face. She could recall times when his eyes were narrowed and nearly colorless with anger and other times when they were turbulent and dark with passion for her alone. She trembled inwardly, amazed at the depth and breadth of Matt Breckenridge.

The cabin, fashioned out of rough-cut logs, reminded her of something from the turn of the century. It stood on a slight knoll, surrounded by oak and pines, its sides grayed and weather-beaten from years of withstanding the storms that struck each winter along the Maine coast. The Piscataquis River moved serenely down below them, sandpipers scurrying the length of the bank looking for tasty morning morsels. Matt took their luggage inside, and she followed him, gazing around the darkened interior.

"It smells musty. How long has it been since you last came up here?" she asked, moving the curtains back and releasing the window lock to allow fresh air inside.

"Last October. With the windows open, it will air out in a few hours," he assured her. "Why don't you get changed into some jeans. I don't think you want to wear those expensive-looking slacks anywhere but in here."

Alanna caught his teasing gaze and obediently unpacked her jeans and a pale pink blouse. Despite the rustic appearance of the cabin, it had every modern convenience. There was a small fireplace at one end with a neat stack of wood beside it. She found the bedroom and wandered into it. The bed was made of brass, and the frame needed to be shined badly. Running her fingertips along the railing, she made a mental note to see if some polish was available. It was a shame not to keep an antique like this shining brightly.

Matt was waiting patiently outside with two fishing rods and a tackle box when she sauntered out of the cabin. He gave her an appreciative look.

"Well, you prepared to catch our dinner for tonight?"

Alanna gave him a startled look. "Me? Why, I've never fished before in my life, Matt Breckenridge."

He grinned. "You'd better hurry up and learn, lady, because if we don't catch something, we aren't eating."

She laughed, following him down a well-worn trail toward the river. Within half an hour, he seemed satisfied with the spot he had found and set the gear down. "This is our old fishing hole. The bottom of the river is muddy, and the black-backed flounder come up here to live."

"The only flounder I've seen is in the meat market all neatly packed in plastic and Styrofoam."

He laughed. "You're in for a surprise then. Spread that blanket out on the bank, and we'll catch a little sun while we're fishing," he suggested.

Soon, silence settled around them, the fishing poles resting on the bank. Alanna couldn't keep the disgust out of her face when Matt used what could only be described as a repugnant-looking worm with a hundred legs as bait. She avoided watching as he calmly placed the multilegged creature on the hook. It was only after he had cast the line into the water that she would take the rod from him. She closed her eyes, enjoying the warmth of the sun as it rose higher into the sky, the call of the birds, the sight of the seagulls wheeling above them, and the lap, lap, lap of the water.

Matt lay on his side, idly watching the tip of his rod. He reached out, pulling Alanna over beside him. Her hair, dark with red highlights, fanned out as she rested on his arm.

"You look like a wood nymph," he murmured, tracing the outline of her jaw.

She shivered as his fingers trailed down her neck, resting gently against her shoulder. "A wood nymph in jeans?" she laughed softly, losing herself in his gray gaze.

His eyes darkened momentarily. "To me you're a magical creature. A woman with an immense range of emotions. And I love to watch each one play across your lovely face. When I first met you, I thought you were just another reporter come to create more havoc at the base camp."

"Yes, and I've been an unknown quantity in your life ever since," she returned, leaning against the strong hand that cupped her face.

He looked away for a long moment, his features becoming less readable. Alanna sensed the turmoil in him, and she waited, watching him wrestle with some unknown emotion. She caught her lower lip in her teeth, her brows moving downward with concern. Finally, she could no longer stand the strain.

"Matt?"

"Hmm?" He turned, as if not really there with her. He managed a small smile of apology. "I'm sorry, I was thinking." He caressed her cheek lovingly. "About Cauley," he said simply.

Her heart beat more rapidly, and she forced herself to remain relaxed. "Want to talk about it?" she whispered.

Again, she saw naked pain reflected in the depth of his eyes and chided herself for causing it.

"With you, yes," he answered, his voice growing husky. He sighed and lay on his back, drawing her nearer until her head rested on his shoulder. "Cauley was so damn worried that you were a spy sent down by Thornton to get to me. He told me how he cornered you in the chopper on the way down from San Dolega."

Alanna grimaced, feeling his body tense. "I know. He warned me off. I think he told me about your wife and child to force me to leave you alone."

"He and I had a few words on that account," he answered grimly.

"I don't think he'll ever believe I'm not a danger to you. But it doesn't matter, Matt. He's a loyal friend. He was worried about you."

"I told him that as far as you were concerned, it was none of his business. Ever. And it won't happen again, Alanna. That was a hell of a thing to hit you with."

She nodded. "Actually, it helped me see another, less harsh side to you," she admitted. "At first, I thought you were that cold monster that the senator had led me to believe in. You *looked* cruel. I tried to hate you like the senator did, but every time I tried, you did something to dispel that myth. And when Cauley hit me with your past, I knew that the senator had to be wrong. There is too much kindness and humanity in you, Matt. So, in a way, Cauley did us both a favor."

He was silent for a moment. Finally, he expelled a deep breath and muttered, "It damn near broke up our friendship. There wasn't a day that went by that he didn't try to undermine my feelings for you, Alanna. Even now he swears that you're pretending to care for me in order to trap me for the senator's sake."

Alarmed, she left the sanctuary of his embrace,

sitting up with an incredulous look in her eyes. "That simply isn't true!" she cried, stricken. "Matt—I don't—I mean I'm useless when it comes to playing games. I just haven't the talent or the training to do it. And I would *never* allow anyone to use me like that!"

He reached over, sliding his hand down her arm and entwining his fingers in hers. "I know that, honey. And I'm sure that if things work out as I know they will, Cauley's attitude will change as he sees the reality of the situation. Don't look so hurt, Alanna. He's only one person, and I'm certainly not avoiding you because of his beliefs." He managed a rueful grin. "Matter of fact, I've had a hell of a time waiting for this moment. Come here. . . ."

Her heart leaped in response as he pulled her down beside him, his eyes glittering as he claimed her lips in a soul-binding kiss. His mouth pressed firmly against her lips, parting them, demanding entrance. A moan of need rose in her throat, and she guilelessly arched her body upward. He groaned, gripping her tightly. Dragging his mouth from her throbbing lips, he growled thickly, "I want you, Alanna. . . ."

Her lips felt bruised with the power of his initial kiss, and she could only stare up into his stormy gray eyes, nodding mutely with consent. She trembled beneath his knowing fingers as he caressed the side of her breast. Lowering his head, he trailed a series of light, fiery kisses down her neck and throat to her shoulder. Heat uncoiled from the center of her body as she felt his hand sliding beneath the blouse, the touch of his rough fingers sending shivers across her supple flesh. Deftly, he unfastened the bra, teasing her breasts until they grew taut, the nipples hardening against his slow, exquisite assault. She entered the realm of his lovemaking as a willing partner, and he encouraged her to participate fully.

She moved her slender fingers across his tightly muscled chest, the dark hair like coarse silk beneath her hand. She felt him tense as he removed the blouse from her shoulders and she instinctively pressed against him. A shuddering sigh escaped from her as her bare breasts brushed against his body. She met his descending, predatory mouth, a column of fire leaping to burning brightness within her. His hand molded her taut breast, and she stiffened against him, a small cry escaping as he leaned over, capturing the hardened peak in his mouth. Her fingernails sank deeply into his flesh, moaning as he pulled her hips against his thighs.

Her breath came in ragged gasps as he forced the jeans off her hips, running his hand lightly across the flat, velvety expanse of her stomach, trailing lower, eliciting primeval instincts that erased all thoughts but one of fulfillment with him. She felt the jeans being pulled from her legs, and she lay back against his arm, glorying in his masterful touch. Her body ached with the pain of longing, and she welcomed him back into her arms as he removed the last of his clothes. Matt brushed her lips with his tongue, tasting them, relishing their sweetness. He wrapped his hand in the dark tresses of her hair, forcing her head back as his tongue traced the swell of each breast. She groaned, straining to make contact with him. It was sweet agony. Each touch . . . each caress. Somewhere in her chaotic mind she remembered he had said that their loving would be on his terms. A soft whimper escaped her as she gripped his shoulders, begging him to complete the union.

Gently, he slid his hand between her legs, parting them, stroking the sensitive flesh of her inner thighs. Blood pulsed and pounded through her; fire swept like a raging inferno through her tense, damp body. She looked up, meeting his dark, stormy eyes.

"Please," she begged, breathlessly. "Now . . . I need you so badly. . . ."

He leaned over her, his knee moving between her thighs. "You're mine," he growled thickly.

She closed her eyes, lips parted, still wet from his last hungry kiss. The weight of his body descended upon her, and she arched her hips upward, meeting, melding with him. Her cry of ecstasy mingled with the soft growl of his voice. She clung to him, unable to breathe, aware only of the aching warmth within her. Cradling her hips against him, he thrust deeply within her, the pleasurable sensation spreading as she matched her own rhythm to the hard movements of his body. Tears squeezed from beneath her lids, streaking down her flushed cheeks as the final, soul-shattering gift was given to her. A sob broke from her, and she arched, frozen against him as the climax shook her body into new heights of frenzied pleasure. Seconds later he gripped her, relishing his own release. Collapsing against his arms, she tasted the salty perspiration of his flesh, nuzzling deeply into his embrace, satiated and fulfilled as never before.

Gradually, ever so gradually, Alanna floated back down to earth. The sun warmed their bodies, the noon wind caressed their skin like a lover. Matt held her close, absently stroking her long, unbound hair, running his fingers through the silken tresses. He studied her in tender silence. Finally, he leaned over, gently parting her lips in a kiss that brought more tears to her eyes. Alanna reached up, caressing his face, her eyes sparkling with joy. He returned the smile he saw in her eyes, briefly running his fingers across her full lips.

"You are mine," he murmured huskily. "I knew that from the moment I saw you. I wanted all of you, Alanna. Not just your lovely body, but you as well."

"How can you be so sure?" she whispered, her voice still wispy.

He shrugged, a smile playing at the corners of his mouth. "Experience maybe."

Alanna shivered deliciously beneath his exploring touch as he caressed her soft curves. Her logical mind was not functioning at all, and she felt almost incoherent, not really listening to his words as much as to the husky tenor of them.

"I love you, Alanna," he said simply, studying her, a slight frown in his eyes. "This is the second time in my life that it's happened, and I don't want to lose you like I lost Rachel." He smoothed a rebellious strand of hair off her damp brow. "You're part of every waking and sleeping thought I have, honey. I was so damn lonely when you left Costa Rica, and then we had to deal with this furor over Thornton's report." He stopped, looking beyond her toward the river. "From now on, I want to see you whenever I please." He turned, watching her. "What do you think?"

Her heart hammered briefly in her chest. Three words, spoken so softly and with such tenderness: He loved her! "Oh, Matt," she whispered brokenly, moving back into his embrace. She sobbed quietly, and he held her for a long, long time until the tears were spent. Finally, she pulled away just enough to shakily wipe her flushed cheeks dry. He gave a low laugh, taking his hand and brushing away some of the tears himself. Placing his finger beneath her chin, he forced her to meet his intent gaze.

"I love you. Now and forever, Alanna."

She blinked, a tremulous smile upon her lips. "And I love you, Matt. Oh, God, don't ask me how or when. . . . One morning I woke up and I knew that I—" She choked back a sob. "I don't ever want to be without you."

They spent a delicious half-hour dressing each other beneath the dappled shade of the tall oak that stood near the bank of the river. Alanna was content to rest against his body afterward as he leaned back against the trunk of the tree, idly watching the green surface of the river swirl and eddy with hidden currents. Her heart mushroomed with an explosion of joy as she lay in his arms, head against his shoulder, eyes closed.

Matt nuzzled her cheek gently. "You know, for the longest time after Rachel died, I thought I'd never love again," he began huskily. "I loved her so damn much, Alanna. I married late because I knew my career in the Marine Corps would be taking me from one base to another, and I just didn't want to subject my family to that kind of stress."

She reached up, resting her hand against his strong forearm. "How long did you know her?" she inquired softly.

"For five years before I married her." He exhaled painfully. "Waiting was the biggest mistake of my life. I should have married her at the outset."

"And how long were you married before the crash?"

He bent his head down, leaning against her neck, his breath warm as it fanned across her face. "Two years. Beautiful happy years, even though I spent all but ten months in Vietnam." Finally, he raised his head, staring off toward the river. "In some ways, she was like you. Rachel had a hell of a temper. You never knew what she would be like on any given day. But she was artistic and had a volatile personality to match. I didn't keep very many of her paintings, but someday soon I'd like to show you the two I did keep."

Alanna nodded. "I'd love to see them. She must have been a woman of incredible depth, Matt."

He turned, kissing her temple. "Like you, honey."

She managed a grimace. "I'm locked into lobbying, statistics, facts and figures. I don't find that very creative."

"Mmm, I think there's much more to you than that job. You just need to be given the room and encouragement to explore the other facets of yourself."

"Sometimes I don't know what you see in me, Matt. I'm afraid I don't see the same potential you do," she whispered painfully.

He tightened his arms around her for a moment. "As a child you said you stayed in your room and wrote story after story. Who knows, maybe you have a hidden talent for writing just waiting to be sprung loose."

A soft smile curved her lips. "You give so many hope and encouragement. I wish I had known your parents, because their strength gave you the courage to do whatever was asked of you. They passed on the will to survive, to attempt anything that you thought you might want to try. God, how fortunate you were, Matt."

"I was," he agreed. "You find a lot of New Englanders are made out of some pretty stiff starch, as they say."

"I never realized just how beautiful Maine is," she murmured.

"Not half as lovely as the woman I'm holding in my arms," he murmured, guiding her chin upward.

Her lashes swept down across her cheeks as her lips met his strong mouth. The touch was tentative, searching, exquisitely gentle with love. She reached around, slipping her arms behind his neck, drawing his body to her. This hour, this day would be indelibly etched in her memory forever.

It seemed as though they had always belonged together, she thought languidly. They spent the remainder of the afternoon talking, sharing, and laughing. The richness of his wisdom continued to amaze her, and she asked more and more questions. Through him another new world was opening up, and it simply awed her. Finally, he urged her to her feet, and taking her hand, he led her down an old trail.

The goldenrods waved their yellow-flowered heads, nodding in the late afternoon breeze as Matt and Alanna crossed a small meadow. The grass was withering with frost but still stood knee high. At the other end of the field stood an old gnarled oak bent with age. Alanna sat beneath its weather-beaten branches while Matt leaned lazily against it just above her. They remained silent, watching the honey bees making their last forays to gather food before the severe winter left the area blanketed in heavy snowfall. The chirping of crickets and the cooing of a mourning dove somewhere in the distance blended beautifully with the drowsy sounds of the afternoon.

Matt finally hunkered down on his heels beside her. "I used to come here with Rachel often after we were first married. It became an even more special place when she brought me here one day to tell me she was pregnant."

Through half-closed eyes Alanna idly watched a yellow and black monarch butterfly waft across the unseen air currents drifting through the meadow. She returned her gaze to Matt, sliding her fingers lightly across his arm.

"I can't begin to understand the depth of your grief," she said in a hushed voice. "I've tried to imagine the loss of—of—" She flushed, unable to complete the sentence.

"Losing Rachel and the baby was indescribable," he whispered. He expelled a painful breath. "Jim Cauley was the chopper pilot assigned to our group at that time. He happened to be there when I received the news of my family's death. If it hadn't been for him, I probably would have lost it completely. He helped me get my gear packed and saw me off to Da Nang, where I boarded a flight back to the States."

She trailed her fingers down his darkly tanned forearm, entwining her fingers within his. "He's a true friend in every sense of the word," she said. "Somehow you survived all of it and are stronger because of it."

He shared a rueful smile with her. "The only way we get stronger is to survive the hardships life throws at us."

She nodded in agreement. "Why is it we only grow strong when we experience pain? Wouldn't it be wonderful if we could develop that sort of backbone from happiness and joy?"

"Fate sometimes plays with a marked deck," he answered. "You weren't exactly dealt a fair hand either, lady."

"I feel like my problems were minimal compared to what you've had to endure," she admitted. "My loss occurred when I was too young to remember."

Matt drew her hand upward, kissing the coolness of her flesh. "Not remembered, but never forgotten. Tell me, Alanna McIntire, what do you plan on doing with the rest of your life?" he asked.

"Work, I suppose." She shrugged. "I know this probably sounds silly, but I'm not sure. Ever since I left Paul, I've felt like a cork floating on the ocean. My world revolves around the Hill and politics."

He was studying her through his thick dark lashes. "You don't dream of rising above your position of assistant to a senator? What about becoming Thornton's chief lobbying associate? You've certainly got the intelligence, education, and moxie to fill that job."

The afternoon breeze blew several strands of hair across her eyes, and she pulled them back, tucking them behind her ear. "Moxie. That's a good word." She looked up and met his warm gaze.

"It suits your Hungarian fieriness. So, what are your ambitions?" he prodded.

Alanna moistened her lips, thoughtfully phrasing her words. "I'd love to be responsible for certain aspects of the senator's work." She had not honestly given it a great deal of thought before. She shook her head. "Since I've met you, my job has become less important. What about you? Are you a thirty-year man, as the military slang goes?"

He rested his head against the trunk, closing his eyes. "No. I've got two more years to complete the mandatory twenty, and then I'm retiring."

"Retiring at age thirty-eight must be nice," she baited.

"Jealousy will get you nowhere," he countered good-naturedly.

"You've earned it," Alanna said, conviction in her tone. "So, are you going to pull out your rocking chair and write your memoirs?"

"No," he said slowly, watching her facial expression intently. "I already have a job lined up with a firm in Colorado to manage their bridge-building division as soon as I get my discharge."

He must have read the surprise etched in her widening blue eyes. "Anything wrong with that?" he demanded, his voice humorous.

Alanna blinked, realizing the effect his plans might have on her life. She had taken it for granted that Matt would always be near. Of course, it was absurd to expect him to stay in D.C. when he disliked politics so strongly. He was watching her, his gray eyes narrowed and unreadable. "No," she stumbled lamely, searching desperately for an excuse for her shock. "It's so hard for me to get rid of the Marine image, that's all."

"It's only an image," he insisted.

She shook her head. "You'll never leave the military behind completely. The squaring of your shoulders and your confident stride will show no matter what you do,

Matt." She forced a smile she did not feel. "There's a sense of authority about you. . . ."

"All civil engineers have that aura of power," he explained with a drawl. "You see, we like to build, mold and shape things out of the natural fabric of the earth and call them our own. I find building infinitely more positive than carrying around a rifle and hand grenades, don't you?"

"Absolutely. I just can't get over the difference between Matt Breckenridge the Marine colonel and Matt Breckenridge the man who is worshiped by children and loves nature so much."

"All human beings have many facets," he interjected softly, pulling her close and resting his cheek against her hair. "Like you. You love children, too, if I'm not mistaken."

"There's been a part of me that's wanted children," she confessed quietly. "I wanted to give at least one baby a chance to be loved by a mother and a father. I may not have known my parents, but I can give the love I missed to someone else."

He brushed her hair with a kiss. "You'd make a wonderful mother."

She felt a new surge of elation coursing through her as she lingered over the thought of carrying his child. How much love would be showered upon their baby!

They remained in each other's arms for another half-hour. The magic of the autumn meadow spun a sense of euphoria about them. Gently, Matt nudged her out of the spell, and she raised her head from his broad shoulder.

"If we want to eat, we'd better get back to fishing," he whispered, pulling her upward.

Alanna fell gracefully back into his arms, swaying against him, relishing the hardness and strength of his male body. Sliding her hands around his neck, she raised her lips to his, initiating the kiss. A groan vibrated deep from within his chest as her lips met his descending, predatory mouth. The world tilted crazily beneath her feet as she drank deeply of his mouth, dizzied by his tantalizing male scent. Her heart sang with so much joy that she wondered fleetingly if it were possible to explode with happiness. His hand moved insistently down the length of her arched spine, capturing her hips, pulling her roughly against him, and making her acutely aware of his arousal. She gazed up in wonder at his fiery, silver eyes, the impact of his passion and desire for her leaving her stunned.

They rested against each other for a moment, overwhelmed at the emotional storm created by their brief contact. Alanna did not have the necessary strength to stand on her own two feet. Finally Matt whispered. "I'm starved, but it's for you."

She nodded faintly, her lashes sweeping downward like thick crescent fans against her ivory skin. "I know," she answered breathlessly.

"You aren't going to be safe in the cabin tonight, lady," he growled in warning. He released her, and they slowly began to walk back toward the river, meandering through the secluded meadow, leaning against one another.

Alanna tried to take the fishing seriously, but Matt's nearness distracted her. After an hour, Matt had hooked a flounder, which he proudly displayed to her. The fish was odd-looking, with both its eyes located on one side of its flat head. Alanna wrinkled her nose.

"I never realized just how ugly flounder is," she confided, catching the laughter in his eyes.

"Don't knock it," he said. "That's our dinner."

She made no attempt to follow him as he took the catch back to the cabin to clean. His parting words were, "You stay here and enjoy the view."

He ambled back sometime later and propped himself

up against the tree, gently pulling her back into his arms. Alanna closed her eyes, content. He leaned over, brushing her hair with a kiss.

"Nice to hear the sounds of nature instead of D.C. rush hour traffic, isn't it?" he whispered.

"Mmm, no traffic, honking horns, fumes, or people giving each other nasty hand signals."

"Think you might survive somewhere other than a city environment? Or are you a hothouse flower who would wilt?"

"So far so good, don't you think?" she asked, opening her eyes and meeting his laughter-filled gaze.

"At least you don't run screaming if a bee buzzes too close or a little dirt gets scuffed on your shoes."

She gave him a playful jab in the ribs. "Matt Breckenridge, after I survived Costa Rica, I don't know how you have the gall to infer I can't survive Maine!"

He laughed deeply, gently depositing her against the fragrant quilt of pine needles. His eyes danced with a sensual invitation as he leaned across her, his face inches from her own. "I'll give you credit, you're one hell of a woman," he breathed, caressing her parted, waiting lips. He traced the outline of her lips, teasing her until she moaned. She instinctively arched against his sun-warmed body in response. Molding his hard, male mouth against hers, Matt deepened the exploratory kiss, his tongue moving into the moist sweetness of her mouth. Her breathing became shallow and rapid beneath his trailing hand as he followed the natural curve of her breast, lazily circling the hardening peak. Slowly, ever so slowly, he lifted his mouth from her, passion written in his eyes.

"Do you know how many times I've dreamed of holding you in my arms and making love to you through the night?" His voice was low and disturbing to her senses. "I've never wanted anyone as much as you, Alanna," he breathed huskily. He touched the stray strands of her hair, pushing them off her brow, studying her with an intensity that created storms of longing within her. "You're the kind of woman I want to see tangled up in my sheets the morning after. You have that kind of power over me. You're in my blood, lady, and I can't think two coherent thoughts without thinking of you." He caressed her flushed cheek. "We were made for one another. There's an indomitable strength in you, honey. I saw it in Costa Rica, and I see it in your eyes now. You're so alive, and you have so much love and affection to give."

She basked in the warmth of his adoring gaze, unused to such love and honesty coming from a man. It moved Alanna deeply, and she tentatively reached upward, resting her hand against his rough cheek. "I love you so much," she whispered tremulously, "and I love the idea of sleeping with you in a tangle of sheets."

Chapter Twelve

The flames in the fireplace licked and crackled pleasantly in the background as they finished their evening meal. Alanna sat on the rug, leaning lazily against the couch, a soft smile playing over her lips. The flounder, dipped in cornmeal and fried until a golden brown, had been delicious. She had eaten with a ravenous appetite, but inwardly another hunger was perfectly sated.

Matt had loved her with infinite tenderness, and even now, hours later, her body remained bathed in that warming glow. When she had whispered, "I love you," she had seen his gray eyes widen with surprise and then tenderness. Never had she taken so much pleasure in lovemaking. She sighed softly, resting her head against his shoulder.

"Good?" he murmured against her ear.

"The lovemaking or your marvelous cooking?" she asked.

"Both. Cooking is just another form of love."

Alanna touched her stomach. "I feel like I've eaten at the very best seafood restaurant," she admitted. "I never knew how delicious fresh fish could taste with potatoes and pan bread. You're an extraordinary cook."

He leaned forward, moving their plates to one side and then joining her, resting against the couch. "My Dad taught us how to make something out of nothing. I can remember as a kid digging a hole out in the back yard, making a small fire, and throwing a potato, some butter, and milk into a tin can to make potato soup."

She stole a look up at his face. "Was it edible?"

"Naturally."

"And how did your mother react when she found out you had dug a hole in the backyard? I imagine she skinned you boys alive."

"No, she didn't. All she asked us to do was fill it in after we were done and to go out beyond the lawn the next time. She was a pretty savvy woman in most respects," he murmured fondly, smiling.

"You were lucky," Alanna agreed. She felt his mouth brush against her cheek, and she raised her chin, offering her lips. He kissed her slowly. When he finally broke contact, his face was scant inches from her own.

"And what about the lovemaking?" he asked, his voice husky and suggestive. "Did that pass muster too?"

She caught the glimmer of mirth deep within his eyes. Her breath caught in her chest as she lost herself within the flame of his ardent gaze. Finally she whispered, "I've never been loved so thoroughly . . . so . . ." A lump prevented her from saying anything else.

He maneuvered her around until she was lying across his lap, her head cushioned against his shoulder. His one hand rested against her thigh as he pressed her against his body. Alanna closed her eyes, dropping little kisses against his neck and jaw, incredibly happy and at peace with herself.

"I love you," he whispered. As if to reinforce the words, his protective embrace tightened momentarily. "And I want to marry you, Alanna McIntire. . . ."

Her heart contracted in joy. She opened her eyes, meeting his warm gray gaze. She saw so much there . . . his love for her, a shadow of fear still lingering from his past, physical desire.

"I made up my mind that I was going to marry you after the first night you spent at the base camp. I had gone over to the chow hall to get you something to eat, and when I came back, you had fallen asleep. I knew you hadn't heard me coming into the room, so I just stood there watching you. I saw for the first time the vulnerability in your face, honey. You looked so damn lost and beautiful in that moment that I knew I loved you beyond any shadow of a doubt." He smiled wryly. "And after you had eaten and we sat there in the darkness talking . . . my God, Alanna, do you realize I'd never spoken to anyone about those emotions before? I was stunned by what I told you of my feelings about war and killing. And you sat there with understanding and sympathy written so clearly in your eyes. . . . At that moment all I wanted to do was take you into my arms and hold you. I wanted to lose myself in you and know, for the first time since all of it happened, that I was going to be all right. You gave me a strength and offered a solace that no one else had been capable of giving me. And I knew that if I were hurting, you would support me emotionally until I could get on my feet again."

Tears glittered in her eyes. The power of his admission shook her very soul.

"And then I went through a stage where I feared losing you as I had Rachel. I seesawed back and forth as to whether or not to let you know how I felt. I wondered if it was better to let you go and never run the risk of losing the person I loved most in the world. I knew I couldn't take it again emotionally. It took me seven years to come to grips with Rachel's death, and it damn near tore me apart. I—" He faltered, his voice growing hoarse. "I never thought I could love again, Alanna. Not until you walked into my life. I had a choice to make: to deal with my fear and admit to wanting you as my wife, or," he murmured quietly, "to give you up because I was too weak and cowardly to go after what I wanted and needed."

A small cry broke from her lips as she reached up, sliding her arms around his neck and drawing him against her. "Oh, Matt," she cried softly, "I love you so much. I can't stand the thought of ever leaving you."

Matt buried his face in her silken, cascading hair. "Say you'll be my wife, honey. Now and forever!" he groaned, his arms tightening around her.

"Yes . . . oh, yes," she whispered.

The temperature had dropped again during the night, covering the trees, grass, and brush with a glistening coat of frost. Alanna stood at the kitchen sink, a cup of coffee in her hand and a wistful expression on her face. The sound of Matt moving around the cabin gave her a renewed sense of joy. She turned slowly, a smile pulling at the corner of her mouth as she allowed her gaze to move to the open bedroom door. A tangle of sheets, she thought, blushing slightly. The bed sheets were rumpled and twisted, the blankets pushed carelessly to the end of the bed. She closed her eyes momentarily, caught up in the memory of his body, his touch, the whispered words of honesty and love shared between them last night.

Alanna heard Matt approaching and opened her eyes. He was clean-shaven, his dark hair still damp and shining from the shower. She inhaled his masculine scent as he stooped to draw her into his arms. He leaned down, kissing her nose, cheeks, and finally, her parted, waiting lips.

"Mmmm," he purred close to her ear, "you taste like sweet clover honey to me."

"And you are my Sir Galahad," she murmured, merriment written in her eyes.

"Without a horse, of course," he teased, grinning. He cocked his head, studying her. "Do you know how incredibly beautiful you look this morning to me? Good loving brings out an inner radiance." He traced her arched eyebrow. "Your eyes are like emeralds with a hint of gold in their depths. I think I might lose myself in them forever." His fingers trailed down the velvet expanse of her cheek, and he outlined her parted lips, sending a shiver of pleasure through her. "And your mouth . . ." He groaned softly. "So soft and inviting, so sweet to taste." He sighed. "I'd better stop, or I'll convince both of us to go back to bed in a moment."

Alanna trembled deliciously within his embrace. "It doesn't sound like a bad idea," she agreed.

"The selfish part of me would love it. But I'd like to spend the morning doing some hiking around here with you, honey. I'm anxious to show my home ground to you, to share my growing-up years. Or does that sound boring to you?"

Alanna shook her head. "It sounds wonderful. After the mud and tropical storms of Costa Rica, I'm up to anything."

"That's my lady. Come on, let's pack two knapsacks, and we'll be off."

They walked through groves of stately pine and climbed the gently sloped earth above the river, the dry leaves of maple and oak crunching beneath their feet. Stepping out into the sun-drenched meadow, Alanna felt her heart soar. She impulsively skipped a few steps and turned, a smile on her lips.

"I feel like running for the sheer happiness of it!" she exclaimed.

He released her hand, sharing her smile. "Go ahead," he coaxed huskily.

"Thanks," she whispered, and then turned, throwing herself into the arms of the long, gently rolling meadow. Her hair streamed across her shoulders like dark silk, and she flew through the tall grass. She was a butterfly, a yellow and black monarch floating on the invisible currents.

Finally, as the meadow narrowed and then ended in another group of oak and evergreens, Alanna slowed reluctantly to a stop. Perspiration dotted her brow, giving her face a glistening sheen. Her cheeks were flushed from the exertion of the ecstatic run, and her breath came in short, shallow gulps as she leaned down, resting her hands against her knees in an effort to catch her breath. Her dark hair framed her features in tangled disarray.

Matt found her, grinning broadly as he sauntered over the small rise above where she stood. Alanna straightened up, lifting her chin and meeting his smiling eyes. She laughed, impulsively running up the small incline to throw herself into his arms. He lifted her off her feet and swung her around, their laughter melting together into a beautiful song that echoed across the meadow.

Alanna gasped for breath, giggling as he returned her to the ground. Matt reached out, taming her hair.

"I told you, you're a wood nymph," he teased, his gray eyes dancing with pleasure as he watched her.

She tried to catch her breath. "I've *never* done this before! But it feels so good!" she exclaimed. "Matt, I've never felt so alive, so happy! This must be love. It just must be," she said, her voice dropping to a reverent whisper as she leaned close and hugged him fiercely.

He tried to remain serious, but that irrepressible smile lurked in his eyes as he led her into the shade of a pine tree. He deposited her on the carpet of pine needles and then joined her, opening up the knapsacks and sharing the lunch.

"I told you before," he said after a few minutes, "that there were other sides of you that were there but had never been allowed to surface. We were just privileged to witness one of them," he murmured, "the earth child, Alanna McIntire."

She blushed beautifully. "I love it! I feel so clean and free inside, Matt. I can't explain it."

"That's why a lot of people like to jog, because it releases inner inhibitions and frees up their emotions."

"And that's why you run every morning when you're at home?"

He nodded, passing her another peanut butter and jelly sandwich. "Yes, although I prefer to release my stored-up tension in a much more creative way with you," he drawled.

Alanna gave him an impish smile, ignoring his comment. "Your job probably produces as much tension as mine," she noted. "I wish I had discovered jogging earlier, it might have helped me take the office pressure in stride, so to speak."

She saw a troubled shadow cross Matt's eyes, and she tilted her head inquiringly.

"Have you given any real thought to what Thornton might do when he finds out you've agreed to become my wife, Alanna?"

The words acted like a bucket of icy water on her ebullient mood. "No—I . . . I haven't," she admitted, then flashed him a tender smile of love. "You've occupied my thoughts day and night, Matt," she confessed. And then she shrugged, suddenly losing the rest of her appetite. Alanna felt his sun-warmed fingers on her arm as if to give her physical reassurance.

"Now you understand why I asked you yesterday what your job meant to you, honey. I know without a doubt that Thornton will get rid of you. If he doesn't fire you outright, he'll create enough pressure and embarrassment to force you to leave." His fingers tightened momentarily about her arm. "That means living with me for two more years in the D.C. area. I know Thornton hates me enough to make sure it's tough for you to get any kind of other job that's connected with the government."

Alanna faced him, gripping his hands. "Matt," she begged in desperation, "please tell me what happened to make him hate you so much!" She swallowed hard, watching the play of emotions on his face. "Please, darling, tell me. I won't say anything. I promise. Help me to understand this damn feud between you and the senator. I—I could take being fired and even barred from the Hill if I only knew the truth of the matter."

A flash of pain and then indecision appeared in his eyes as he stared at her. Alanna felt his inner torture, and she tightened her grip on his fingers. "All of it, Matt. Don't spare me the details just because I may find them hard to take," she urged throatily.

His mouth became thinner, that same grim line that she had seen before when the weather had prevented the rescue efforts at San Dolega. He bowed his head, chin resting against his chest, and the silence grew around them. "When I was asked never to divulge the true story, Alanna, I meant to keep that promise," he said, his voice oddly devoid of emotion as he raised his head to study her. His brows formed a downward arc. "But it wouldn't be fair to allow you to walk into the field of fire without knowing how things stand."

She remained motionless, noticing that he had

dropped back into military terminology. Field of fire. . . . It sent a shiver down her spine, and an ugly, unsettling sensation replaced her sunny mood. Matt looked away, his profile rugged and withdrawn as he stared at the beauty of the meadow in the noon light.

"You'll need some background information," he began in a faraway, detached tone. "I went back to Vietnam after viewing the graves of my parents and Rachel and our baby and threw myself into the most dangerous Recon activity that I could find. That meant operating behind enemy lines for more than ten days at a time. I don't know how to explain the stress of such duty except to say that we lived with death twenty-four hours a day. Our job was to melt into the enemy's homeland, gain information, and then radio for a chopper to fly us back to base on the other side of the DMZ, where we delivered our reports.

"I hadn't been able to release the grief I carried with me, so it compounded my problems. Inevitably, I put my team into an untenable position. It happened because I was still too caught up in Rachel's death . . . in the death of my child, whom I'd never seen." He closed his eyes, his face expressing the anguish of his next words. "I had put the lives of six other Marines in danger. The enemy had discovered us, and we had our backs to the river. We were all wounded to some degree or another, and that was when Jim Cauley came out of nowhere and rescued us. He went against my express orders by flying into that withering blanket of fire. He disregarded them and saved all our lives." He halted again, his face becoming less readable. "Thank God no one died. I don't think that I could have lived with that on top of everything else."

"Is that how you got your shoulder wound?" she asked softly.

"Yeah. I recuperated in-country at a hospital in

Saigon and then got orders cut to the I Corps area again."

Alanna watched him, amazement evident in her wide-eyed gaze. "Why? Surely you could have gone home at that point?"

He turned, regarding her moodily. "Home to what? My parents were dead, my wife and baby . . . hell, Alanna, I was empty inside and at the same time filled with so much hate, anger, and bitterness that it was eating me up alive. In my own convoluted way, I was trying to release that hatred against a known enemy. I couldn't face my brother and his wife or their kids yet. I just didn't have the emotional stamina to stand on my own two feet."

"How did you and Tim Thornton meet, then?" she urged gently.

Matt ran his fingers through his hair in an aggravated gesture. "My company commander, who was also my best friend, wouldn't let me go back to the Recons because my shoulder was not fully healed yet. So he put me in charge of a company of Marines instead.

"Morale was at an all-time low. We were trying to extricate ourselves from an embarrassing little war that we had no business being in. But orders kept coming down to continue our search-and-destroy raids and our ambushes. It was then that Tim was transferred into my company. He had enough rank to take certain responsibilities for his squad, a group of ten men. But he was high on grass most of the time, and once the gunnery sergeant found him shooting up." Matt's face became grim and battle-hardened.

"I have no use for a soldier on dope or drugs. He's a threat to everyone, not just to himself. I was ordered by my superior to take the company out on one of the last search-and-destroy sweeps. Tim, in the four months he'd been with us, had become a real albatross.

He knew he had his father's political clout behind him. He pulled things that no one else would dare and got away with it."

Alanna moistened her lips. "Somehow, I can't envision you letting him get away with it too often, Matt," she began slowly.

He gave a derisive snort. "If I had had my way, he would have been sent flying back stateside so fast it would have made his head spin," he growled. "He was just one of those rebels that would eventually get a lot of people hurt, and I knew it. . . ." He rested his arms against his long muscular thighs, clasping his hands in front of him. "In retrospect I realize I should have done something about it sooner," he muttered.

"What stopped you?"

Matt remained silent for almost a minute before answering her. "My company commander, Bob Green, told me he was getting pressure from headquarters staff to give Tim a good report. Bob and I had grown up together in Maine, and when he joined the Marine Corps I went away to college. He worked up through the ranks, and when I joined up after graduation we renewed our close friendship. When I needed someone, Bob used his authority to get me under his command, and I was grateful. Neither of us expected Tim Thornton to be dumped on us.

"Bob asked me to be patient with the kid because the staff threatened to ruin his career otherwise, and he was sitting in a good position to become a general himself someday. I agreed to try to ride the situation out. But Tim kept eroding the morale of the men. Finally I said to hell with it and flew to Da Nang to see what I could do. I tried everyone, from the colonel on down, hoping to take their attention away from Bob and focus it on me instead." His face grew hard. "And that's where I got my hatred for politics, Alanna. I was told that Tim was the son of an influential senator who held the purse strings to the military via the committee on defense spending. They didn't want the boat rocked. The Chiefs of Staff were afraid of large defense cutbacks and didn't want Thornton's son implicated in *anything* which might set the military up as a target of his father's vast senatorial anger and power. God, I can still see myself standing stiffly at attention while that panel of officers explained their reasoning to me. I was told that if I intended to remain a career officer I'd better learn to live with the kid. Not only that, they threatened to destroy Bob's career if there was any trouble. It was an effective maneuver. I might have destroyed my own career, but they were betting high stakes that I wouldn't jeopardize his." He sighed raggedly. "They were right," he whispered.

Alanna stared at Matt disbelievingly. "It sounds like they blackmailed you," she murmured.

He gave her a cutting smile. "They did. It was on that final sweep that everything went to hell," he said, tiredness evident in his voice. "When we stopped to make camp on the fifth night, LPs, or listening posts, were set out around the perimeter of the company. The men in the LPs were on watch for four hours at a time. It was their job to warn the company if the enemy was getting ready to launch a surprise attack. Tim had the post at the northern side of the camp. According to the surviving Marines in his company, he had taken a couple of uppers before going out," Matt snarled softly. "The LPs were supposed to radio at any sign of danger so I could call in air strikes and get assistance to protect my men."

Matt rubbed his palms against his thighs, straightening up. "To make an excruciating story very short, Tim, after being "up," promptly came down and fell asleep at his post. The enemy did launch a ground assault against us early that morning. Tim apparently awakened after the sappers, who carry explosives, had passed by him. I don't know whether he was disoriented or just plain scared, but he got out of the foxhole and ran into the jungle."

Alanna inhaled sharply, her hand across her mouth as she stared at Matt. "Are you saying he deserted his post?"

Wearily, Matt nodded. "Exactly. He left our entire company vulnerable to attack. Our first warning was when the sappers started blowing holes in the concertina barbed wire and the enemy began to pour through those holes, attacking the awakening men." He rubbed his face, shaking his head. "God, it was the worst nightmare I've ever survived, Alanna. We ended up rallying enough to throw back the first wave. But the second wave came, and we had so many casualties, I—" His voice halted. Finally, his words came out in anguished tones. "I had to call in an air strike on top of our own position in order to save us."

"Oh, no," Alanna cried softly, large tears blurring her vision. She resisted the horrible image of an air strike being dropped on both the enemy and the Marines.

"It's a last-ditch procedure when you're being overrun." He gave a painful shrug. "Not one that we like to employ, but—if it hadn't been for Tim leaving his post, it would never have happened. Never." The final words were grated out with such coldness that Alanna felt her stomach knot.

"I launched an investigation as to what had happened. We found Tim's body almost a quarter of a mile away—he had been killed by the enemy. I interrogated his squad mates . . . or what was left of his squad. The two men who survived told me he had been drinking alcohol before going out and popped the uppers just before leaving for his post. I had Thornton's body flown directly to Saigon for autopsy. At that point, I didn't care any longer. The press was hounding headquarters, and the pressure was on Bob because he was the officer in charge. I was going to make sure Thornton got credit for the massacre and that Bob's name as well as my own were cleared in the process. I had all the proof I needed because the autopsy report from the hospital showed significant levels of alcohol as well as drugs in his bloodstream."

"They stopped you," Alanna stated hoarsely, her eyes round with disbelief. "Oh, my God, Matt, you mean all these years you've taken the blame for what happened, and it wasn't your fault?" she cried.

He managed a bitter smile. "Let's just put it this way, honey. Orders came down, unofficially, that my commander was to cover up the whole sordid affair. I was so distraught at that point, I allowed Bob to make me promise to go along with the phony story. In essence, we were both ordered to go along with the cover-up. And if we didn't, then we could expect our careers to be ruined. And the blame for the massacre would be squarely laid on Bob."

She could only sit there in shock. "I can't believe you would sacrifice your convictions in such a situation."

"Frankly, when I look back on it, I can't either," he admitted. "But you have to remember my emotional instability, the shock of losing so many Marines, and the fact that my best friend was begging me not to spill the ugly truth. And the truth wouldn't really help anyone. Tim was dead—he couldn't be taught a lesson." He turned, grasping her hand and squeezing it. "We all do things we'd never thought we would do when the pressures are great enough, Alanna. Maybe you've never been beaten down so far you couldn't separate right from wrong. Looking back on it, I realize I should have insisted on an investigation that would put the blame squarely on Tim Thornton. Hindsight is always more accurate," he muttered, shaking his head.

"So you've lived with this cover-up during the rest of

your military career," she said. "And you've taken the brunt of Senator Thornton's hatred because he thought *you* caused Tim's death."

"Yes, and the ironic thing is that ever since Bob became a general, he and Senator Thornton have constantly been at each other's throats over the defense budget. I guess everything goes full circle."

Alanna straightened up, recalling the bitter feuds between the senator and the military in the finance committee. "You don't mean General Robert Green?" she breathed.

"Yes." He gave her a sidelong glance. "See how messy a political problem it has become?"

She had automatically put her hand against her breast. "My God," was all she could stammer out. "Can you imagine the scandal that would explode on the Hill if this ever got out? The senator is a dove, and he hates the military for so many reasons. If his son's memory were dragged through the mud that way, he'd become rabid in his hatred."

Matt got to his feet, taking both her hands and pulling her up. "It would be political disaster for the military," he agreed grimly.

"And it might ruin your career and reputation, too," she stammered, looking up at him worriedly.

He laughed softly, sliding his arms around her hips and drawing her against him. "I've only got two years left, honey, and there isn't much they can do to hurt me now. The only reason I continue to take Thornton's abuse is because I'm what is known as a 'short-timer' now. I can see the end in sight, and I have the strength to bear that load until I get my discharge papers." He leaned down, caressing her lips in a long kiss. As he drew away he muttered, "Besides, I'm in love, and I'm happy for the first time in many, many years. And your love and understanding will make it easy to carry this damned albatross the last two years."

Chapter Thirteen

Alanna stood in the foyer of her apartment, unable to move away from Matt. It was late Sunday evening, and she was feeling tired, but happy.

"Look, you get some rest, lady," Matt ordered gently. "I'll call you tomorrow evening, and we'll make some plans for the next week. Fair enough?"

She thrilled to even the slightest touch of his hand upon her body. How could a weekend go so quickly? It all seemed like a beautiful dream that was fading away, and now she was beginning to wake to the cold, harsh reality of living once again. But he was standing there, that arresting gaze caressing her with unspoken love. Mustering a small smile, she nodded. "It sounds wonderful," she whispered.

"Good. Maybe, if we get lucky, I can steal you away to my home in McLean for next weekend. Deal?"

Her heart thudded at his husky invitation. "I'd love that, Matt."

* * *

The senator's office was in a flurry of preparations as Alanna entered the suite of bustling, busy rooms. Aides and secretaries were walking quickly back and forth, and the air was charged with an indefinable electricity. She stopped by Peggy's desk as a matter of habit to pick up her weekly assignments.

"What's going on?" she wanted to know.

"Plenty, believe me," the secretary responded, giving her a full smile.

Alanna had never particularly cared for Peggy. Why was it that when Peggy smiled like that it brought a picture of a barracuda to mind? Shifting her briefcase to her left hand, Alanna asked, "What's on my agenda for the week, then?"

Peggy reached into her bottom left drawer and pulled out a heavy manila envelope with Alanna's name neatly typed on it. "You mean two weeks, my dear. Here are your airplane tickets and a packet of information on your assignment. The senator was so pleased with your lobbying efforts in California that he's sending you to the state of Washington to confer with several companies that have defense contracts with the federal government. You'll be meeting with representatives of several major aeronautics corporations and gathering data that he needs in order to develop a better picture of the defense budget requests due up for vote in the next several months. All the info is there. You'd better rush home and pack a bag because I've got you leaving on an eleven-thirty flight to Seattle."

Alanna moaned inwardly, staring at the packet. Without a word, she turned and went to her office, picking up pertinent telephone messages and then leaving the Hill. Disappointment transformed her ebullient mood into a spiraling depression. Two weeks away from Matt? Her heart twinged with real pain at the thought of the unforeseen separation. She set her briefcase down after entering her apartment and went directly to the phone. Dialing Matt's office, she was connected with his secretary.

"I'm sorry, but Colonel Breckenridge is in a meeting all morning. May I take a message?"

Alanna caught her lip between her teeth, unsure. What if certain people over at the Pentagon found out that she had called? Would it create an embarrassing situation for Matt? The story he had told her on Sunday was fresh in her mind, and she wanted to protect him from any possible problems. "No—no thank you. I'll just try at a later time. Thanks."

To her despair, when she got to the airport she discovered she had not packed her personal telephone book, which contained his home phone number. In her hurry to catch the flight, Alanna had literally thrown her clothes into a suitcase and called a taxi. It had been a miserable oversight on her part. His home phone, she found out, was unlisted. Once in Seattle, Alanna was caught in meeting after meeting, and the few times she tried to call Matt's office, he was not at his desk.

Finally, the following Friday, she got a chance between meetings to place a call to the Pentagon.

"I'm sorry," his secretary answered crisply, "but Colonel Breckenridge will be out of his office until Monday. May I take a message?"

Alanna grimaced, her fingers gripping the phone more tightly. "No—I, uh, guess not." She slowly let the phone drop back down on the receiver cradle, staring at it for a long, long time. She threw herself into her meetings, using both Saturday and Sunday to cut short the number of days she had to spend in Seattle. The men and women she met with were only too happy to hold business discussions in the evening, as long as the senator's office picked up the tab. Alanna neither read the newspaper nor watched television because of the accelerated itinerary. By twelve each night, she fell into an exhausted sleep, too tired to care what was taking place in the world around her.

Early Thursday morning, Alanna placed a call to Peggy. "I'm coming home early, Peggy. The work is completed, and I'll have the report on the senator's desk by Monday morning."

"Oh, that's great! I'm so glad you called in! The senator is anxious for you to return and wants to see you the minute you land. I'll pass the word along that you'll be arriving at Washington International at three this afternoon."

Alanna hung up, on the verge of mental and emotional exhaustion. She ignored Peggy's bright mood, not stopping to wonder why the woman was suddenly being so friendly. Right now, all she wanted to do was get to her apartment, find Matt's home phone number, and contact him. God, how she missed him!

The flight was bumpy, making her even more irritable by the time the jet landed. It was cold and rainy; the winds buffeted the plane strongly from the northwest. She hadn't slept well for several days, worrying about being out of touch with Matt. What would he think? He couldn't know she had forgotten his phone number. And, afraid of the Washington grapevine, she hadn't wanted to mail a note to his Pentagon office. Would he be worried? Angry, perhaps? No, she told herself, he would understand. She got up, joining the line of people trudging out single file from the plane. After she explained it to him, he would understand. A tired smile pulled at her mouth. They would both laugh at her silly mistake later over a drink at her apartment. As she emerged from the congested boarding area into the main airport, Alanna was mentally planning the logistics of spending the evening with Matt.

She was so enmeshed in her thoughts that she failed to see the wall of photographers, television cameras, and other media representatives who were waiting like anticipating vultures as she walked into full view. Flashbulbs popped, the blinding strobe lights of the portable television cameras snapped on, and reporters crying out Alanna's name brought her to a stunned, shocked halt.

"Ms. McIntire! Ms. McIntire!" one aggressive reporter yelled, thrusting his microphone ahead of the wall of human bodies as they surged forward toward Alanna. "Is it true? Have you finally ripped open Colonel Breckenridge's black market ring down in Costa Rica? Tell me, how did you find out he was stealing medical provisions?"

Alanna's eyes widened enormously, and her lips parted. A tidal wave of fear consumed her as she stared open-mouthed at the reporters and television crews. They swirled around her like buzzards circling a dying animal. More microphones were thrust at her like weapons. The brightness of the lights caused her to shield her eyes momentarily.

"How did you do it, Ms. McIntire?"

"Senator Thornton says you were responsible for proving Colonel Breckenridge's complicity. Do you have a comment for us? Do you find the colonel's actions as despicable as the senator does?"

"The senator says you were responsible for gathering the evidence and would testify before the special investigative committee looking into this matter."

Panic struck her, and adrenaline surged through her body, making her want to run and hide from their relentless attack. Stunned and confused, she made a half-turn, bumping into another reporter, a red-haired woman who smiled brightly at Alanna.

"How did you gather this evidence in Costa Rica?" she asked.

Alanna wanted to scream. This couldn't be happening! No . . . oh, God, no! Her mind was blanking out from shock. Matt, she screamed silently, Matt, I need to talk to you! Oh, God, what's happened? There wasn't any evidence against you! What happened?

"Please, give us a statement!" someone else shouted over the noise.

Alanna felt the growing silence as all eyes and cameras were trained upon her. The woman reporter at her elbow reacted first.

"Did you gather evidence?" she pressed.

Alanna glanced at her, her eyes wide and startled. "I—uh, yes, I did, but—"

"Isn't it true Colonel Breckenridge gave you a hard time right after you landed in Costa Rica?" another reporter shouted.

"Yes, but I—"

"And didn't you find pieces of medical crates in the highlands a few days later?"

Her nostrils flared, and she felt real paranoia. "We found crates, but they didn't belong to the San Dolega effort!" she nearly shouted. "Matt—I mean Colonel Breckenridge was with me, and we both agreed that the crates weren't from San Dolega," she repeated, her voice charged with raw emotion.

A television crew shoved their way forward, and Alanna recognized a man from one of the local stations. "Ms. McIntire, the senator says that he has evidence to prove that those crates *were* from the San Dolega relief effort and that a missionary had brought evidence to him prior to that. What do you have to say to that? Was Colonel Breckenridge trying to lead you off the trail?"

She looked around wildly for some avenue of escape. She *had* to find Matt! The initial shock had worn off, and now the adrenaline that had been pumping so strongly through her body took over. She glared at the television reporter, pushing by him.

"Colonel Breckenridge never lied to me!" she

snapped, and then she shouldered her way through the crowd as quickly as she could, hurrying down the long tiled corridor toward the baggage claim.

They followed her, hounds on the scent of their quarry. To her relief, Alanna spotted Senator Thornton's chauffeur waiting in the baggage area. She ran forward to meet him, her breath coming in sharp gasps.

"Stephen, please drive me to the office. Immediately. You can come back and pick up my baggage later."

The white-haired chauffeur nodded briskly, taking her airline folder.

"Of course, Ms. McIntire. The senator wanted me to take you to his office as soon as your chat with the reporters was finished."

Alanna shot a look over her shoulder; the group of reporters was fast closing in on them. "Just get me out of here," she whispered tightly. "Now!"

Distraught, Alanna walked quickly by Peggy's desk and twisted the handle of the door to the senator's inner office.

"Alanna," he greeted warmly, putting his pen beside the document he had just signed. "Thank you for dropping by. I'm sure you must be exhausted after the jet flight and your interview with the press. I'm afraid you'll have to get used to this in the future, but please, sit down, my dear. We have several topics to discuss."

She ran her fingers tensely through her dark hair.

"Senator, what is going on? I didn't find Colonel Breckenridge guilty of *anything* at San Dolega!" Her voice rose in pitch as she asked the question. He gave her a paternal smile, as if he were dealing with a precocious child who had just thrown a temper tantrum.

"My dear child, you are white as a sheet. Here, have some brandy. I'm sorry that Peggy forgot to inform you that the press would be there, but surely you knew about all this? After all, it's been on the evening world news on all the networks for the last three days."

Alanna felt dizzy suddenly, gripping the edge of the desk with whitening fingers. "What?" she whispered hoarsely.

Thornton ambled around the desk to his liquor cabinet, pouring her a small snifter of brandy. Handing it to her, he continued smoothly, "And because of your thorough investigation I want to be the first to congratulate you on your new post as my chief lobbying associate." He raised his snifter, clinking the side of her glass in toast. He watched her through hooded eyes as he took a sip. "I believe a ten-thousand-dollar raise also goes with your new position."

Alanna's hand trembled badly, the apricot brandy sloshing against the sides of the crystal snifter. "Oh, my God . . ."

Thornton guided her to the rich, plush expanse of his sofa. "Certainly you deserve the position, Alanna. I've watched you for two years and have admired your stamina and loyalty to me and the public. And you've enabled me finally to bring Breckenridge to justice. I can't think of a better way to reward you than make you my right-hand man . . . person in our lobbying efforts." He leaned over, patting her shoulder and smiling confidentially. "Congratulations, my dear. You've given me the murderer of my son, and I'm gratefully indebted to you because of that. All that remains now is the enjoyment of watching him stripped of his falsely won honor and medals. You do know that the entire investigation is going to be picked up by all the major networks and broadcast after the eleven-thirty news each night? I've seen to that." He turned away, setting the snifter down and rubbing his fleshy hands together. "And I owe it all to you," he murmured.

Her heart pounded like a thrashing, mortally wounded bird in her chest as she rose unsteadily to her feet. Her throat was scratchy with tears. "This is a mistake. All a terrible mistake, Senator. Those crates weren't from the San Dolega mission. I had photographs of them. . . ."

Thornton was regarding her silently from beneath his bushy eyebrows. "Yes, I had prints made from the one roll of film you gave us," he commented smoothly.

Alanna froze mid-stride. "There were two rolls, not one."

"When you handed me that manila envelope, my dear, there were twenty-five pages of your report and one canister of film."

Alanna stared at Thornton, stunned. "No," she cried. "No, there were two! I know, I put them there myself. That other roll had all the shots of the crates and their numbers. Those numbers didn't match the numbers on the relief supplies flown into San Dolega. The policemen who were with me saw them. They can swear to you that the crates weren't from San Dolega!"

Thornton smiled patiently, reaching for a thick folder on his desk. "You'll find in here notarized statements from those very policemen affirming that those crates *were* from San Dolega, my dear. Furthermore, the police commissioner was kind enough to send a letter testifying to his men's unimpeachable character. He has also uncovered a bank account containing ten thousand dollars in Colonel Breckenridge's name at the main bank in San Jose. It definitely links him with the stolen supplies. Listen, you go home, take tomorrow off, and go through the contents of this envelope. The hearing starts Monday, and I want you well rested and your thoughts in order when it begins." He put his arm on her shoulder, escorting her to the door of his office. "After all, this is the first of many important steps in your new job, and I wouldn't want you to be too tired

213

to testify in our behalf. I'll have Stephen drive you to your apartment."

In a state of shock, Alanna walked woodenly up to her apartment. Several copies of the *Washington Post* lay randomly piled near her door, and she froze as she saw the banner headline on one of them: Marine Hero Investigated. Relief Fraud. Shakily, she scooped up the newspapers and unlocked the door before going inside. Throwing them all on the couch, Alanna ran to her phone. She leafed through her address book with renewed urgency, looking for Matt's number. She broke out in a cold sweat waiting for an answer from his home phone. It rang and rang. In despair, she finally hung up, biting her lower lip until she tasted blood in her mouth.

Her mind whirled with renewed anguish. She closed her eyes, burying her face in her hands, and drew an unsteady breath. It was Thursday. . . . Her mind focused on the cabin up in Maine. What would Matt have done as soon as he found out about the investigation? Would he have flown north and stayed at the cabin? Alanna gripped the phone, and she desperately foraged her memory for John's and Evelyn's address. Contacting information, she finally got their number.

Evelyn answered. "Hello?"

Alanna gripped the phone tightly, her voice coming out in a tumult of anguished words. "Evelyn, this is Alanna. Please, for God's sake, don't hang up on me. I've got to find Matt. There's been a terrible mistake—"

"Well—I—"

Alanna clenched her teeth. "Where is he, Evelyn? I've got to talk to him."

Silence lengthened on the phone line, and Alanna held her breath. "I didn't know about this, I swear," she rattled on. "I was in Seattle for nearly two weeks.

When I landed at the airport only a few hours ago, I found out. Please help me, I don't want to lose him, Evelyn. I love him."

Evelyn's voice softened slightly. "He isn't here, Alanna. I believe he's at his home in McLean. At least, that's where he was the last time John and I talked to him. What's happened, Alanna? My God, we just can't believe the horrendous stories that are being leaked out of Senator Thornton's office. They've made Matt a scapegoat, and you're supposed to be testifying against him next Monday."

Pain lacerated her heart, and she fought back the tears. "We both thought that Senator Thornton was going to let my report die, Evelyn. This is as much a shock to me as it is to all of you." A ragged sigh escaped her lips. "Give me Matt's home address, will you? I'll drive out there and see him. Somehow, I've got to make him understand I didn't do this to him. There's something strange going on. Thornton has lost one of my film canisters—the one with the film that will clear Matt. Oh God, I hope I have the time. . . ."

"Alanna, I believe you," Evelyn confided, her voice growing warm once again. "I told John you weren't capable of doing something like that. I just instinctively knew it."

Alanna's stomach knotted at the mention of instinct. It brought back searing memories of her and Matt walking along the jungle trail discussing logic and intuition. And right now, all her instincts were screaming at her to get to Matt as soon as possible. She scribbled down his address and thanked Evelyn. Hurriedly, she left the couch and ran to her bedroom, throwing off her two-piece wool suit.

Chapter Fourteen

𝒟ressed in jeans, a long-sleeved blouse, and a light jacket, Alanna opted for the stairs instead of the elevator. As she ran to her car, rain slashed relentlessly at her face, the wind tugging at strands of her hair to lift it from beneath the collar of her jacket. Sliding into her Ford Mustang, she shakily opened a map of Virginia while the car warmed up.

She wasn't the adventurous sort, and trying to negotiate the intricate street system of D.C. made her nerves fairly scream with a new level of impatience. Finally, she was on the main interstate, darkness falling more rapidly than usual because of the torrential rainfall.

It was near 9 P.M. when she finally found his home. It was a ranch-style house that sat on the outskirts of the city ensconced within a grove of pine, ash, and elm trees. Her spirits were beginning to pick up as she drove slowly down the long asphalted driveway, moving past the split-rail fence. Her mouth grew dry when she realized that there was only one light on in the house. One car was parked in front of the double garage: a low-slung red sports car. Her palms grew damp, and her fingers became icy as she shut off the engine. She sat there gripping the steering wheel for a long moment.

Forcing herself out of the car, Alanna walked slowly up the concrete path, oblivious to the rain which was soaking her lightweight jacket. Her throat ached with unrelenting tension as she moved up to the small porch and knocked on the heavy oak door. She waited, nervously clutching her handbag. Again she knocked, only this time louder. The door was jerked open.

Alanna gasped, taking a step back, her eyes wide.

"You," Jim Cauley said, his voice barely above a snarling whisper. He glanced over his shoulder and then stepped outside, shutting the door quietly behind him.

Alanna felt the rage emanating from Cauley and automatically stepped off the porch back into the rain. She blinked, the rain stinging her face. "Where's Matt?" she demanded, her voice betraying her fear.

Cauley stood there, his hands resting tensely on his hips as he glowered down at her. "Haven't you done enough damage?"

The cold didn't matter; she wasn't aware she was trembling. "Jim, I've got to see him! There's been a terrible mistake and I—"

"He made the terrible mistake by falling in love with you," he hissed. "And you led him right over the edge. You're the kind of woman that survives real well on the Hill, you know that? I warned him about you, and he said no, that you were sincere and not a spy for Thornton. I knew better. I saw right through your little ploy. Are you enjoying your new status up there? It must make you feel real good to know you've destroyed one of the finest men in the Marine Corps."

His attack transformed her fear into galvanizing anger. No one had ever spoken to her with such hatred. Alanna took a step forward.

"Look, Cauley, I don't care how much you hate me. Matt loves me, and I love him. I don't give a damn how much you dislike me. I don't care if you think I was a spy. I'm here to see Matt, and I intend to do that one way or another."

He glared at her darkly, his blue eyes narrowed pinpoints of malevolence. "He's sleeping," he snapped.

"Then wake him up. I'm not leaving," she said with chattering teeth. She wrapped her wet arms across her chest.

Cauley wavered for an instant, as if mentally reviewing his options. "Look, dammit, he's passed out. I got here about an hour ago, and he was drunk as hell, trying to drink the pain away." His voice lost its steely edge, and his shoulders slumped downward. "He's dead to the world. Why don't you let him have these few hours of peace, because when he wakes up he'll go through the same hellish pain all over again."

A lump grew in her throat. Pain . . . oh, God, the anguish Matt must be feeling. "Over—over the indictment?" she ventured.

Cauley snorted. "You've hurt him in the only way possible. I saw him go through this same kind of hell when Rachel died. Jesus, you've destroyed him emotionally by telling Thornton—"

A strangled cry erupted from her. "I've said nothing to the senator! I love Matt, for God's sake."

The officer shook his head, looking beyond her, his mouth set in a grim line. "Yeah, and he used to love you once. But that's all over now." He glanced down at her, tiredness evident in his voice. "You'd better go, there's nothing else to say. I don't know how you can live with yourself after what you've done to Matt."

Alanna clenched her hands, anguish in her tone. "Cauley, tell him I was here. Ask him to call me when he gets up. I still love him! I don't want to lose him. Please . . ."

"Yeah, sure! See you Monday at the hearing," were his parting words.

She stood there another minute before she could think coherently enough to move out of the rain. Chilled and shivering, she slid into the Mustang, digging unsuccessfully in her purse for the keys. Hot tears rolled down her face, falling silently onto the wet fabric of her jeans. Somehow, she found the keys in the darkness. Vision blurred, Alanna backed the car out of the driveway and onto the street. Her mind was numb with shock and outrage. Matt no longer loved her. He believed she was going along with the senator's plan to implicate him. And she was sure Cauley was using the situation to make the final rend in their relationship. Shakily, she tried to concentrate on driving in the gloomy downpour. The windshield wipers moved steadily back and forth, and she drove home in a state of shock.

Alanna stumbled into her Georgetown apartment near midnight. Shivering with cold, she ran a tub of hot water and tried to soak out the feeling of sickness invading her heart and body. Crawling into bed, she curled up into a fetal position, feeling feverish and nauseated. Closing her eyes, she let her body tremble every few seconds with another shudder. Inwardly, she wanted to die. There was no life without Matt. No joy. No love. . . .

She rose before dawn Friday morning, feeling sluggish and lethargic. A depression worse than any she had ever known swamped her. Three different times she had picked up the phone to call Matt, and three times she had lacked the courage to do it. She knew Cauley would be there and would intercept the call.

Cauley had probably also neglected to inform Matt that she had driven out to see him. Rubbing her pale features, she finally got off the couch and stumbled into the kitchen to make coffee.

At six-thirty the phone began ringing. She flew across the living room, thinking it might be Matt calling. Instead, it was only the first of a series of reporters and newsmen inquiring about the investigation Monday morning. By ten, Alanna was experiencing a degree of anxiety she had never felt before. She was torn between taking the phone off the hook and angrily telling the reporters to leave her alone. But if she did take it off the hook, Matt might not be able to get through. To take her mind off the dilemma, she dressed and tore open the packet Senator Thornton had given her at the office.

Her stomach tightened into a huge knot as she read with disbelief the report she had submitted to Thornton after returning from Costa Rica. Paragraphs had either been deleted or changed to implicate Matt. She read the report slowly, making notations where she knew the material had been changed. Examining the black and white photos, she saw with remorse that one of the crates had been taken from the wrong angle, so that the lettering was unreadable. It was the only one featured in the pictures. Matt was leaning over the crate, and her heart squeezed with anxiety. What would the other senators think when they saw it? Would they believe she had caught him in the act of stealing the supplies?

By noon her temperature had risen dramatically, and she was feeling ill and weak. Gathering up the annotated report, she dressed in a pair of woolen slacks and a warm sweater and slipped on her winter coat. The weather was ugly outside, with rain falling in a steady drizzle as she drove to the Hill. Alanna ignored all the social amenities once she arrived at the office and went directly to Peggy's desk. The secretary looked up.

"What are you doing in here? I thought Senator Thornton gave you the day off."

"I have to talk to him, Peggy." Her voice shook with barely controlled anger.

"Well—"

Alanna looked toward the closed door of Thornton's office. "Right now," she grated.

"He's out to lunch, I'm afraid," she answered briskly, arranging a stack of papers.

A wave of dizziness swept over Alanna, and she closed her eyes for a moment. Taking a deep breath, she planted her feet apart to steady herself. "When will he be back?"

Peggy took her time in consulting his appointment book. "Oh my, I forgot. He's taking part in a vote up on the Hill this afternoon. After that he and his wife are flying down to North Carolina to stay with Representative Benton over the weekend." She gave Alanna a weak smile. "Sorry."

It was almost impossible to think rationally due to the fever. "Who worked on the final preparation of the hearing report, then?"

"Why, I believe the senator's two attorneys."

"Bill Sullivan and Henry Bauman?" she demanded, frowning.

"Yes, I believe so. Why?" she asked sweetly, fixing a saccharine smile on her mouth.

Alanna wearily leaned against the door of her apartment, physically exhausted by the short trip to the Hill. She dropped the briefcase near the couch and shrugged out of her damp coat. Going to the bathroom, she opened the medicine cabinet and swallowed two aspirin. Determined to get in touch with Matt, she returned to the couch, dialing his number.

The phone rang eight times before Alanna reluctantly set it back down into the cradle. Tears gathered in her eyes. She slipped off her shoes, lying down on the couch and sobbing softly. Her body shook with spasms as the pent-up frustration and anxiety flowed from her. A horrible sense of dread washed over her when she analyzed the situation. Various sections of her report were missing or changed, and the film which would vindicate Matt had disappeared. She had never trusted Bauman; there was nothing she could put her finger on, but the feeling was a strong one. She had worked closely with him and Sullivan before, and a new sense of spiraling dread made her already nauseated stomach churn even more.

Finally rising, Alanna took a hot bath and climbed back into bed, exhausted. As sleep came, she thought of Matt and how much she loved him. Each time Jim Cauley's words rang in her mind, a new flow of tears streaked down her cheeks. "He used to love you once," Cauley had said. Gripping her pillow with renewed anguish, she gave in to the exhaustion and slept.

She awoke late Saturday morning with the phone ringing. Stumbling blindly out of bed, Alanna made it to the living room. She coughed heavily, a deep rattle in her chest as she picked up the receiver. Her heart thudded with despair when she discovered it was another nosy reporter calling.

Alanna slammed the phone down. She had another coughing attack, gripping her chest and gasping for breath. She felt hot again and decided to take more aspirin. After making coffee, she phoned Matt's house.

"Hello?"

Her heart sank. It was Jim Cauley. Taking a deep breath she said, "This is Alanna. I want to speak to Matt."

"He isn't here," came the terse reply.

"Where is he?"

"Over at the Pentagon with General Green preparing his opening statement for Monday. Why don't you quit trying to reach him, he doesn't want to talk to you."

Alanna gasped softly, gripping the phone. "No—that isn't true! Didn't you tell him I drove over to talk with him?"

"I did, and he said he doesn't want to see you. Is that plain enough for you, Ms. McIntire?" The line suddenly went dead, and Alanna shakily lowered the phone from her ear, staring at it. A tidal wave of anguish slammed into her, and she dropped the receiver, a cry breaking from her lips.

Monday morning dawned, funeral-pyre gray in color. The freezing drizzle continued. The clouds were a turbulent, angry mass, and the wind rose and fell erratically. Alanna woodenly went through the motions of dressing in a dark navy blue wool suit and white silk blouse, barely conscious of pinning her dark hair back into a severe chignon at the nape of her neck. She had fought the cold all weekend, but she felt even worse now. On Sunday she had tried to concentrate on the report, memorizing passages that were incorrect. A heaviness pressed against her chest, making breathing difficult. She looked into the bathroom mirror. Her jade eyes were dark with torment, sunken against the paleness of her features. Two pink fever spots showed on her cheeks, and bruised shadows were visible beneath each of her eyes, making her appear haggard and drawn. Even her mouth was thinned, the corners pulled in, indicating the severity of emotional pain that she was experiencing. Alanna was too exhausted to put on much makeup and chose a pale pink lipstick for her mouth. In less than two hours she would see Matt. Her brows moved downward at the thought, and she felt tears gathering in her eyes. No, she mustn't cry. Not anymore. Every time she whispered his name or pictured him in her mind, her heart wrenched with new-found pain. A chill shot through her, and Alanna felt deathly cold. Picking up her navy blue jacket, she slipped it on.

At exactly nine o'clock she arrived at her office and grimly moved toward the Senator's door. Peggy smiled cheerfully as Alanna walked by her desk.

"This is your big day, Alanna. Just think, you'll be on every national newscast by this evening giving your testimony. Aren't you excited?"

Alanna barely gave her a glance as she strode into Thornton's office. He was meeting with the two attorneys and a number of other aides when she entered. A knife of dread twisted in her stomach. Thornton looked ecstatic, laughing and smiling genially with Sullivan and Bauman. Compressing her lips into a single line, Alanna walked silently up to the group of men, her briefcase tightly clenched in her left hand.

"Senator, may I speak to you alone for a minute?" she asked, her voice husky with strain.

All three men turned simultaneously. Thornton eyed her critically for a second, frowning.

"Are you all right, Alanna? You look pale."

She waved it off. "Just a chest cold, nothing more."

Henry Bauman, the head attorney for Thornton, smiled. "Your voice sounds an octave lower. Just don't go hoarse on me up there today."

"Don't worry, I won't. Senator, may I have a few minutes of your time? This is important."

"Of course, anything for our star witness. Gentlemen, I'll see you later."

She remained standing, feeling lightheaded. It had to be from the tension, she thought. Thornton smiled warmly, motioning her to sit down.

"Have a seat, Alanna. Sorry you're feeling under the weather. By tonight you'll be a national celebrity. That will be quite a coup for you, my dear."

She remained on her feet. "I've gone over that report you've given to the investigation committee, Senator, and I've noted several errors in the text," she began as evenly as possible. A lump formed in her throat, and she swallowed against it. "My report has been drastically changed, and I want to know why."

"New information came to our attention after your initial report arrived, Alanna."

"Then why wasn't I put in charge of piecing it together?" she asked, her voice husky with restrained fury.

Thornton shrugged. "Look, you were on the road, and I decided to turn it over to Henry. He's had extensive experience with this sort of project, and I felt he was the best one to make subsequent changes in light of the situation."

A wave of dizziness swept over her, and she was forced to sit down, the briefcase resting tensely across her thighs. "That still doesn't explain where the missing canister of film went."

He gave her a perplexed glance. "There was only one, Alanna. I've told you before." He suddenly laughed and came over, patting her gently on the shoulder. "My dear, you were thoroughly exhausted when you arrived from Costa Rica. And after reading your report, I can see why you might have been out of sorts upon your return. Don't look so disappointed, it happens to the best of us."

Her fingers tightened on the handle. "I don't care what anyone says, Senator Thornton, there was a second roll of film. Somehow, it has gotten misplaced or—"

Thornton swung around, his eyes black and ominous. "I've waited too long for this moment, Alanna," he purred silkily. "You're an intelligent girl. Just read the report which has been prepared, and let Henry present the affidavits from the various Costa Rican officials."

He gripped her elbow, gingerly escorting her out of the office. "After all, my dear, you've just been promoted and given a very handsome raise. Stephen," he called, motioning for the chauffeur to come forward, "please escort Alanna and Henry over to the Senate chambers." He consulted his watch. "In thirty minutes the proceedings begin." He smiled wolfishly at her, motioning for her to take the lead.

Once in the limo, Alanna took the opposite side of the seat from Bauman. Her heart pounded in her chest just before she spoke.

"Henry, I think you ought to know something."

Bauman turned, studying her closely. "Yes?"

"I won't go through with this. I think you know that. I won't allow my report to be altered by lies and deceit."

One eyebrow rose in reaction, and he managed a smile. "Weren't the pay raise and promotion enough, Alanna?" he inquired softly.

"I've never accepted a bribe," she hissed.

"How long have you been up here on the Hill? Goodness, I'd think you'd know by now the power and importance this position you've been given commands. You'll have this city at your feet."

She compressed her lips, glaring at him. "I won't do it!"

"I think you will," he began. "Do you realize that Colonel Breckenridge has told us about your little affair with him in Costa Rica, my dear?" He rubbed his palms together and gave her a smile of satisfaction. "Don't look so surprised. When heat's applied, you'd be surprised what people will do to save their own skins. Your dear colonel and his blessed attorneys will use that fact to try to discredit you. They'll call you a woman scorned out for revenge. If you try to claim the report fraudulent, you're going to get caught in the crossfire. Breckenridge has already declared you one of the enemy. You'd better stick with your friends."

Alanna gasped, the full implication slamming into her. "I can't believe Matt would do that," she cried hoarsely. She gripped her briefcase. "He wouldn't," she protested. Bauman looked supremely confident, cool, and collected as she searched his bland face for some hint that he was lying.

"My dear, we also know about Colonel Breckenridge and how Tim really died out there in Vietnam. So you see, the whole messy bucket of worms has been spilled. And if you think you're going in there to call this report a fabrication, you'd better think twice."

Alanna sat back, feeling faint. My God, how had it all happened? "How—"

"We told Colonel Breckenridge that you spilled the goods on Tim's death," Bauman added.

"I said nothing!"

"Who's going to disprove it? The Marine advisers on Colonel Breckenridge's case believe it. As I said, if you claim fraud, we'll say that the report was amended to include later evidence. My dear, if you agree to go along with the report as I've edited it, I'll make sure you're properly defended so that your reputation and job are secure. It's obvious the colonel has no feelings for you."

She squeezed her eyes shut, the world spinning crazily around her. Did Matt believe she had told Senator Thornton? That would explain why he never tried to phone her before the hearing!

"And don't forget the bank account under the good colonel's name down in Costa Rica. We've got him," Bauman growled. "Right where we want him." He glanced over at her. "You look positively white, Alanna. I'd go powder my nose once we get to the chambers, and try to look a little less frightened. It won't look good on television, you know. . . ."

Her head was throbbing in pain when the crush of reporters and television cameras descended upon them the instant they left the safety of the limousine. Helplessly, Alanna was propelled along, Bauman at her arm. A sense of utter unreality chilled her as they swept into the large hearing chamber. She had no time to look toward the other block of seats and tables where she knew Matt must be sitting. Instead, Bauman deftly deposited her at the front table, which stretched like a crescent before the awesome tribunal of senators sitting above them. Two microphones were pushed at her, and Alanna pulled the chair closer. Bauman gave her a brief, cutting appraisal and then set about digging out an incredible array of affidavits, papers, and long, yellow legal pads.

Her heart was hammering wildly in her breast, and she remained frozen, staring up at the senators. Another chill ravaged her fevered body as she watched Thornton shake a few hands and seat himself as one of the investigating committee, a smug smile on his mouth.

Regardless of the pain it might cause her, Alanna lifted her chin and let her gaze sweep across the other half of the crowded room. Her breath lodged in her throat as she spotted Matt sitting at the front table surrounded by military officers. The memory of meeting him at the San Jose Airport exploded inside her head. It was the same Matt, incredibly handsome, eyes narrowed with concentration and mouth thinned with tightly leashed emotions. The dark green wool uniform he wore only strengthened the image of a warrior ready to do battle. The ribbons on the left breast of his uniform attested to his brilliant service career as well as to countless personal sacrifices. But Alanna looked beyond the impressive exterior and saw a man who once more was prepared to combat the dictates of fate with a stoic acceptance that she could not comprehend.

The situation had nearly paralyzed her with conflicting emotions and uncertainty. Yet Matt looked serene and quietly confident in the face of it all. His strength awed her, left her despising herself for her own weakness. Matt's courage was a beacon of hope. Gazing at him, she knew she must protect him, no matter what the cost to herself. She broke out in another cold sweat, her eyes widening as he lifted his head after conferring with an officer at his left. It was as if he were uncannily aware that she was watching him.

Their eyes met and locked. Alanna's lips parted, and she wanted to scream and warn him that he was being framed by Thornton. His gaze was cool and unreadable as he assessed her. She felt heat rushing into her cheeks and tears blurred her vision. Perhaps it was her imagination or the raging fever that was clouding her mind, but Alanna thought she saw his gaze flicker with concern. Her heart wrenched in that split-second, and she tore her eyes away from him, unable to stand the pain that she saw in his expression. Alanna had expected hate and anger. Instead, she had sensed something quite different—something that left her confused and shaken. There had been no animosity in Matt's eyes. He didn't hate her! Wildly, she tried to name the emotion she had seen there. Empathy? Certainly not a look of pity. She clasped her perspiring hands in her lap, unable to make sense of the silent communication that had taken place in that one, brief glance.

Her head pounded with throbbing pain, and she was barely cognizant of the opening remarks from Senator Seale, who chaired the investigative committee. Once again, Matt was being crucified for something he had not done. Matt no longer loved her because he thought she had divulged his secret to the senator. And Jim Cauley was constantly at his side, feeding him more lies about her. Now, as never before, Alanna began to understand why Matt had hated politics and the power associated with it. Alanna clenched one fist, pressing it against her chest as a feeling of suffocation overwhelmed her. She was intent on steadying her breathing, trying to calm her hammering heart.

Then something came together deep within her, and Alanna felt a calmness spreading out to all parts of her hot, trembling body. She was ill, but that no longer mattered. A new determination came into being within her. *This time,* a voice howled within her head, *they aren't going to get to Matt. I won't let them. I'll tell the truth and force them to close down the investigation because of conflicting evidence.*

She heard Bauman's cultured baritone voice listing the evidence against Matt. Desperately, she closed her eyes, pushing back the feeling of disorientation. She must be able to present her own evidence coherently in order to neutralize Bauman's convincing delivery. Futilely, Alanna realized that it would be her word against the senator's. It would mean the loss of her job . . . her status on the Hill. . . . But that no longer mattered. She had lost Matt's love, and each time she allowed that thought to hit her, she wanted to die. Morosely, she remembered Paul's droning words: "This is reality, Alanna, dreams don't come true."

Tears blurred her vision, and she took a deep, unsteady breath. She had had a dream come true. Matt had loved her. And because of that, she was prepared to lay her entire career on the line for him.

The morning dragged by with Bauman and Sullivan trading the spotlight as they pieced together the story of the relief effort. Each affidavit, each piece of evidence was duly filed with the senatorial committee. At lunch, Bauman quickly propelled her through the encroaching mob of reporters and led her into an empty chamber across the hall and out another door to an awaiting limousine. Her legs felt wobbly, and she gratefully fell back into the deep, cushioned seat, closing her eyes.

"You look terrible, Alanna," Bauman muttered. "Think you'll make the firing line this afternoon?"

She nodded, compressing her dry lips. "I'll make it if it's the last thing I do. Don't worry."

"You know that not every senator on this investigative panel is after Breckenridge's career. You're going to get some heat from Seale and Forester because they're confirmed hawks."

She gave him a fleeting smile. "I'll give it my best shot," she promised. But what I have to say may surprise you, she added silently.

Her heart wrenched with renewed agony as she reentered the chamber and saw Matt standing in the center of the room conferring with a Marine general. Again, he halted his conversation, lifting his chin to study her, his gray eyes quickly scanning her features. Alanna tried to choke down the desire to run into his arms. Oh God, his arms. . . . She felt Bauman's fingers gripping her elbow.

"Alanna?" he asked, an edge to his voice.

If it hadn't been for his bodily support, she might have lost her balance. Placing her fingertips on her brow, she forced a smile.

"I'm fine," she whispered, "just the tension."

"Dammit, you didn't eat anything for lunch. You don't look good at all. You're going to be questioned closely late this afternoon," he growled unhappily, leading her to the chair. "Maybe you ought to get to the doctor's office or an emergency room after the session today. What the hell did you do, catch the Asian flu?"

She touched her chest. "Just a little lung congestion and a fever," she murmured. "I'll be fine, I took two more aspirin, and that ought to clear my head enough for what I'm going to do this afternoon."

Bauman remained unconvinced. "The senator won't

like it if you're not in top form. This is a lousy time to get sick. Damn."

She slowly took the marked report out of her brief-case, thinking that if she dropped dead Bauman would be more worried about the loss of testimony than about her. So much for humanity, she thought bitterly, suppressing a cold growing rage within her.

By two-thirty Matt had completed his testimony, which contrasted sharply with Bauman's presentation. Bauman, like a true lawyer, was taking objection when Thornton smiled wolfishly at the rest of his assembled panel.

"I think, Henry, it would help to hear from someone who was actually there, don't you?" he suggested silkily, his gaze turning to Alanna.

She saw the gleam in Thornton's eyes, and she sensed his barely controlled desire to twist the knife more deeply into his victim.

Bauman looked sharply to his right, studying her. "Well—of course, Senator," he responded lamely.

Alanna sat on the edge of the chair feeling the glaring pressure of the spotlight. Thornton had jerked the string, and like a puppet, she was supposed to dance for him. She leaned forward, both hands planted on the table top, knuckles whitened. "There has been a grave injustice done here, Senator Seale, and I want to set the record straight." She gulped hard, and then a torrent of words spilled from her lips. "Colonel Breckenridge has been implicated in this crime with falsified evidence. Someone at the senator's office has taken my report, cut out substantial portions of it, and replaced them with outright lies!"

Bauman jerked the microphone from her. "Senators, I think you should keep the following fact in mind during Ms. McIntire's further testimony. She spent twenty-four hours a day with Colonel Breckenridge down in Costa Rica. Not five hours or even twelve. But all day and *all night*. Unfortunately, we were unaware of their liaison at the time the report was handed in to us. Naturally, when additional information reached the senator's office, he chose someone less—uh—*biased* to revise the report."

Alanna felt the explosion of disbelief around her, and she fell back against the chair, one hand across her mouth. Whispers flew through the room, and then suddenly she heard Matt's voice slice through the buzz of speculation.

"Mr. Bauman, I don't know who gave you that information, but your conclusions are erroneous and unforgivable under the circumstances."

The room hushed immediately, and Alanna jerked her head up, staring at Matt in stunned disbelief. He was angry, his gray eyes stormy and narrowed. Her heart raced as he glanced at her for a brief, melting second.

Bauman shrugged eloquently. "It may be unforgivable, Colonel, but it is true."

"Under the circumstances," Matt snarled, "she had no choice, and neither did I. Senators, I received orders to take Ms. McIntire up to San Dolega immediately. We drove part of the way, then hiked the last five miles to the village and arrived at nightfall. The area was completely destroyed by earthquake, and if it hadn't been for my own equipment, we both would have spent the night out in the rain. The fog had us socked in, and there was no transport available. As it was, we did spend the night in the same tent together."

"Colonel," Bauman chided, "we have a sworn affidavit that you also spent other nights together, including the time you were searching for those crates." He picked up the papers. "It's all here, senators, the three policemen have sworn to what I've just said."

"Again, Mr. Bauman, it was an unfortunate necessity since we were out in the middle of a jungle. But to suggest that Ms. McIntire's testimony is worthless because of our supposed indiscretion is ridiculous."

Senator Seale looked down at Alanna with new interest. "And what do you have to say about all this, Ms. McIntire?"

She pulled the microphone from Bauman, glaring at the attorney. Her throat ached with tension. "Senator Seale, there is something even more disturbing about this investigation," she blurted out unsteadily. Dizziness washed over her, but she forced the words out. "I had taken two rolls of film with me to that meadow where the crates were discovered. On the first roll were four photos of the meadow itself. On the second roll were photos of the colonel and the police investigating the ten crates that had been broken open. I had pictures of each crate number, and none of them, I repeat, none of them corresponded with the numbers on supplies intended for San Dolega. We found out later that they had been stolen from a shipping dock by three men who are political enemies of Costa Rica. They had trucked those crates to an area where the supplies could be utilized by guerrillas in Nicaragua." She gulped hard, glanced at Thornton's reddening face, and then rushed on in a breathless voice.

"As you can see, there are only five photos with this report, and the story I got from the Senator's staff is that the second canister of film was not found with the material that I turned over to them upon my arrival home."

Seale gave Thornton a look of triumph. "It's obvious if you only had four photos from that one canister, Ms. McIntire, that only four pictures should be here with us today. Is that not correct?"

An icy feeling was spreading through her body, and she felt lightheaded. Of course! They had to have the other canister in order to have produced a fifth photo! Seale was smiling broadly, and she nodded. "That's correct. Furthermore, I've underlined sections of my report that have been changed or deleted to reflect badly upon Colonel Breckenridge. The few supplies being stolen from San Dolega were tracked down by the colonel when we flew back to San Jose. The Costa Ricans responsible for the theft are now in jail."

She felt Bauman's fingers gripping her elbow, and pain raced up her arm. Half turning, she jerked away from him. Not to be outmaneuvered, Bauman took the microphone.

"Senator Seale, we still have irrefutable evidence that Colonel Breckenridge has a bank account in San Jose with considerable money in it—money that was gained by selling stolen medical supplies."

"Mr. Bauman, I think that we have evidence that will disprove your allegation," Matt thundered. He looked up at Seale. "With your permission, Senator, I'd like to supply you with the signature on my supposed bank account and my true signature. I flew down to Costa Rica last week and investigated the bank account and gathered evidence to prove it is not mine." He handed them to an aide who took them up to Seale.

Alanna held her breath, her gaze fastened on Matt. He had been down in Costa Rica last week! She gasped. Cauley had lied! Matt hadn't been home at all when she had driven over to talk with him. Her heart wrenched with new-found agony when she realized Matt was defending her despite the fact that he thought she had told Senator Thornton about Tim's death.

Seale was analyzing the signatures intently. He raised his eyebrows, nodding his head. "Senators, I've just been handed a sworn statement by one of the most widely recognized graphologists in the United States, and it appears that Colonel Breckenridge did *not* open that bank account in Costa Rica. Take a look."

Thornton blustered. "Let's get on with it! I want to

know why my boy's death was covered up by the Marine Corps."

Alanna forced herself to move, gripping the microphone with both hands. "No! The reason for this hearing was to investigate the theft of medical supplies from San Dolega." She no longer cared about anything. Her breathing was uneven, and she gasped to find sufficient air to inhale. "Senator Seale, I appeal for your help in vindicating Colonel Breckenridge. He *is* innocent! The real investigation ought to center around those other photos and why they weren't introduced as viable evidence."

Matt's voice rose above the gathering pandemonium. "Senator Seale, I would also offer this photocopy of a receipt from a local photography service. The receipt is for developing two rolls of film with a total of twenty-four pictures. The signature on the order is Senator Thornton's secretary's. The date the secretary left these photos to be developed corresponds to the date Ms. McIntire turned over the initial report to the senator. I believe some explanation from his office is necessary on this small but important point."

Bauman was offering protests, and Sullivan had leaped to his feet. The banging of the mallet striking the hardwood base sounded like a pistol shot through the confusion of exclamations and cries.

"Let's call a recess," Seale droned. "I think it appropriate for this investigative committee to discuss the need for further testimony. Gentlemen, shall we retire to our chamber and look at our options in light of this new evidence?" He slammed the mallet down again, emphasizing his point.

Chapter Fifteen

A deluge of reporters, television cameras, and commentators descended upon Alanna. She sat helplessly entrapped by the crowd of newspeople. Bauman elbowed his way past, throwing her one last glaring look. Sullivan muffled an oath, shoving his way clear so that she sat there alone.

Numb and confused again by fever, she felt the grip of a hand on her arm. Stupidly she looked up. Up into the face of Matt Breckenridge. Her lips parted, and tears rolled silently down her cheeks.

"Come on," he urged. "Can you stand?"

Blindly she rose, a feeling of utter weakness making her lean heavily against his strong body as he made a path for their exit. Once inside a small side room, he closed the door, locking it behind him. Alanna stared up at him, lips parted, unable to say anything. How could she? What could be said to salvage their destroyed relationship?

"Here, sit down before you fall down," he ordered

tightly, guiding her to a straight-backed chair. She sat, and he knelt down on one knee, touching her hot, fevered cheek. "You're burning up," he growled, searching her face worriedly. "I knew there was something wrong. Damn. Come on, I'm taking you to the hospital."

Alanna reached out, gripping his arm. "Matt—I never said anything to Thornton," she croaked, tears blinding her vision. "They—they said that you told them about us sleeping together in Costa Rica and you wouldn't return my phone calls, and when I came to see you—"

He looked at her sharply as he rose. "What are you mumbling about?"

"That—Cauley said you—"

"That's a damn lie! Come on, you're ready to faint. Just hold on, Alanna." He helped her to stand, his mouth a thin, compressed line. "Hang on, Babe," he whispered tightly, "and we'll get this straightened out between us."

She sobbed quietly, burying her head against his shoulder, incredibly weak. "Oh Matt," she choked, "I love you. . . . I never said any of those horrible things. They tried to blackmail me and—"

"Hush," he ordered. "No matter what happens, Alanna, just know that I never stopped loving you for an instant. Not one second."

She was only vaguely aware of the reporters when Matt led her to the awaiting dark olive green car. Lying back against the seat, she closed her eyes, allowing the fever to take her into a semi-delirious state. The motion of the car and the warmth of Matt's arm holding her tightly against him lulled her to sleep.

At the hospital Matt never left her side for a moment. She had a fever of one hundred and three degrees, and they promptly gave her antibiotics. Afterward, on a bed in the emergency room, she weakly sat up when the doctor left.

"Where do you think you're going?" Matt demanded, putting a restraining hand on her arm.

She gave him a confused look. "Home."

"There will be a million reporters sitting on your doorstep waiting for you, Alanna."

She searched his stony features. "Where then?"

"My home. . . . Our home."

"But—"

He shook his head, a slight smile curving one corner of his mouth. Taking her into his arms, he pulled her tightly against him. "You're very sick, honey. You need rest, and you need someone to take care of you for a while. I want you home with me. You stay here, and I'll get your coat and the prescription. Promise you won't leave?"

She muffled a sob against his chest, aware of his hand stroking her unbound hair. "Never. . . ."

It was raining when they left the hospital, and Alanna found herself exhausted by the drive to McLean. At some point, she rested her head against Matt's broad shoulder and fell asleep immediately. He gently woke her, guiding her from the garage into the rambling brick home. Leaning tiredly against him, she let him take her into the master bedroom.

The room was large and airy with another antique brass bed, delicately carved oaken dressers, and beveled glass mirrors on the closet door and the bureau. Royal blue curtains were drawn aside to allow the natural light from the sun to filter through the large floor-to-ceiling windows. An enormous Boston fern graced one corner.

Matt took off her coat and made her sit down on the bed. She unbuttoned the blouse and skirt, slipping out of them. Matt brought over his large, thick, terry cloth robe, wrapping her warmly within it, and then drew a tub of steaming hot water. She loved his thoughtfulness and reached out, catching his hand as he brought in a bath towel from the other room.

"I'll be all right," she urged, squeezing his fingers and offering a smile she didn't feel. "I'm just a little tired."

He observed her critically, standing in front of her with his hands resting casually against his lean hips. "You should see yourself. Your skin looks so damn translucent I can practically see your bones. And the darkness is coming back to your eyes, which means a fever." He pressed his cool hand against her brow, pursing his lips. "Just as I thought. Time for another round of antibiotics."

Alanna groaned. "Let me have my bath, and I'll take them afterward," she muttered.

The warm water revived her slightly. Dressed in a warm flannel shirt, she stepped from the steamy bathroom into his bedroom. Matt was there waiting with several pills and a glass of water. Alanna wrinkled her nose, taking them without further protest. Urging her into the bed, Matt drew up the fleecy quilts and shut off all but the bathroom light. "Go to sleep, honey. I'll be nearby if you need me. I've got a few phone calls to make."

Alanna nodded wearily, her eyelids feeling like lead weights. One part of her longed for his embrace, but her body needed sleep. In moments, she had spiraled into a dreamless world, content.

She had no idea how long she slept, but when she awoke, Matt was sitting on the side of the bed watching her. He offered her an encouraging smile, reaching out and touching her damp forehead.

"Your fever's down," he said, taking a cool cloth and gently dabbing it against her cheeks and neck. "How do you feel?"

Her mouth tasted gummy. "Better," she managed. "I'm thirsty. . . ."

He nodded and got up, pouring some orange juice into a glass. Coming back to the bed, he slipped his arm beneath her shoulders, drawing her upward. Alanna rested against his body, drinking the cool, sweet liquid. Matt put the glass on the bedstand, cradling her within his arms.

"Better?"

She nodded, closing her eyes, needing his closeness. "I had horrible nightmares. . . ."

"I know, honey, you've been delirious the last seven hours." He touched her shirt. "Let's get you into some dry clothing, you've soaked everything." She nodded mutely, unprotesting as he wrapped her in a dry blanket and then carried her into the living room. A huge gray dog sat near the couch where he placed her. Alanna's eyes widened in alarm.

"That's Megan," he explained. "She's been watching over you, too. Just lie here until I can get the sheets changed and find a pair of pajamas for you." He tucked her in, making sure she was comfortable. Straightening up, he looked over at the Irish wolfhound. "Stay," he ordered the dog. "Megan won't hurt you, honey. She's just big."

Alanna managed a broken smile, closing her eyes. "After all the hell we've been through, the dog could be nine feet tall and I wouldn't care."

She drifted off to sleep again and awoke when Matt carried her back to the bedroom. Megan followed, wagging her tail in friendly fashion. Alanna offered no resistance when Matt stripped the soaked flannel shirt from her body. Like a child, she allowed him to redress her in a pair of his own pajamas. Once back within the warmth of the bed, she felt better.

"Feel like some tea?" he offered.

"Sounds good."

"We'll be back in a minute," he promised.

Matt sat on the edge of the bed holding his cup of tea and watching as she drank her own. "You look better," he noted.

"I am." Alanna carefully set the cup down on her lap, resting against the pillows he had arranged behind her head. "Matt, we have to talk. I've got to unravel everything—"

He reached out, capturing her hand. "While you were asleep I made a few important calls, Alanna." He set his cup down, his face reflecting the pain she heard in his voice. "From what I can piece together so far, Jim Cauley went to Thornton and told him about us and how we had spent those nights together." His nostrils flared, and he stared down at the carpet for a long time before continuing. "Cauley also told Thornton what happened to Tim over in Vietnam."

Alanna gasped, nearly spilling the contents of the cup. Matt reached over, taking it and placing it on the bedside table. "Why?" she cried softly. "Oh, my God, why, Matt?"

He shrugged painfully. "It's hard to explain, Alanna. Men who go to war together share a very special camaraderie unlike anything I've experienced elsewhere. And because of that, Cauley felt he had earned an important place in my life. He never let go of the war, and I did. You saw that down at San Dolega the night he wanted me to go after those children trapped up on the mountain. For him, it was like going to war all over again. Another chance to get high on adrenaline and risk his neck in some dangerous condition. He lives in the past, and he expected that same closeness of me even now. And I can't give that to him. Getting older means continuing to grow, not just living in the past. Jim just never left the war behind, that's all."

Alanna swallowed, her heart aching with new anguish. "And he saw me as a threat?"

"Exactly. The night you came over to talk to me he just happened to be there to feed Megan while I was down in Costa Rica. He made up the whole thing, Alanna. I wasn't home asleep after drinking myself into a stupor. I had decided to fly down to Costa Rica to investigate that phony bank account myself."

"And he never told you I had come over?" she asked in a small voice.

Matt slowly shook his head. "I just found out about it by confronting him on the phone." He looked up at her, his gray eyes tender with love. "In my heart I knew you would never tell Thornton. I knew you hadn't done it, Alanna. But I was so wrapped up in getting the information together for the hearing that I didn't have time to contact you. I tried calling your apartment over and over, but all I got was a busy signal."

"It was those stupid reporters calling," she explained, her voice flat with distaste.

"The first week you were gone I found out where you were staying in Seattle and left at least three phone messages at the hotel. You never returned them."

She touched her forehead shakily. "Lord, that was when I was holding those evening meetings. I would stumble in around midnight or one in the morning, Matt, and literally fall into bed. I never thought . . ." Her voice faded, and she stole a look up into his tired face. "I never expected you to call. I've been so jumpy ever since you told me the real story about Tim's death that I never gave it a thought. I'm so sorry. . . ."

He squeezed her hand. "It's understandable, honey."

She chewed on her lower lip. "Matt, what about Tim's death? What's happening because of that?"

"It means a full investigation," he admitted heavily. He leaned over, kissing her cheek. "But you're not to worry about that. First things first. Let's get you well."

"But—"

"Shh, it's one in the morning and time for sleep. Remember what I told you before; we'll live one day at a time. And right now all I want to do is take a shower and then hold you in my arms all night."

She lay awake waiting for him, restless with questions about the turn of events. But before she realized it, she had dozed off, her body giving in to the ravages of the illness.

Alanna awoke slowly, glorying in the sensation of Matt's arms around her. She barely opened her eyes, her head tucked beneath his jaw, listening to the even cadence of his heart and his softened breathing. She had slept against him, their legs tangled, her arm thrown across his naked torso. Drawing her hand up, she lightly skimmed the surface of his muscled, hard body, delighting in the breadth of his chest where the hair was a silken carpet beneath her exploring fingertips.

She felt him awaken. His hand moved around her slender waist, then pulled her hips daringly against him.

"Don't wake a sleeping lion," he growled, his voice thick with sleep.

She smiled gently, arching against him suggestively, her breasts pressed tantalizingly against his chest. "Is that an old Chinese saying?" she teased softly, raising her chin and kissing him lightly.

A smile tugged at the corner of his mouth as he barely opened his eyes. "No, an old Marine saying," he growled, the reverberation of his voice sending a thrill through her.

Alanna suppressed a smile. She reached up and

brushed back a lock of hair that lay against his forehead. "I thought that was a jungle bunny saying." She tensed, waiting for his reaction to the derogatory nickname given the Marines.

Matt grinned, gently pinning her beneath him. "You know, you're getting pretty bold for this time of the morning. It must be a sign of recovery."

She laughed softly, reaching up and slipping her arms across his shoulders, glorying in the texture of his back. "No, it's love, darling," she whispered, mesmerized by the flicker of light in the depths of his gray eyes.

He sobered, resting on his forearm above her. "Lady, I'm having a hell of a time keeping my hands off you," he muttered huskily. "If you weren't so damn ill I'd—"

She placed her fingertips against his strong mouth. "Then love me, Matt," she pleaded softly, "love me as if there will never be another tomorrow."

He groaned, sweeping her into his arms. Alanna was keenly aware that he was holding himself in check. She felt fragile and breakable, yet, at the same time, her spirit overflowed with joy. She trailed her hand down the line of his lean waist to his thigh. Matt stiffened, gripping her tightly against him.

"Don't," he groaned. "I don't want to hurt you, honey."

She relaxed within his embrace, hypnotized by the silver flame blazing within his eyes as he hungrily gazed down at her. "I'm not some kind of doll that can be broken. I want you, darling, like I've never wanted anyone in my life. We nearly lost one another," she whispered throatily.

Without a word, he cupped her face within his scarred, callused hands, his mouth descending in a fiery kiss against her parted lips. It was heated, blazing steel meeting the sweet coolness of water. His tongue forced an entry between her teeth and she moaned with pleasure as he tasted her with tantalizing slowness. Simultaneously, his hand traced the curve of her breast, stroking the hardening peak like a feather. She whimpered softly, arching against his hand, begging to be touched and tamed.

His mouth left her wet lips, finding the tautness of her breast. Alanna sighed languorously as his mouth claimed the nipple. Her fingernails dug into his back muscles. An uncoiling warmth spread throughout her lower body, and she responded to the urging of his masterful touch. She felt his hand slide between her thighs, stroking the velvety expanse of her flesh, asking entrance. She was mindless, reacting only to primal instincts. The urgency mounted within her, and Alanna rose to meet his descending body as he parted her thighs with his knee. He slid his hand beneath her hips, guiding her upward to meet his thrust.

An explosion seemed to roar through her, and a small cry broke from her lips as their bodies moved in throbbing unison. A sudden wave of pleasure melted the last barriers of thought, and she stiffened against him, arching, a low moan coming from her throat as she threw back her head in ecstasy. It seemed only seconds later that she felt him grip her tightly, in the throes of his own release. She fell back against him, her body damp from the fulfilling climax. She tasted the saltiness of his jaw as she reached up to kiss him.

Matt groaned, pulling up the quilt to protect her from the coolness of the air. Their hearts still raced madly, and a trickle of sweat curved along the outside of his corded neck. She felt the pounding pulse where her cheek lay against him and smiled, caressing his arm and shoulder.

Words were a primitive form of expression compared to the tender touching and lingering kisses they gave to one another afterward. Her hair lay damply against her temples, and Matt idly ran his fingers through the silken threads. "You have the most beautiful mane of hair I've ever seen," he murmured. "You're a sleek panther, so graceful and lovely. . . ."

"And you are a lion."

A smile teased one corner of his mouth. "Not a jungle bunny?" he teased warmly.

She opened her eyes, laughter sparkling in them. "No one would dare accuse you of being anything less than a complete man, believe me," she said earnestly, reaching up and stroking his rough cheek. When she thought of how she had nearly lost him, her eyes must have darkened, because his smile faded.

He gently erased the small lines that had gathered on her brow with his thumb. "A penny for your thoughts, honey?"

"It's nothing. . . ."

"Anything that suddenly makes you look like that isn't 'nothing.' Now, what is it?"

She snuggled into his arms and he lay back, bringing her against him. Absently, she touched the curling, damp hair on his chest, trying to assemble her scattered thoughts.

"These next few weeks aren't going to be easy," she murmured, her eyes moving upward, meeting his gaze.

He exhaled slowly, running his fingers through her hair in a caressing motion. "No, they aren't." He managed a partial smile. "Feel like getting up and eating breakfast? We'll talk about it then."

The sun poured warmly through the green curtains in the kitchen as they dawdled over a breakfast of eggs and sausage. Alanna leaned back against the rattan chair, closing her eyes momentarily. Already the phone had rung eight times, and it was only seven o'clock. It had been reporters calling to find out something about the impending investigation. Finally, Matt took the phone off the hook and left it in the living room. He poured them each a second cup of coffee and sat down.

"Are you sure you still want to marry me?" he asked, sitting down across the table from her.

Her heart leaped in response, and she looked up, lips parted. "More than ever," she whispered, her voice tremulous.

He reached across the table, capturing her hand. "The press will jump on this, making us both scapegoats if they can." He frowned. "I'm more worried for you than myself, honey. I've taken this kind of heat before, and to tell you the truth, I'm glad it's finally out in the open. But you . . ."

She squeezed his hand gently. "We have nothing to hide. And we have the truth on our side."

"It won't be easy," he repeated. "The press won't attack you as much if you don't marry me. We could wait it out—"

"No, I'm in love with you, Matt, and I want to be by your side during the whole investigation. Don't ask me to wait. Please."

He gave a rueful shake of his head. "I wanted to give you a choice, Alanna."

"To me, there never was a choice to make," she said. "You stayed by me when I needed someone to lean on. You gave me support without my ever having to ask for it." She reached out, her hand resting upon his. "I can do no less for you. Isn't that what love is all about, helping one another?"

He gripped her hand in response. "That's a big part of it," he agreed huskily. "And I love you for your courage. Not every woman would be willing to go through the hell this hearing is going to stir up."

"It's so unfair," she whispered tightly, referring to the investigation.

"Nobody said anything about life being fair."

She lowered her gaze. "What about Jim Cauley?"

Matt rose, moving over to the sink and staring out the window toward the open field that had been recently harvested of corn. "I had a long talk with him last night over the phone." He turned to watch her, pain evident in the depths of his eyes. "We've gone over the reasons for his actions. Our friendship will never be what it was. Maybe time will help heal the wounds."

She felt his anguish. His best friend had suddenly turned traitor, divulging their deepest shared secrets. "You must have conflicting feelings over what he's done."

"I do. I—" He shook his head, compressing his mouth into a thin line. "God, I'd never have thought he'd do something like this, Alanna. I mean . . . we've saved each other's lives so many times in the past." He shrugged his broad shoulders, looking suddenly older. "I guess a strong friendship is like marriage: there's a fine line between hate and love. Jim stepped over that boundary."

Alanna got up, moving to his side, slipping her arms around his waist and resting against him. "Maybe your friendship can still be salvaged, darling. In his own way, I guess he wanted to protect you from me and the investigation."

Matt embraced her tenderly, resting his head against her hair. "I understand what he did, honey, but it's going to take me a while before I can forgive him." He kissed her temple. "Enough of this, we have happier things to talk about." He touched her cheek with his finger, tilting her chin upward. "Such as a date for a wedding and where you would like to honeymoon."

She smiled gently, encircling his neck with her arms, reaching up on tiptoe and kissing his mouth.

"By the time we get married and this investigation is over with, it will probably be around Thanksgiving," he said. "We could spend the holiday up with John and Ev."

"And we could stay at the cabin for our honeymoon?" she returned softly.

"Why not? Fishing season will be over with. Guess we'll have a lot of time on our hands," he suggested huskily.

Alanna took in the incredible tenderness burning in his gaze. Matt leaned down, his mouth gently touching her parted lips. She closed her eyes, aware of his heady male scent, the aura of strength about him. Despite the investigation to come, she wanted to be near him. Fate had brought them together, and now no man would tear them apart.

"I love you," she whispered, her voice trembling with emotion.

Silhouette Classics

COMING IN APRIL...

THORNE'S WAY by Joan Hohl

When *Thorne's Way* first burst upon the romance scene in 1982, readers couldn't help but fall in love with Jonas Thorne, a man of bewildering arrogance and stunning tenderness. This book quickly became one of Silhouette's most sought-after early titles.

Now, Silhouette Classics is pleased to present the reissue of *Thorne's Way*. Even if you read this book years ago, its depth of emotion and passion will stir your heart again and again.

And that's not all!

Silhouette Special Edition

COMING IN JULY...

THORNE'S WIFE by Joan Hohl

We're pleased to announce a truly unique event at Silhouette. Jonas Thorne is back, in *Thorne's Wife*, a sequel that will sweep you off your feet! Jonas and Valerie's story continues as life—and love—reach heights never before dreamed of.

Experience both these timeless classics—one from Silhouette Classics and one from Silhouette Special Edition—as master storyteller Joan Hohl weaves two passionate, dramatic tales of everlasting love!

COMING IN APRIL

NAVY BLUES
Debbie Macomber

Between the devil and the deep blue sea...

At Christmastime, Lieutenant Commander Steve Kyle finds his heart
anchored by the past, so he vows to give his ex-wife wide berth. But
Carol Kyle is quaffing milk and knitting tiny pastel blankets with a
vengeance. She's determined to have a baby, and only one man will
do as father-to-be—the only man she's ever loved...her own
bullheaded ex-husband! Can the wall of bitterness protecting Steve's
battered heart possibly withstand the hurricane force of his Navy
wife's will?

You met Steve and Carol in NAVY WIFE (Special Edition #494)—
you'll cheer for them in NAVY BLUES (Special Edition #518). (And
as a bonus for NAVY WIFE fans, newlyweds Rush and Lindy Cal-
laghan reveal a surprise of their own....)

Each book stands alone—together they're Debbie Macomber's most
delightful duo to date! Don't miss

NAVY BLUES
Available in April,
only in *Silhouette Special Edition*.
Having the "blues" was never
so much fun!

Silhouette Special Edition

**MORE SPECIAL THAN EVER,
SAY THESE TOP AUTHORS:**

JO ANN ALGERMISSEN

"To me, writing—or reading—a Silhouette Special Edition *is* special. Longer, deeper, more emotionally involving than many romances, 'Specials' allow me to climb inside the hearts of my characters. I personally struggle with each of their problems, sympathize with the heroine, and almost fall in love with the hero myself! What I truly enjoy is knowing that the commitment between the hero and heroine will be as lasting as my own marriage—forever. That's special."

TRACY SINCLAIR

"I hope everyone enjoys reading Silhouette Special Editions as much as I enjoy writing them. The world of romance is a magic place where dreams come true. I love to travel to glamorous locales with my characters and share in the excitement that fills their lives. These people become real to me. I laugh and cry with them; I rejoice in their ultimate happiness. I am also reluctant to see the adventure end because I am having such a good time. That's what makes these books so special to me—and, I hope, to you."

SSE-A2

5

MAURA SEGER

A compelling trilogy stretching from the Civil War to the twentieth century and chronicling the lives of three passionate women.

SARAH is the story of an independent woman's fight for freedom during the Civil War and her love for the one man who kindles her pride and passion. $3.95   ☐

ELIZABETH, set in the aftermath of the Civil War, is the tale of a divided nation's struggle to become one and two tempestuous hearts striving for everlasting love. $3.95   ☐

CATHERINE chronicles the love story of an upper-class beauty and a handsome Irishman in turn-of-the-century Boston. $3.95 U.S.   ☐
$4.50 Cdn.   ☐

Total Amount	$ _____
Plus 75¢ Postage	.75
Payment enclosed	$ _____

Please send a check or money order payable to Worldwide Library.

In the U.S.A.	In Canada
Worldwide Library	Worldwide Library
901 Fuhrmann Blvd.	P.O. Box 609
Box 1325	Fort Erie, Ontario
Buffalo, NY 14269-1325	L2A 5X3

Please Print

Name: _____

Address: _____

City: _____

State/Prov: _____

Zip/Postal Code: _____

 WORLDWIDE LIBRARY